THE RATTLESNAKE SEASON

A Josiah Wolfe, Texas Ranger Novel

LARRY D. SWEAZY

BERKLEY BOOKS, NEW YORK

THE BERKLEY PUBLISHING GROUP
Published by the Penguin Group
Penguin Group (USA) Inc.
375 Hudson Street, New York, New York 10014, USA
Penguin Group (Canada), 90 Eglinton Avenue East, Suite 700, Toronto, Ontario M4P 2Y3, Canada
(a division of Pearson Penguin Canada Inc.)
Penguin Books Ltd., 80 Strand, London WC2R 0RL, England
Penguin Group Ireland, 25 St. Stephen's Green, Dublin 2, Ireland (a division of Penguin Books Ltd.)
Penguin Group (Australia), 250 Camberwell Road, Camberwell, Victoria 3124, Australia
(a division of Pearson Australia Group Pty. Ltd.)
Penguin Books India Pvt. Ltd., 11 Community Centre, Panchsheel Park, New Delhi—110 017, India
Penguin Group (NZ), 67 Apollo Drive, Rosedale, North Shore 0632, New Zealand
(a division of Pearson New Zealand Ltd.)
Penguin Books (South Africa) (Pty.) Ltd., 24 Sturdee Avenue, Rosebank, Johannesburg 2196, South Africa

Penguin Books Ltd., Registered Offices: 80 Strand, London WC2R 0RL, England

THE RATTLESNAKE SEASON

A Berkley Book / published by arrangement with the author

PRINTING HISTORY
Berkley edition / October 2009

The Rattlesnake Season is based on a short story, "Rattlesnakes and Skunks," which originally appeared in issue #1 of *Out West* Magazine (June 2006, 1018 Press).
Cover illustration by Bruce Emmett.
Cover design by Lesley Worrell.
Interior text design by Laura K. Corless.

For information, address: The Berkley Publishing Group,
a division of Penguin Group (USA) Inc.,
375 Hudson Street, New York, New York 10014.

ISBN: 978-0-425-23064-0

BERKLEY®
Berkley Books are published by The Berkley Publishing Group,
a division of Penguin Group (USA) Inc.,
375 Hudson Street, New York, New York 10014.
BERKLEY® is a registered trademark of Penguin Group (USA) Inc.
The "B" design is a trademark of Penguin Group (USA) Inc.

PRINTED IN THE UNITED STATES OF AMERICA

10 9 8 7 6 5 4

To Rose: For believing all along

ACKNOWLEDGMENTS

This book would not have been possible without the help of a number of people. First and foremost, a heartfelt thanks to Ed Gorman, who asked me to write a short story a few years back with a main character who was a Texas Ranger. Even after living in Texas for nearly five years, I don't think I would have tackled the Texas Rangers on my own. Thanks again, Ed, for lighting the way.

There is not enough room here to say thank you to all of my writer friends and family members who helped me over the years, either with a critique or an encouraging word, when I needed it the most. You know who you are.

Special thanks goes to John Duncklee for helping me with the Spanish translations. Any mistakes are my own.

I can't thank Carolyn Morrisroe enough for taking a chance on me, and Sandra Harding and Rick Willett for seeing me through the process.

And, finally, I can't ever thank my agent, Cherry Weiner, enough, for sticking with me, and never giving up on me or my work. That means more to me than you know.

AUTHOR'S NOTE

It has been argued that there is no other American law enforcement agency as legendary as the Texas Rangers. That argument weighed heavily on my mind as I wrote this book. I have created a fictional character, and at times placed him in a fictional setting, among real people. In doing so, it is my hope that I have captured the essence of the Texas Rangers, and Texas of the 1870s. Hopefully, I have helped tilt the argument further in favor of the Rangers. I have the utmost respect for the Rangers, past and present.

For historical works concerning the Texas Rangers, the following books served me well, and might be of interest: *Lone Star Justice: The First Century of the Texas Rangers*, by Robert M. Utley (Berkley 2002); *The Texas Rangers: Wearing the Cinco Peso, 1821–1900*, by Mike Cox (Forge 2008); *Six Years with the Texas Rangers, 1875–1881*, by James B. Gillet (Bison Books 1976); and *A Private in the Texas Rangers: A. T. Miller of Company B, Frontier Battalion*, by John Miller Morris (Texas A&M Press 2001).

PROLOGUE

July 1872

The midwife, a short, rotund Mexican woman, who went by the name of Ofelia, stood over Lily's lifeless body and shook her head. "She is dead, señor."

There was no blood, no struggle. Lily did not have the strength to bear a child. She had battled for days between the labor of childbirth and the onset of influenza. She lay flat on the bed, her belly protruding, beads of sweat still on her forehead. A bowl of steaming hot water sat next to the bed, and the room was filled with an odd sour odor.

Josiah Wolfe could barely breathe. He staggered to the bed, past Ofelia's helper, a scrawny young thing with saucer-shaped brown eyes, rimmed with tears, that the midwife referred to as *niña*, girl, and never by name.

Lily's skin was still warm to the touch.

He closed his wife's dull eyes and kissed her forehead without fear of contracting the sickness. Life was too painful. He was willing to die that very moment himself, willing to join his wife in the land of heaven, even though he was not much of a believer. Not now. Redemption and resurrection seemed to be nothing more than a folktale. The sickness had shown no mercy, a devil that could not be fought. Where was God's hand in all of this? Josiah had wondered more than once, especially after the preacher man from Tyler had refused to come to the house out of fear for his own health and well-being.

Josiah Wolfe had never felt so empty, or so angry, in his entire life. It seemed that death was everywhere he looked. He ran out of the house yelling, screaming, venting his rage into the darkness of the night.

A coyote answered back, mocking him.

He fell to the ground in a bundle of tears and spit, and began to pound the dirt. He didn't know how long he was there, how long it was before someone laid a hand on his shoulder. It was only minutes, but seemed like eternity.

"The baby lives, señor, but we do not have much time." Ofelia stood over him, staring down with the eyes of a sad mother. "I cannot reach the feet."

Josiah caught his breath, filled his lungs, but he could not speak. Everything seemed so hopeless—even the suggestion that life somehow still existed did not, could not, touch his heart.

"I will need a butchering knife to save the baby," Ofelia said. "Can you get it for me?"

Ofelia's voice sounded like it was coming out of a well, even though the wind had whipped up, pelting his face with dry Texas dirt. In a stupor, he pulled himself up, staggered to the barn, and found his skinning knife. Ofelia grabbed the knife from his hand and disappeared back into the pine cabin that once held his dreams and love, but now only held the lifeless body of his one and only Lily.

By the time he returned to his marriage bed, there was blood everywhere.

The *niña* could not take the sight of Ofelia cutting open Lily's belly—she had run from the foul-smelling room in a panic when she saw the midwife's intent. Josiah could barely stand the sight himself. He stopped and hunkered in the corner, his eyes glazed with tears, his stomach in tatters.

Candles flickered on the table next to the bed, and Ofelia muttered under her breath as she slit Lily's pure white skin. It took Josiah a minute to realize that the woman was praying. "*Perdoneme, Dios . . .*" Forgive me, God.

After making a long cut down the center of the stomach, Ofelia motioned for Josiah to come to her. "I will need your help, señor."

Josiah's knees and hands were trembling. He could not look at Lily's lifeless face, or bring himself to speak. The words *I can't* were stuck in his throat.

"Pronto, señor."

Ofelia shook her head with frustration and mumbled a curse word under her breath. The knife tumbled to the floor. Josiah had never seen so much blood in his life. He wanted to scream at the Mexican woman and make her stop—but he knew she was doing the right thing. The baby deserved a chance to live. Lily would want him to fight, to do whatever was necessary to save their child.

Slowly, Josiah made his way to the side of the bed.

Ofelia took his hands gently into hers and guided them to Lily's belly. "I am sorry, señor, this must be done to save your baby. You must pull back the skin with all your strength."

Josiah took a deep breath, fighting back the bile that was rising from the depths of his throat.

In a swift motion, Ofelia thrust her hands deep inside Lily, tussled and turned her arms, and just as quickly, pulled a nearly lifeless baby up and out of the body. She placed the baby, all covered in blood and dark blue as a stormy summer sky, on the bed and cut the cord.

Josiah staggered back as Ofelia swatted the baby on the behind. Nothing happened. It looked dead. She swatted again. And again nothing. Finally, she blew into the baby's mucus-covered mouth and smacked the baby on the back, just between the shoulder blades. The baby coughed and heaved, and began to cry.

"You have a son, señor. You have a son."

CHAPTER 1

May 1874

Josiah Wolfe sat atop his Appaloosa stallion, Clipper, and watched a rooter skunk push through a dry creek, searching for anything that moved or anything that held the slightest hint of green.

The skunk, black with a broad white stripe down its back and a nose that looked like it ought to be on a hog, didn't see the four-foot-long diamondback rattlesnake sunning itself on the bright side of a big boulder a few yards ahead of it.

Wolfe rubbed the butt of his gun, a .45 single-action Peacemaker, then thought better of interfering. He'd wait it out, see what happened next, though his betting side told him not to count out the skunk.

He gently edged the stallion back up the trail so he'd be downwind when all hell broke loose.

The snake hissed and wiggled its tail, setting its alarm in motion, but that didn't seem to deter the hognose. In the blink of an eye the skunk recoiled and without warning jumped straight at the snake, capturing it just behind the eyes with a determined set of iron jaws.

There was no time for the snake to spit or smell the foul stink that escaped from the skunk's defensive gland. Without so much as a shiver, the reptile succumbed with no chance of a fair fight, its head smashed flatter than a johnnycake. The rattle quickly subsided, a tiny echo in the wind, like the last bell ringing on a funeral coach.

Josiah had little use for snakes or skunks, and even less for their human counterparts.

If it wasn't for one such critter, Charlie Langdon, he'd be home right now, readying the hard ground for planting even though the dry north winds had yet to stop blowing.

Winter had been slow to let go, and spring was hesitant to come on fully—not that winter was much of a worry in East Texas, not like in the Dakotas, but the wind still raged cold and fierce at times, and the leaves still fell off the trees.

Once in a blue moon, snowflakes fell from the sky on Christmas. But spring was near . . . The smell of renewal was in the air, and honestly, Josiah Wolfe wished more than anything that he was back home to welcome it, instead of being on the trail to bring a killer to justice.

Josiah watched the skunk drag the snake off, probably to a den nearby loaded with babies whose hungry mouths and eyes had yet to see the light of day.

He had been on and off the trail since the day he had become a lawman within the confines of Seerville, the town where he'd been born and raised. Like his father before him, Josiah had worn the marshal's badge. Life was fine until the town up and died, when the railroad curved and went through Tyler instead. There wasn't much left to marshal after nearly everyone moved on or was foreclosed on.

But Josiah had the deed to the family homestead, and pulling up stakes was something he wouldn't consider—not with all his kin buried on the back forty.

He wasn't much of a farmer, and his land wasn't real hospitable to much of anything of use, since most of it was floodplain and swamp, but he made do with what he had.

When the opportunity to become a Ranger came his way, he'd leapt at the chance. Josiah had listened to tales about the Rangers since he was a little boy, peering from behind the cupboard when he should have been tucked in bed, as his father and his deputies gathered around the fire and sipped whiskey.

The heroics of the Texas Rangers in the Cherokee War in 1839, and the Battle of Plum Creek, when more than a thousand Comanche warriors were faced down, were seared into Josiah's memory. Not long ago, after Reconstruction, the Rangers had fallen out of favor, replaced by the Texas State Police—a halfhearted unit, formed by then Governor Davis, that was never afforded the respect of the Rangers.

The Rangers still existed during that time, but they weren't funded very well, or at all, and mostly disappeared. But word went out that the newly elected Democrats, and specifically the new governor, Richard Coke, in Austin had recommissioned the Rangers, giving them more stature and power, and a healthy budget.

Six companies, consisting of seventy-five men each, were quickly being assembled. Now that this Frontier Battalion was being formed, the Rangers would be responsible for the whole state, and not just for responding to the Indian troubles in the West.

Josiah had ridden in a posse with Captain Hiram Fikes in the years since Reconstruction took hold, and when

Fikes heard that Seerville no longer needed a marshal, he'd sent word to Josiah that he would be a welcome addition to the company of former Rangers who were to cover East Texas.

Josiah would be an official Ranger—which seemed odd, considering their lack of real organization in the recent past. He'd be on the dockets, something more than a side-kick to Captain Fikes, helping out when he was called on by the shadowy group of men who had called themselves Rangers during the years after the War Between the States.

He would be a member of Company B, since he lived near Tyler. Headquarters were eventually going to be in Garland, over one hundred miles from home, but since the companies were still forming, they had all been called to a camp along the Red River. There was a task to complete first, before making that trek: Bring in Charlie Langdon.

Luckily, the Rangers could live just about anywhere they chose—as long they didn't mind being away from home for long stretches at a time.

Josiah didn't mind traveling so much when he was younger.

When he first joined up with Captain Fikes, life was pretty much an adventure. He had a pretty wife, Lily, whom he'd been in love with all his life, and three fine-looking daughters. The money he made with Captain Fikes wasn't much, if there was any at all, but it helped keep a couple of cows in the barn, and between that and his hunting skills, there was always meat on the table for his family.

Sometimes, riding with Captain Fikes and the other Rangers took him away for months at a time, but when Josiah returned home it was always to a hero's welcome.

Lily always made a big to-do when he entered the pine cabin, and the girls giggled and clapped like he was the

King of England or somebody equally important, returning from a great exploit or conquest. He liked that word then, "conquest." It made him feel important.

Lily loved books, and filled the girls' heads with a multitude of story ideas.

Several seasons passed, and they all got lulled into a comfortable rhythm—until the influenza struck. First, the fevers took Fiona, the youngest. After weeks of battling the sickness, the poor little thing slipped away in her mother's arms. And then, like a wild boar rampaging carelessly through the small cabin, the fevers took his other two daughters, Claire and Mavis, only days apart.

For the first time in years, Josiah and Lily were left alone, their emotions and hope all but drained out of them. They pretty much wanted to die, too—but they held on, fought off the flu with tonics and sheer determination for one simple reason: Lily was pregnant, and the baby was nearly due to birth.

Wolfe shook his head . . . tried to force the thought of Lily from his mind as he brought the horse back up to pace, leaving the stink of the skunk behind him, heading toward his new life as a Texas Ranger—and leaving his young son behind.

Traveling was not such a welcome adventure these days, but it was a relief not to look up on the hill and see a row of graves that had yet to settle into the ground.

There was no escaping the loneliness on the trail. Even the birds were silent. Somewhere in the distance he heard a growl and a yelp, and figured it was the skunk celebrating the snake kill with its brood.

The ridge Wolfe had been riding on flattened out, and

he spotted a few puddles of water up ahead in what used to be a creek. It had been a good while since he'd watered Clipper.

He glanced up at the sun and figured he'd be in San Antonio by nightfall, even with a stop.

It didn't take long to venture down to the water.

Vultures soared overhead, and he could hear the first frogs of spring croaking for a mate. The grasses were still tender, their tips still a little brown. Bluebonnets, red buckeye, and paintbrush were slowly setting into bloom, coloring the dull landscape in all the colors of the rainbow. The fragrance from the wildflowers was overwhelming.

Lily had loved spring.

The Appaloosa took to the water like it had been trudging through a desert for days. Wolfe hadn't ridden the horse hard, but he had kept up a steady, headlong gait, stopping only to relieve himself and watch the skunk do away with the snake. It had been a good while since he'd asked Clipper to make such a long trail ride. The horse was a bit out of shape.

With the sun beaming down from a cloudless sky, the air was beginning to warm.

Josiah Wolfe propped himself against a boulder the size of a good bull and closed his eyes, with the thought of resting.

It was as if he were snakebit himself.

Memory gripped him, and the image of Ofelia standing over Lily's body with the skinning knife flooded lifelike through every corner of his mind. It was like it had just happened. He could still smell the blood.

Josiah opened his eyes quickly and tried to think of something else, tried to force away the image of Lily lying dead on their marriage bed. Even thinking of Lyle, smiling and laughing, his eyes just like Lily's, did little to relieve his mood.

He mounted Clipper and headed toward San Antonio.

The thought of Charlie Langdon, the man the Rangers were to bring in, dangling from the end of a rope, didn't bring him out of this funk, either, as Josiah let his mind wander back to the present.

Charlie was a low-down scoundrel if ever there was one. For a time, Charlie had been his deputy in Seerville, after the two of them had fought together in the war, but Josiah caught on pretty quickly that Charlie was the kind of man that liked to walk on both sides of the law, and couldn't cast away the confederate demons who urged him to steal, and kill.

Charlie Langdon made things up as he went, twisted the law so it suited whatever con he was knee-deep in at the time. And that's what got Charlie in trouble. After Wolfe fired him, Charlie left Seerville, and went on a cheating and robbing spree that claimed four innocent lives in Tyler over the next two years—and then Charlie disappeared.

Josiah had no authority in Tyler, so Charlie's crimes were out of his jurisdiction, but he would have given anything to have gone after the double-crossing snake at the time.

Some said Charlie went to Indian Territory and was hiding out in the canyons, while others just hoped he was dead. Neither was right. Charlie had changed his name and gotten another badge pinned on his chest. But skunks can't change their stripes any more than a rattlesnake can sneak up quietly on a man, and before long, Charlie was walking on both sides of the law again. It was his bad luck to come up against a small group of men finishing up a fight with a band of Kiowas, the Texas Rangers—most notably, Captain Hiram Fikes.

Fikes had sent word to Wolfe and told him Charlie Langdon was in custody. If Josiah wanted the charge, he could come to San Antonio and take Langdon back to Tyler for sentencing for the four previous killings. Once he delivered Langdon to the jail in Tyler, he would have little time to head back to the camp along the Red River for indoctrination into the formal ranks of the Rangers.

In Captain Fikes's eyes, Josiah was still a Ranger. Now, with the changes being made in Austin, his past experience as a Ranger was needed even more. It was a hard decision, leaving Lyle with Ofelia, but Josiah felt he had no choice. He needed a new future, for himself and for Lyle. And he knew the citizens in and around Tyler were beating the drum to see Charlie Langdon hang. But that wasn't Josiah's immediate concern.

His main concern was returning home to his son as soon as possible.

The rest of the ride was uneventful. It was dusk when he rode into San Antonio. The liveliness of the town shocked his system. City life always did.

After Lily's death, he stayed as close to home as possible. The silence of his land, of Seerville, which was now nothing more than a ghost town, host to only a few Mexican squatters, including Ofelia, was comforting. He had never been one for the pleasantries of society—manners and conversation were Lily's gift—so he did not miss being around people on a daily basis. But he did mind the loneliness more than he'd thought he would.

Oddly, the noise of the streets, of wagons and horses coming to and fro, piano music banging out of the saloons, *was* a tad bit comforting to Wolfe. His dull mood did not lighten, but for the first time in a long while, he began to think about the pleasure of a bath and shave.

He found a livery near the jail and stabled his horse. Most people paid him no mind. Wolfe was just another face in the crowd, since the Rangers didn't wear a badge. The organization was more akin to a brotherhood, and though it wasn't a secret society, it felt like it at times . . . though recently, with Governor Coke installed in Austin, after President Grant refused to oust him, the Rangers were out in the open, a welcome sight to most Texans. Many of the Rangers were war heroes, and they operated on the legend of their name, like Hiram Fikes.

Josiah hadn't been with the organization long enough for people to recognize him—he had no legend attached to his name. Not yet thirty-four, in comparison to Fikes he felt he was still green behind the ears, and had become more tepid and reclusive since Lily's death. But he had a strong interest in seeing justice served.

It only took a little asking around, and Josiah found out the whereabouts of Captain Hiram Fikes. He was playing poker in the Silver Dollar Saloon, two doors down from the jail.

"Pull up a chair, Wolfe." Fikes was a short and skinny man with a head full of solid white hair, barely taller, it seemed, than a whiskey barrel. His skin was leathery and wrinkled, and from a distance he looked like a stiff wind could blow him straight away into Indian Territory.

More than a few brash and arrogant outlaws had underestimated the captain and found themselves six feet under without the chance to beg for forgiveness. The captain was one of the best shots Josiah Wolfe had ever met. It was as if the new model Winchester Fikes carried was an extension of his arm instead of a weapon all to itself.

"Just checking in, Captain. I'll take my leave if you don't mind. I'd like to get the trail dust off my neck."

Fikes shook his head no, pointed insistently to the chair, puffed heavily on the cigar that dangled from the corner of his mouth, and said nothing further to explain his command.

The other three men at the table looked impatient. It was the captain's turn to deal, and by the size of the chip stacks, it looked like he was cleaning out some deep pockets.

The music and laughter seemed foreign to Josiah. He tried not to stare at the two painted women standing next to the piano, or at the picture of a naked woman over the bar. It had been a long time since he'd been in a room with women, even the lowly kind, and it stirred a deep longing inside him that almost made him blush.

Aside from going into town, Ofelia was the only woman he came into contact with these days . . . and not once had Josiah let his mind wander to the fence of desire since the day he buried Lily next to his three girls.

"I've been waiting for you, Wolfe, and we haven't got much time." Fikes shuffled the cards like a professional dealer, a smile growing on his face as he turned his attention back to the game. "I know you might be wondering why I had you ride all this way, other than that Charlie Langdon has a history with you."

"I was, sir, but I'm glad to fulfill the request. It came at a good time."

Fikes flopped out five cards to each man, then stared up at Josiah, the smile gone from his face.

"It's time for you to decide if you want to keep Rangering. The last couple of years have been tough for you, but it's time to realize there's people that still count on you, Wolfe. There's going to be more Rangers now than ever, and you've been around me long enough not to be considered a greenhorn. I'll need you one hundred percent. There's a lot at stake. The legislators in Austin are wasting no time in setting up the companies, and Governor Coke's going to want quick results to prove we're worth the money."

"I understand, Captain."

"I hope you do. There's trouble brewing up your way, and I'm gonna need every man I can count on to keep a spark from turning into a wildfire. Ain't none of the men I got are as familiar with that country up there as you. Some are going to be mighty disappointed because they signed up to fight with Comanche in the counties out west. They might not have their heads where they need to be, thinking an outlaw ain't near as dangerous as a redskin. They're going to need a strong hand, a strong aim, these new recruits, not a man with calluses from a plow."

Wolfe understood the tone, the underlying meaning of the words just spoken. Captain Hiram Fikes wasn't sure he could trust him in his current state of mind because he hadn't fully committed to Rangering. He was still in mourning for his family, his demeanor was as black as widow's weeds, and Fikes was telling him to snap out of it, or go home and be a farmer.

Josiah couldn't blame the captain. You had to trust the man you picked to cover your back. He knew right then that the request to escort Charlie Langdon back to Tyler was a show of faith as much as anything else. There were other Rangers Fikes could have called on to make the trip.

"I don't mean to be anything else other than a Texas Ranger, Captain."

"Good. That's what I was hoping to hear. There's a room for you at the hotel across the street."

"The Menger is a little out of my league, Captain. I was planning on staying down by the livery."

"You let me worry about the hotel room this time around. You've had a long ride. Feders and Elliot are keeping an eye on Charlie Langdon for now, and I'd just as soon he not see you until he needs to. He's got men all over town, and I hear he might try to bust out of jail. He's got a grudge against you a mile long, and I figure he's marked you with his boys. I'd rather you be at my side than at the smoking end of the barrel of one of those scoundrels."

CHAPTER 2

Josiah left the captain at the Silver Dollar, the big pile of gambling chips getting bigger. He didn't bother to introduce himself to Fikes's card mates. Their identities were none of his business, and they looked like locals—but for all he knew, they could have been fellow Rangers that he did not know. Everything was changing pretty fast since Governor Coke took office. In any case, Captain Hiram Fikes was the last man in Texas who needed looking after.

Josiah paused, and thought it was a little odd that the captain was wasting away the night while his men were standing guard outside the local jail, but he figured even an old Ranger needed to blow off steam.

He made note of Feders and Elliot, one on the roof, one by the door, both about as inconspicuous as that skunk on the trail. He'd met Feders, a lanky true Texan like himself, before and ridden with him briefly on one of the early sojourns with Captain Fikes. He didn't know Elliot at all. He was a new recruit. But they were both Rangers, and he was glad to see them, glad to know Fikes wasn't just relying on the locals to keep an eye on Charlie Langdon.

If Charlie Langdon did have a gang in town, they knew there were Rangers to contend with, too, and might think twice about busting Charlie out. Neither Feders nor Elliot noticed Josiah; they looked bored, none too concerned about Charlie Langdon, or much else for that matter. But for all he knew, that could have been a ruse.

Josiah, on the other hand, was aware of every sound, of every man, woman, and child bustling about, and unsure of who was who since the captain told him he might be a marked man.

Having to think about the safety of his own person was enough to give any man pause, but Josiah instantly thought of Lyle, and what would happen to his young son if Langdon's men carried out their intent.

Lyle would be an orphan—plain and simple. The boy would more than likely be pulled from the small pine cabin that had always been his home, out of Ofelia's arms, and taken to the county orphanage. It was a thought Josiah could barely stand to consider, so he pushed the thought away and refused to consider it any further.

He headed quickly to the Menger Hotel, and stopped once he stepped inside the grand lobby.

It was a magnificent sight, three storeys of opulence—white tiled floors, with intricate geometric designs that looked like a sharp-edged number eight repeated over and over again, and ivory pillars, gilded with gold leaf paint, that held up a mezzanine and another floor. Plants of the like he had never seen before were scattered about the lobby, tall and jungle-like, as big as trees, but fragile-looking, adding to the expensive airs the hotel decorators had successfully put on.

It would have been the highlight of his life if he could have brought Lily to a place like the Menger Hotel, all fine and fancy, just the two of them, holding each other's hand like they did when they were courting.

But that was not to be, and Josiah knew it.

His heart ached for Lily every day, and he still forced himself to think of her as living and walking on the earth, bustling about at home, taking care of the girls and Lyle, while he was away. He knew it was a lie to himself, but the matters of love, and of the future, were subjects he'd desperately tried to avoid, until lately. He kept telling himself that he had a job to do, a son to look after—that was enough for any man to worry about.

But for a brief moment, he allowed himself a glimpse into the past, into his imagination, and watched Lily, dressed in her Sunday best, stroll across the lobby floor of the Menger Hotel, like a queen.

He shook his head, cleared his mind, and made his way to the registration desk.

The clientele of the Menger Hotel was more apt to be businessmen and formal ladies than a Ranger fresh off the trail.

Josiah immediately felt self-conscious, and almost decided to head down to the flophouse by the livery, but he just couldn't bring himself to leave. He didn't want to insult Captain Fikes by declining his generosity.

Fresh pomade glistened in the hair of the mousy-looking man who stood behind the registration desk. There was not a speck of dust on his dark blue double-breasted uniform. Gold buttons tinkled on the little man's sleeves as the clerk lifted a pen, a look of disdain rising on his face.

"May I offer some direction, sir?"

"A room is all I need at the moment."

The clerk hesitated. "We are full up. You may want to check the other hotels for your needs, sir."

Josiah stiffened, knew he was being looked down on, and he didn't take too kindly to the man's attitude. "I'm with Captain Fikes. He said there was a room reserved in my name."

The clerk's eyebrows arched with immediate recognition. "My apologies. Name, sir?"

"Wolfe. Josiah Wolfe."

The man ran the pen down a piece of paper in a fancy big book that looked more like a ledger than a guest book, and nodded.

"That'll be room 210. We usually ask our guests to check their weapons at the desk, but I understand that you're a Ranger." The man looked over his shoulder, then leaned in and whispered, "I voted against that snake Edmund Davis in hopes he'd be run out of the state. In all that commotion, we've all been wondering where the Rangers were." The clerk smiled and squared his shoulders. "Welcome to the Menger Hotel, sir. I hope your stay is a pleasant one."

Josiah smirked, even though he didn't mean to, and took the key. He was more than a little uncomfortable with public discussions about politics, but the recent fracas in Austin obviously had everyone talking.

The election of Richard Coke was a good thing for the Rangers, and Josiah was more than enthused about the formation of the Frontier Battalion, but his political views were privately held. Even though he agreed with the clerk, he wasn't about to let on to a stranger that he was happy to see Governor Coke take office.

Davis's loss signaled the end of Reconstruction, and

honestly, Josiah hoped the final curtain was about to fall on the War Between the States.

Those scars needed healing, just like his own, though he wouldn't admit that the war had scarred him . . . but it had had an affect on every man who picked up a weapon and left home to fight for a cause he believed in. Or, like him, fought because it was a duty to his family and to his state.

The only strong feeling Josiah had about slavery was simple: A man was a man, regardless of his skin color, and how he lived was more important than where he lived. One man owning another had always seemed odd to him, and his family had never had the wealth to engage in such an idea, so it had never been an issue of true consideration for them, never mattered one way or the other. Folks had been forced to take a public stand on something private.

Some men still carried a torch for the Confederacy, but Josiah wasn't in that crowd. And neither, obviously, was Governor Richard Coke.

Josiah made quick arrangements for a bath, then headed up the ornate staircase in search of his room. It had been a long time since he'd made the trip to San Antonio, so he was a tad bit saddle sore, and could still taste the trail grit between his teeth. He had a fresh set of clothes wrapped in his bedroll and was anxious to soak in a tub of hot, steaming water and get the stubble shaved from his face.

The room Captain Fikes had reserved for him was easy enough to find.

It was like walking into a palace suite. A brass bed with fresh linens took up only part of the room. A sitting chair, upholstered in thick red material that looked soft as a short-haired cat, sat regally in the corner. A writing desk and chair sat next to the bed. A pitcher with chunks of ice in it sat in a porcelain bowl with designs glazed onto it that looked like the lobby floor. A large hand-carved mirror was centered above the bowl and pitcher, reflecting a version of Josiah, and the room, back at him.

Josiah favored his father, tall, lanky, a head full of hair the color of summer wheat, and eyes the color of blueberries. He had always walked in the shadow of his father, from his gait, to his quiet beliefs, to his perception of good old right and wrong. But he was more similar in looks than any other way he could think of.

He did not recognize himself so much anymore. His face had gone gaunt, sunk in with grief, his eyes trail-worn, and his skin looked like it lacked elasticity, or the properties that exhibited a good diet—and that would be true. Since Lily's death, he had taken little pleasure in food. It was only sustenance, something to burn in the fires of the daily chores.

Josiah decided a bath and a bit of rest in a fancy hotel would do him some good.

There was a hint of lavender in the air. The room was almost too pretty to step foot in, to muck up with his filth. Josiah was glad the window looked out over the street. He could see Feders in his spot on the roof, his Winchester propped against the false front of the dry goods store, in the direction of the jail. The Alamo was out of view, but at only a scant twenty or so steps from the Menger, it was always on the mind of even the least reverent Texans when they visited San Antonio.

Evening was coming fast as the sun set in the west, the sky on the horizon a deep red, with pink fingers reaching into the gray sky over the hotel. Josiah was still tense, but starting to relax. He dropped his bedroll on the floor, left the beauty of the room, and headed for the bath.

An attendant, a wiry old Mexican with hair as white as a roll of fresh cotton, nodded. "Señor Wolfe?"

Josiah returned the nod, and the Mexican jangled a ring of brass skeleton keys, found the lock, and opened the door to the bath.

Steam met Josiah as he walked into the small room. A tub full of hot, vaporous water sat in the middle of the room. It was a welcome sight. Just the stay in the hotel almost made the long trip worth it.

"I will be right outside if there is anything you need," the Mexican attendant said in English, but with a thick Spanish accent. "Here is soap, fresh towels, and a variety of sundries that are gifts of the hotel. You will need a shave afterward?"

Josiah took a deep breath. "Yes, *sí*," he said. Using Spanish came unnaturally to him, even though Ofelia chattered away constantly at home and he understood more of the language than he cared to admit. "Thank you."

The Mexican stared at Josiah expectantly, and it took him a moment to realize that the man was waiting for a tip. He handed him a single bit, then waited for him to leave before he deposited his Peacemaker and Bowie knife, a gift from his father when he went off to war so long ago, on a shelf within reach of the tub. But the Mexican did not leave.

"For the shave, señor?"

Josiah handed the man another coin. This time the old Mexican smiled and hurried off, firmly closing the door behind him.

The sole window in the tiny room was barely cracked open. Josiah could hear piano music from across the street. Wagons were still coming and going, but not as frequently now that evening had set in. A horse whinnied, then trotted away on the hard dirt road. Voices were dim, mostly male, and unthreatening.

He disrobed, glad to get the dirty clothes off his skin, and climbed into the tub, gently at first, then fully, deciding to get the shock of the hot water over with as quickly as possible.

It did not take him too long to relax. Josiah rested his head against the rim of the tub, closed his eyes, and fell asleep before the tips of his fingers began to prune.

A loud blast woke Josiah out of his deep sleep.

Water lapped over the side of the tub as he jumped up, reaching for his gun. It was gone from the shelf, as was his knife.

Panicked, he immediately sought to dry himself, peering out the side of the window as he did.

Smoke roiled from the front of the jail. Feders was still in his spot, the Winchester aimed tensely at the heavy wood door of the adobe building, but Elliot was nowhere to be seen.

The door to the jail was standing wide open, and Josiah could see two men standing just inside, the light too dim to tell much of what was going on. It was not quite dark, the light of the day gasping gray, fading quickly from the sky as night quickly approached.

Elliot walked out of the alley and across the street, holding a blazing torch with one hand, his six-shooter in the other.

Josiah could see inside the door now. Captain Fikes just under the arch, the barrel of his gun pressed against Charlie Langdon's temple. He could see the glitter off the pearl handles of the captain's gun in the light of Elliot's torch. It was the first time he'd seen Charlie Langdon in years. The sight made his stomach tumble, tie up in knots, and it was impossible to restrain the distaste he felt.

There was a group of men, across the street, engaged in a scrap of some kind, and Josiah figured it was Langdon's men going at it with some of his fellow Rangers and the local deputies. He was anxious to join the fight, and a little relieved to see that the captain had Charlie in his grasp.

Shouts rose from the crowd, from the mob, a mix of definable noise, punches being landed. No horses or wagons were running through the street now. The only evening commerce in San Antonio was blood, explosives, and anger. Everything else had come to a full stop.

Obviously, Fikes had been right about the jailbreak attempt, and the card playing was likely a ruse, along with Feders and Elliot's coy attempt at boredom, to convince Langdon's men that the captain didn't take the job of overseeing the outlaw too seriously. Bad choice on their part, not to see through Captain Fikes's wiliness and trap setting.

For a second, Josiah almost smiled—until he remembered that his own gun and knife were missing, and he was standing naked and unarmed in a hotel bath without any way to signal for reinforcements if they were needed.

He quickly gathered up his clothes, put on his pants, made sure he had not overlooked his weapons, then cracked open the door of the bath, slightly—and came face-to-face with the barrel of his own gun.

CHAPTER 3

The official name for the Peacemaker was Colt's Single Action Army. Josiah had also heard it called the New Model Army. He didn't call it the Peacemaker—it was just his gun. But he was proud of the gun, proud that he was able to purchase such a weapon a year after its introduction, with a little money he'd saved up. It had been bought just before the trip to San Antonio, in an attempt to excite himself about the prospects of the future—but that effort had failed at the time. The newness of the gun was just a reminder of what was lost to him.

His Colt 1860 Army was retired, put away for Lyle, and that action had brought a rush of memories to the forefront of his mind that nearly crippled him for days. The old-timers called his affliction Soldier's Heart, a sickness that followed many a man home from the war, but Josiah just called it regret, grief from seeing and being the cause of so much death and destruction. He was little more than a teenage boy when he joined up with the 1st Infantry, and now, as a man, he barely spoke of those days. Regardless of the victor, war was a nightmare he hoped never to see again.

He was not sure how many men he had actually killed after he joined the Confederate cause, but he was sure it was quite a few. Sometimes at night, in his dreams, he saw men wandering in a foggy field, bandaged, bleeding, searching for help. The only way Josiah could end their suffering was to wake—but for him, he carried the dreams throughout the day, every day, combined with his grief for his family. There was no escape from the ghosts he'd left on the battlefield and in his marriage bed.

The precision of the Peacemaker was not what Josiah had hoped it would be after the purchase from Ham Wilbur's Dry Goods in Tyler.

The weight was nearly perfect, and it felt comfortable in his hand, but after some practicing, he found that the maximum effective range was about seventy-five yards. The gun grouped its shots pretty well in a six-inch circle at fifty yards, but anything beyond that scattered wildly. A target at over two hundred yards would be a lucky shot, and the shooter would likely have had to aim several feet over the head of the target.

He wasn't quite sure yet how he felt about the new addition. The gun would never be his friend, but he would have to rely on it as a protector, a constant companion. Other than his horse, Clipper, the Peacemaker was nearly the only thing in his life he would allow himself to trust. And it would take time for the Peacemaker to earn that trust.

None of that mattered, of course, dead-on, nose-to-nose, when you were looking down the barrel of a gun. Especially when it was your own.

The point-blank range would splatter the back of Josiah Wolfe's head throughout the fancy, lavender-smelling bath at the Menger Hotel, and his life's journey would come to a sudden, unfulfilled end . . . if he just stood there and did nothing.

It was impossible to see who was holding the gun. The barrel was aimed square at his forehead, and luckily Josiah had his wits about him, because he immediately pushed his bare foot against the bottom of the door, making it a little harder for the person on the other side to force it open.

"Hands up, where I can see them," came a shout from behind the door. The voice grumbled, determined and unrecognizable.

The Peacemaker jiggled up and down, as if to make a point that the person holding it was serious.

Josiah could see a hand, a shadow in the hall—somewhere close, a flame flickered in a hurricane lamp and he could smell the coal oil like the lamp had just been lit. The man was bigger than he was.

"I'm moving them slowly now," Josiah said.

"Don't try nothin' funny."

Josiah shook his head no as he raised both hands slowly up his side. When they were even with his shoulders, he thrust forward as quick as he could, slamming the door and trapping the intruding hand and gun with as much force as he could muster.

The thrust and slam were followed by a loud scream, and by the thud of metal falling onto the floor as the Peacemaker tumbled a few feet out of Josiah's reach.

When he let go, the door popped back, recoiled. He flung it open the rest of the way and threw a hard punch at the first thing he saw.

Just as he'd thought, it was a face Josiah didn't recognize, but that didn't matter.

The man, shaped like a boulder, was shaking his hand, cursing like he'd bit his tongue. The punch had surprised him, but it had hurt Josiah as much as it had the man. His fist stung, like he'd just punched a big rock. The man stumbled backward, reaching for his own weapon, a six-shooter dangling from his side.

Josiah jumped and tackled him headlong, sending them both crashing into the wall. The man was strong, and rolled them both over, punching Josiah so hard against the chin that his teeth felt like they'd been rattled out of place and then set firmly back where they belonged.

He was no match for the big man, and he was in danger of being pinned, of being subdued to the point of fulfilling his attacker's intention. He could only assume the man meant to kill him. He could only assume he was one of Charlie Langdon's gang, come to claim his mark.

That thought made him fight even harder, but the man responded by grabbing Josiah by the throat and ramming a knee into his chest.

Josiah swung wildly, losing his breath, but oddly, he was never afraid . . . just numb and downright angry.

His energy was falling away quickly. The man obviously had the upper hand in the fight, was stronger, more prepared. If there was a way out, Josiah couldn't see it . . . All he knew was that he had no choice but to keep fighting.

Seconds turned into minutes. Minutes seemed like hours. The man squeezed Josiah's throat harder, completely blocking the airway. In one last attempt, Josiah focused all of his strength and energy below his waist, hoping to buck the man off of him. His right hand was pinned now by the big man's ham-hock knees. His left hand was free, but his punches were like a flyswatter on the big man's marble back. He stopped swinging, and lurched his chest forward with all his might.

The man did not notice, did not seem to care.

Just as the light was starting to dim, the big man heaved and tumbled off Josiah. A gasping sound filled the hallway. It was a sickening sound, a rasping, intruding sound, that Josiah had heard before. It was the sound of death reaching out to snatch someone away.

That someone wasn't him . . . this time.

Confused, he sat up, and saw the old Mexican he had tipped for the bath and shave, standing over the big man with Josiah's Bowie knife, fresh blood still on the blade.

The big man was not dead yet . . . but he would be soon if someone didn't help him. He was gasping like a fish out of water. The Mexican had been careful not to cut too deep . . . just deep enough to put an end to the fight. Left to his own devices, the man would surely bleed to death.

"Are you all right, Señor Ranger?"

Josiah rubbed his own throat, nodded yes, grabbed the big man's gun, and looked up and down the hall. "He was alone?"

"I think so, señor."

"All right. Run out and get the doctor. This man needs some attention."

"Señor, are you sure? He tried to kill you."

"Justice is not ours to dole out, my friend. I appreciate what you did, but this man doesn't answer to us. If we watch him die, then we are no better men than he is. I have enough to live with, don't you?"

The Mexican stared at Josiah like he had never heard such words before, smiled slightly, then hurried down the hallway.

Josiah was left there alone, standing over the dying man, wondering how a person could come to disregard life so much that he would try to kill a man he did not know, for a reason that was not his own, as if it were just a job, just another task to be fulfilled.

He hoped he would never come to understand that kind of reasoning.

CHAPTER 4

Captain Fikes was waiting for Josiah in the lobby. "Heard you had some commotion down here for yourself, Wolfe."

The upstairs was full of deputies. A doctor worked on the boulder-shaped attacker. The last Josiah had seen of the big man, it didn't look promising.

Josiah had very little time to get himself together. He cleaned up as quick as he could, anxious to flee the Menger and join the captain and the other Rangers at the jail. His long-overdue shave would have to wait.

"It was one of Langdon's men, I assume."

Fikes nodded. "Burly Smith. Sent to kill you, I expect. That Mexican did you a great favor."

"I'm indebted. The old Mexican saved my life. I told the deputies that, but I don't think they heard me too well."

"I'll take care of it. He's an old friend. I asked him to keep an eye on you, for me. I was pretty certain Charlie would set somebody after you."

"Rightly appreciate that," Josiah said. "The old man deserves a reward." He wasn't really surprised Fikes and an old Mexican were friends. There was a tale there that he would remember to ask the captain about someday, but today was not the day. In a world where Mexicans were reviled, thanks in part to the Cortina War, and Cortina's continuing forays into South Texas to steal cattle, it was good to see the captain didn't lump all Mexicans into a hated category because of the color of their skin.

"I doubt he'll see it, if there is one," the captain said.

Josiah nodded in agreement. "He disappeared once the deputies arrived."

Captain Fikes cleared his throat and looked to the door of the lobby, signaling he was ready to leave. "Don't worry about Juan Carlos. He'll show up when you least expect him to. Always does."

"It's good to have friends like that."

"It is."

"Funny thing is, I thought Charlie Langdon was my friend once upon a time."

"We all make mistakes," the captain said. "Charlie's safe and secure in shackles. Sheriff Patterson has the jail under control . . . now. We'll be heading out in the morning, just like I planned. I was fixin' to check in on you before everything went wild on us. Patterson—" The captain stopped mid-sentence, and twisted his lip into a snarl. His eyes narrowed, then he looked away from Josiah, shaking his head in disgust.

Josiah decided quickly that Captain Fikes was not fond of Sheriff J. T. Patterson. Josiah had never met the man, but had heard he was none too liked in town, so he could only assume Fikes was more than a little irritated about the jailbreak attempt, especially considering the captain seemed to know ahead of time that it was going to happen. Combined with Burly Smith's visit to the Menger that went unimpeded, it didn't speak too highly of the local law enforcers, or J. T. Patterson's ability to keep the peace.

Josiah wasn't about to set fire to the captain's kindling, so he kept his mouth shut, and left Sheriff Patterson's reputation to simmer quietly on Hiram Fikes's tongue.

As if he could read Josiah's state of mind, the captain headed out of the lobby without saying another word. His swagger was a little more pronounced, and his steps were heavier than usual. There was nothing like seeing a man fully in charge and chagrined at the same time. Josiah followed quietly in step. He figured he might just sleep with Clipper at the livery, all things considered, and shave himself.

Pete Feders and Scrap Elliot were waiting for the captain just outside the Menger. They introduced themselves to Josiah, even though he and Feders had ridden together a few years back when the Rangers were trumped by the State Police.

Feders was nearly as tall as Josiah, and was built lean, too. He was almost the same age, a veteran of the War Between the States, and came from a county in West Texas where he'd fought the Comanche and the Kiowa more times than he liked to talk about. A thin scar ran from the corner of Pete's right eye to his ear, and Josiah tried not to stare at it or wonder if it came from an Indian fight.

Josiah thought it was interesting that Pete Feders was not going to fight directly on the frontier, since that was his home territory. But he knew that Feders was loyal to Captain Fikes, and the two had been partnered together pretty much since the onset of the war. In fact Pete Feders had been with the captain when they'd caught up with Charlie Langdon.

Scrap Elliot, on the other hand, was young, probably twenty years old, if that. In Josiah's mind, that made Scrap a kid who hadn't quite made the transition from boyhood to manhood. He had soft skin, barely any facial hair to speak of, and if there were muscles on Scrap's lean arms, they couldn't be seen. But in some ways Scrap reminded Josiah a lot of Captain Fikes, and he cautioned himself not to underestimate the boy just because of his apparent scrawniness. Even though Scrap was a new recruit, he seemed ready to jump right into the thick of things.

Three other men, whom Josiah assumed were Rangers new to Captain Fikes's command, stood off to the left.

With companies forming so quickly, it was hard to know who was a Ranger and who wasn't. No one wore a badge like the sheriff and his deputies. There was no formal uniform as of yet, if there ever would be, and most men were responsible, like Josiah, for obtaining their own weapons, horses, and clothes.

However, the state did value every Ranger's horse and promised to replace it with another horse of like value if something should happen to the animal while on duty. They also provided a ration of food and forty dollars a month—which would go a long way in helping raise a young son. A son Josiah dearly missed. The money was important to him, but it came at the cost of being away from home again for long periods of time. Lyle favored Lily in looks and action, and that made some days difficult to stomach.

The three new Rangers didn't seem too interested in meeting Josiah.

Two of them had been sitting at the table, gambling

along with Captain Fikes at the Silver Dollar. The third one was a stranger to Josiah, a dark-eyed man with rough hands and pants that still bore creases in them—store-bought and new, which immediately made Josiah a little suspicious of him.

It only took a brief pause to consider that the man might have just come into the first bit of money he'd seen in a while, once he signed on with the Rangers.

There was a small sum of money paid up front once enlistment was accepted, and horses were generally being valued at a hundred and twenty to a hundred and sixty dollars. That was quite a roll for a man who, judging from the looks of his hands, was probably accustomed to working on cattle drives.

One of the Rangers who'd been gambling with the captain mumbled something about meeting up after the way was clear and riding on into Tyler. Then they'd all take the trip back to the Red River to train with the entire company by the end of the week.

The men were scouts. Used to being alone. They split up after a nod and agreement from Captain Fikes, and disappeared into the crowd that had gathered in front of the jail.

Torches lit the street like it was noon on a Monday.

Shadows danced on the hard adobe walls of the jail and on the vacant Alamo, like ghosts milling about, looking for a way home. Horses were nervous. Voices were hushed. No one really moved about much. They all just stood in front of the jail, like they were waiting, hoping, for something else to happen.

Children in nightclothes huddled in front of their parents, watching the jail intently. A group of little boys caught Josiah's eye. They were surely hoping to see an explosion for themselves, or a shoot-out between the Rangers and the outlaws.

That didn't seem likely to happen. There were no local deputies to be seen in or around the crowd, and Josiah could tell Captain Fikes was growing more tense by the second about J. T. Patterson's absence.

"We'll meet up with those fellas at the intersect of the Old San Antonio Road near Neu-Braunfels in a matter of days. Sooner, if they see trouble lying ahead. That is if we get Charlie Langdon out of here alive," the captain said.

"Trouble's not quelled?" Scrap asked.

"Hardly," the captain answered. "Patterson and his men are about as inept as a three-legged hog in humping season. Might have a sympathizer or two in their league if they know anything of Langdon's war record." He was staring straight at Josiah.

Josiah understood the captain's gaze. He knew Charlie Langdon better than anyone around.

"Langdon claimed to kill more Union soldiers than any other member of the Texas Brigade. While that may or may not be true, I was among the men of the First Infantry, and Langdon was a respectable soldier who thrived on killing."

Pete Feders looked to the ground, kicked a bit of dirt with the toe of his boot.

"He's a mad dog, then, who got a taste of blood and liked it," Scrap said.

"Maybe that's it," Josiah said. "But he saved a lot of men, too. You have to remember how the Texas Brigade worked. They were first in the advance, and then the rear guard in retreat. First in, last out. Only the bravest of the brave can withstand a life of that kind of fighting. Charlie

Langdon survived a lot of battles because he was willing to lay down his own life. He fought in Chickamauga, Knoxville, and Suffolk, and probably more that I don't know of. The Brigade was highly favored by General Lee. Charlie wasn't a criminal, but he was a cunning soldier, always looking for a way in and a way out. He saved my life more than once."

"So, you knew him then, in the war?" Scrap asked.

Josiah nodded. "Yes, I was there."

"In the Brigade?"

Josiah nodded again. "But the war's been over for a long time. What Charlie went on to become afterward has no bearing on his deeds then. The law's the law. Theft is theft. Murder is murder."

"But if there are men in San Antonio that think Charlie is a war hero . . . ?"

"Or men in the Rangers," Captain Fikes added.

"Then we could be up against some unknowns? Some that would do us harm could be within our own ranks?" Scrap said.

Pete Feders had remained quiet throughout the whole exchange, watching everything around them, noticing anything that moved. Josiah was glad Feders was standing next to him. It had been a long time since he'd been in a group of men where he thought his back was covered.

"More than one of Charlie's gang rode with him in the war," Josiah said. "So he has his followers. But for as many men as he saved, he led ten times that to their death. Those that follow him are loyal out of fear as much as they are out of respect."

"Like Burly Smith," the captain said.

"I didn't know him. Never seen him before in my life, so I can't say if he rode with the Brigade or not. Like I said, what we all did in the war was a long time ago. The Brigade didn't breed bad men. A lot of them came out and put the badge on and wore it, or still wear it, with pride and honor. Others went back to the farm . . . or just faded away."

"I wish I could have been there," Scrap said.

Something had caught Pete Feders's attention. Josiah noticed it, too. The crowd had begun to part. He glanced quickly back at Scrap and said, "No, you don't."

"Well, it's about damn time," Captain Fikes said, pushing toward the man Josiah assumed was Sheriff J. T. Patterson.

CHAPTER 5

The confrontation between Captain Fikes and Sheriff J. T. Patterson seemed to go on for an hour. Patterson was a short, stout man with a belly shaped like a whiskey barrel. Fikes wasn't much taller, but he was lean, and a fair fighter with little tolerance for any man who challenged his authority. No one in the crowd had the capacity or, it looked to Josiah, the desire to interfere between the two.

The men stood inches apart, belt buckle to belt buckle, shouting at each other, cursing at each other, accusing each other of being the cause for the attempted jailbreak.

When the sheriff called Captain Fikes a Nancy-boy, Josiah thought he'd gone too far. To his credit, the captain restrained himself, though it appeared to be a difficult task. There was no question the captain was particular about his dress and hair, but there was nothing the least bit feminine about Hiram Fikes.

At one point, Scrap Elliot started to join the captain's side. "He needs our help," he said. And just as swiftly as

Scrap had started to pull away from the small group of Rangers and jump into the fray, Pete Feders pulled him back like he was a baby bird trying to leave the nest too soon.

"Captain'll do just fine on his own, thank you."

Scrap was immediately dejected. The young Ranger hung his head down like a ten-year-old and sulked back behind Josiah. "He ain't no Nancy-boy. Somebody needs to make that polecat take it back," he muttered.

It was all Josiah could do to keep a straight face. He had seen a lot of eagerness in new soldiers before, but he couldn't remember one who seemed to match Scrap's unbidden enthusiasm. The boy had obviously earned his nickname the hard way.

Just when Josiah thought Captain Fikes had had enough of Sheriff J. T. Patterson's tirade and was going pull back his arm and punch the man square in the jaw, the captain jutted his right hand out, offering a handshake and putting an obvious and immediate end to the dispute.

A distinct sigh of relief rippled through the surrounding crowd.

The two men shook hands. Patterson was reluctant, but finally seemed to be glad that the confrontation had come to a fair end. They spoke a few more words that no one could hear or understand, then the sheriff headed inside the jail. Captain Fikes strode back to Josiah, Pete Feders, and Scrap.

"Damn Austin. This new Ranger law gives the sheriff more power than he ought to rightly have. Especially a fool like Patterson," the captain said. He was disgusted, but trying to remain reasonably quiet, as he could sense the crowd was dispersing around him cautiously. "He needs to ask for our assistance before we have any jurisdiction. And right now he doesn't think he needs anything from us. Not one lick of help. Not one Ranger outside the jail. Says we can escort Charlie Langdon out of town, but anything before then is in his hands as far as he's concerned. Last thing I need right now is word to get back to Major Jones that I've stepped out of line and gone up against the new law. Damn it. This just beats all. And calling me a Nancy-boy to boot. Any other time, I'd've given him a good fist and introduced him bone-to-flesh to Miss Nancy herself."

The captain made a fist, gritted his teeth, and let out a long sigh.

Josiah was fully aware of the power Major John B. Jones wielded at the moment. Jones was a member of Terry's Texas Rangers in the War Between the States, had been put in charge of the Frontier Battalion by Governor Coke, and had, as Josiah had learned from Captain Fikes, little tolerance for disorder or showmanship.

Josiah knew that Hiram Fikes had served under Major Jones in the 8th Infantry—Terry's Texas Rangers—and fought with him until the last engagement at Bentonville, North Carolina; hence the quick appointment to the rank of captain in the Frontier Battalion. It was interesting now to view a different, political, and uneasily restrained side of Captain Fikes.

Since the rules were all new to him, Josiah just stood back and watched it all play out, trying to figure where he fit in. The last thing he wanted to do was get involved in a fight between a badger and a skunk.

Josiah snuck in the back way to Clipper's stall, for fear that there were more of Langdon's men on the lookout for him.

Burly Smith was one less man to worry about. Word had come back to the crowd that he'd died from the wound the old Mexican had inflicted on the big man's throat. Now Josiah was worried about the Mexican's safety. Regardless of the circumstance, a Mexican killing an Anglo was sure to set some embers ablaze. There'd likely be a posse rounded up.

Knowing there was nothing he could do, and hoping the captain would be able to keep his old friend Juan Carlos out of trouble, Josiah rolled out his sleeping blankets in the corner and found himself more comfortable on a bed of hay than he thought he would be. Clipper seemed glad for the company, nudging Josiah slightly just after he settled in.

The familiarity of the open air, the smell of the livery, and Clipper's acceptance allowed a veil of calmness to fall over Josiah, but he did not slip off to sleep at first, not like in the bath at the Menger.

The Peacemaker was tucked next to his belly, and his long gun, a Sharps carbine, lay within reach.

He was a little more comfortable with the Sharps than he was the Colt, but the Sharps had been a constant companion for a matter of years. He knew what to expect when he pulled the trigger. Like everyone else, he had his eye on a new model Winchester, but the purchase of the Peacemaker had put the popular rifle out of his reach, for the moment.

The Rangers preferred their men to use a Sharps carbine, but Josiah figured once he and a lot of other fellas got a little regular money in their pockets, the Sharps would quickly be replaced by the Winchester by most every man in the Battalion. But for today he'd had enough of guns and blood.

He closed his eyes, and in his mind he reached out and unfolded a patchwork quilt of memories.

He kissed each of his girls good night; Fiona first—always first. Then he tickled Claire and Mavis like he always did. The memory of their laughter was his reward for living another day. From there he walked into a tiny room that held his only son, his only living child, and touched Lyle gently on the forehead, asking an unseen and unnamed God to look after his son and Ofelia while he was away. That was his nightly prayer, if it could be called that, his nightly routine.

Now he could rest.

Sometime near dawn, Clipper stirred and woke Josiah. Josiah barely moved, just enough to catch his breath and gain his senses.

Short fingers of dim gray light reached into the livery. A bird whistled and cleared its throat in the distance, then launched into full song, willing, it seemed, the sun to rise so Josiah would have the clarity of vision to see what was coming his way.

It surprised Josiah that morning was so close to breaking. He had figured Langdon's men were cowards, comfortable in the ways of darkness, using it as a shield and a weapon. He had expected they might pay him a visit before the night was over.

He gripped the Peacemaker as quietly and subtly as he could, then flicked open his eyes just in time to see a shadow duck across the gate of the stall.

Clipper snorted.

Whoever it was, he was behind Josiah, in between stalls, probably searching each one for his presence.

He hoped he was far enough in the corner to be out of sight.

As quietly as he could, Josiah propped himself against the outside wall, pushing himself into a mess of spiderwebs, and then fought the instinct to push the crawling critters off his bare arms. There were few things in the world he feared more than a spider. Sneaky, poisonous bastards could leave a good man lame with nothing more than a pinprick bite. He hoped like hell they weren't brown recluses.

As slowly and quietly as possible Josiah fully cocked the Peacemaker.

He'd learned early with the gun that leaving a chamber empty under the hammer was a good idea, almost a necessity, with the Peacemaker. The last thing he needed was a damaged gun that could go off at any time and a hammer that wasn't functional when he needed it most.

He had enough confidence in his shooting ability to give up one shot for the sake of his own well-being and the preservation of his weapon. Another hard lesson learned from the war: Protect your weapon at all times—there could be a time when it was the only friend you had, more trustworthy than any human being could ever hope to be.

"Señor, are you here?"

Josiah let out a sigh of relief. He recognized the voice immediately. It was the old Mexican's, Juan Carlos.

"Yes," he whispered, as he relieved the gun of its ready position. "I'm in the corner of the last stall."

Juan stepped out of the shadows and appeared at the gate. Clipper huffed a snort through his nose, then kicked up a bit of straw.

Josiah stood up and patted the Appaloosa on the shoulder. "Relax, old friend, there's nothing to worry about."

"Ah, Señor Ranger. It is good to find you well."

"Josiah. Josiah Wolfe." He extended his hand to the old man for a handshake. "I believe I am in your debt."

The Mexican looked at Josiah curiously, then grasped his hand firmly. A slight smile came to his leathery face. His wrinkles looked like crevices in the dim, gray light.

"I was just doing my job."

It took Josiah a moment to understand what the man had said. "Job" sounded like "yob." Deciphering Mexicans when they spoke English came relatively easy to Josiah, since he spent so much time around Ofelia, but his Anglo ears were just shy of fully awake, and a good, hot cup of coffee would go a long way to clear his head.

A spider crawled up his forearm. Josiah flicked it off and ground it to a quick death with the heel of his boot. The eight-legged carriers of pain and disease didn't deserve any more justice than they gave, as far as Josiah was concerned.

"My name is Juan Carlos. It was the charge of my friend, Captain Fikes, to keep you safe. I have come to apologize for my failure, señor."

"But I'm fine." Josiah held his voice just at a whisper since he did not want to draw any undue attention to the stall. He had made it through the night without an encounter with Charlie's gang, and he wanted to keep it that way. "If you wouldn't have sliced Burly Smith's throat, he was going to kill me."

"*Sí*, but I was led away, tricked, I think," Juan Carlos said, a forlorn look on his face. "They were carrying in the holy cross for the new *Sancti Antonii*, and I was distracted by a man, another Mexican I do not know, to witness the event."

Josiah shrugged; he did not understand.

Juan nodded. "The church should be complete before

the fall winds blow. The diocese will be here now. Along with all of the glory and the beauty of the Savior, change will come to the church itself."

Like in Austin, Josiah thought, but didn't say aloud. There sure seemed to be a lot of change going on in the world.

"They did not want a crowd," Juan Carlos continued, "until the cardinals are present. They will be on the grounds this morning as they lift the cross to its perch, to its resting place for the ages. But I will not be here. I will be riding in the length of Captain Fikes's shadow."

"You're a scout for the captain?"

"You could call me that. But that is not important, what I am for the captain. I only sought a moment for myself, and while I was away from my post you were . . ." Juan Carlos stopped and rolled his eyes upward as if he was searching for the right word. "Attacked," he finally said. "I beg your forgiveness."

Josiah stared at the old man and knew he was being truthful, that Juan Carlos's action had indeed caused him a lot of grief.

He understood. On the battlefield, when he was truly green and afraid, he had made shortsighted and selfish decisions that had caused a great deal of harm and pain, the loss of limbs by fellow soldiers and even death. The outcome of Juan Carlos's failure did not seem to be so severe in the end, but the man was weighted down by it.

"Really," Josiah said, "there is nothing to forgive. But I hold no ill will if that is what you seek."

"*Sí*, it is. Forgiveness is the journey of my soul. I have learned that the man, this Burly Jones, has died. I have committed a mortal sin, and now I must await my judgment. *Mi destino está en las manos de Dios*—My fate is in

God's hands," Juan Carlos said, translating himself as if it were a habit.

There was nothing else to say as far as Josiah was concerned. The matters of religion and faith left him feeling cold and empty. Some men found it easy to find God in the loneliness of the trail, in the wide-open spaces, in the fear of violence or on the battlefield. While for other men, like Josiah, God was lost there just as easily, after seeing the reality of life and death, the pain and suffering that came uninvited to the innocent.

For Josiah, there was no explanation of war to be found in a new church. A child dying in his arms did not seem natural to him, either—or right. How could a god of any kind allow something like that to happen?

It was not a question that Josiah was going to pose to Juan Carlos, even though he felt the old Mexican just might try and answer it. There seemed to be a different spirit about the old man, in the gray light of dawn, that gave Josiah just a little bit of comfort.

A moment of silence passed between Josiah and Juan Carlos. They stood face-to-face, each waiting, it seemed, for the other to say something of importance.

Outside the livery, the sun had broken over the horizon and the birds began to sing in earnest. A chorus of clucks, chirps, and pure song signaled that the day had started and darkness had been conquered once more.

Juan Carlos reached up and put his hand on Josiah's shoulder. "A long time ago, in another life, my failure caused the death of a good man, but it also brought me into the company of a man who is now my truest friend, Captain Hiram Fikes. It was a blessing and a curse at the time of my greatest sin. I have sought forgiveness since the day I fell from grace. Now I have committed another act against a fellow man."

Josiah looked at Juan Carlos curiously. "You saved my life."

"The sheriff will not see it that way."

"Captain Fikes will stand up for you."

"My salvation is not his fate. I shall not ask him to tarnish his horizons with the blood on my fingers."

"What will you do?"

Juan Carlos looked to the rafters of the stall, then back to Josiah. "I feel as though I have happened onto the dark circumstance of my own violent nature once again. As long as I am alive, Señor Josiah Wolfe, I will be in your debt, and I hope that we become fast friends, but I must face what comes."

"I would like that . . . being your friend," Josiah said, as he walked over and began collecting his bedroll. The captain would be waiting in front of the jail once the sun rose above the horizon.

When he turned around to ask Juan Carlos if he would join him for a bit of breakfast, there was no sign of the old man. He was gone.

CHAPTER 6

Charlie Langdon stood on the steps of the jail, his feet shackled, his hands bound by metal bracelets, connected by a three-link chain. A keyhole sat at the base of the bracelets, and Charlie's hands looked a little big for them to be comfortable. It was obvious he was not going to show one ounce of discomfort to the small crowd that had assembled to see him ridden out of town.

Someone had given Charlie a fresh shave, but it did not appear as though he had been afforded a bath or a fresh set of clothes. His clothes were ratty and worn, the knees sliced open and stained like he'd run through a berry patch trying to escape something, or someone. Still, if he had been let out of custody and left to wander the streets of San Antonio, the man whom Josiah and the other Rangers were charged with returning to Tyler for trial would have fit in without any notice. Nothing about Charlie made him stand out.

In age, Charlie Langdon was only a year or so older than

Josiah, near on thirty-five years old, though he looked like he could have been ten years older. His hair was solid black with gray streaks at the roots and on the sideburns. A thin scar ran under Charlie's right eye, a mark he'd gained in Chickamauga, in a blazing sword volley that left three men dead, and left Josiah stunned and intimidated by Charlie's level of skill with the long blade.

First in, last out, Charlie paid the price of being in the Brigade more than once, and Josiah was usually not too far behind him, running into battle in the shadow of one of the bravest, craziest, men he'd ever come to know. You had to respect any man with Charlie's dedication and fearlessness—regardless of whose side they fought on.

If the end of the war, Reconstruction, and running as an outlaw had taken a heavy toll on Charlie, it was in the physical form. He had always been a big, but spry, man—almost a head taller than most—but he seemed to have lost a little heft. He was far from bony, but he looked stiff, and his eyes were dull, lifeless, and a little sunken in.

Josiah would have judged him as tired and beaten if he hadn't known the man personally. But that might have been precisely what Charlie wanted everyone to think—that he was consumptive, ill, tired of being on the run, his life as an outlaw finally over.

Charlie Langdon was not beyond spinning a spidery ruse like the one Captain Fikes himself had spun to quash the jailbreak. Josiah made a mental note to clue in the captain, in a subtle way of course, about Charlie's talent for deception.

He'd seen Charlie play dead and feign injury more times than he could count, then watched in awe and horror as he rose up, almost as if resurrected by some preordained miracle, to fight hand-to-hand with an unsuspecting Union soldier as the rest of the Brigade retreated to safety.

Last out. Charlie Langdon was always the last man to lay down the sword, and along the way there was no right or wrong, no rules of fairness on the battlefield, just the swift delivery of his own brand of justice and, finally, the satisfied smile that always came to his face as the death of his victim—his sworn enemy the Union soldier or whoever it was at the moment—occurred at his hand.

Josiah was convinced that Charlie Langdon was born with a deep and abiding hate in the pit of his stomach and had never known a moment of love or tenderness.

The jail sat at an intersection on the northernmost corner of the street. Josiah was comfortably mounted atop Clipper, watching for a signal from Captain Fikes to proceed forward, to physically accept custody of Charlie Langdon from Sheriff Patterson. His view encompassed both events that had put a stranglehold on the streets of San Antonio—Charlie Langdon being escorted out of town and the cross being erected on the new diocese.

Josiah was focused as closely as possible on Charlie Langdon.

The captain and the sheriff were huddled in a conversation, standing behind Charlie—who looked bored, expressionless. A deputy stood slightly off to Charlie's right, brandishing a new Winchester. The rifle gleamed in the morning sunlight.

Down the street, a larger crowd had gathered in front of the church that was being constructed. It was no mistake, Josiah decided, that Charlie was being moved on such an eventful morning. The street beyond the jail would be clear, the focus of the populace on the cardinals who had come to bless the cross. There, the crowd could watch the heavy hand-carved stone cross hoisted high above the street, high above the parishioners and nonbelievers alike, and set on its perch for eternity. It would be a spectacle not to be missed.

Josiah was glad to be leaving San Antonio. But the competing crowds at the church and the jail made him nervous. He was not sure who was who—since Rangers didn't wear a badge or anything more to distinguish themselves than Charlie Langdon's gang did. He tried to watch everything—the rooftops, the horses, wagons, and stagecoaches coming and going—but there was too much to take in.

He was certain shots were going to ring out at any moment, that a rush of men would appear, their mission to rescue Charlie, their lack of concern about spilling blood clear in their approach—guns blazing, explosions going off that would make the one the night before pale in comparison, and the street littered with the bodies and blood of innocent onlookers whose only crime was curiosity and thrill-seeking.

Josiah knew his imagination was running free, but he had considered, thoroughly, what Burly Smith's intent was. If it wasn't for Juan Carlos, he'd be a dead man for sure.

Josiah shuddered at the thought.

Finally, the signal was given from the sheriff, and the handoff to the captain went smoothly.

Josiah sighed, holding a deep breath in his chest, so no one could see his physical reaction to the new responsibility. Taking custody of Charlie Langdon was akin to stepping in a rattlesnake hole. Sooner or later you were going to get bit.

Two of the three men who had been sitting with Captain Fikes at the gambling table in the Silver Dollar had returned from their scouting trip to Neu-Braunfels. They were sitting patiently in the lead of Charlie Langdon's horse.

As Josiah had assumed, the two men, Sam Willis and Viola "Vi" McClure, were new to the Rangers. They had been cattle hands and were now anxious to use their navigation skills at fighting the Comanche.

Neither seemed too happy about heading to Tyler, north instead of west—away from the conflicts with the Comanche, instead of headlong into battle. Ridding the land of rustlers and thieves was one thing; redskins, so Willis and McClure said, were another. Each man held a grudge against the Indians as deep as a water well.

Willis sat on a coal black stallion, a white star shining prominently on its narrow nose and a hand-tooled Mexican saddle, decorated with silver buckles and studs, secured to its strong back. McClure's horse strained under the weight of the large man, and he kind of looked like a big child riding a small blond pony.

Josiah saw no need to rush into battle with anyone, but he silently acknowledged both men's lack of fighting experience. They would come to understand that fighting to the death was something not to be taken lightly—or they would die in the process.

Scrap Elliot and Pete Feders sat at opposite sides of the horse Charlie was to ride, waiting patiently for the captain to mount his own horse and give the command to depart San Antonio once and for all. It wasn't Josiah's place to question the captain's tactics, but he hoped there were more Rangers than just the six of them to escort Charlie Langdon out of town.

Josiah held the captain's horse, a tall chestnut mare named Fat Susie—who was anything but fat—at the rear. The origin of the horse's name was not much of mystery to anyone who knew Captain Fikes, and much to the chagrin of the captain's wife. Fat Susie was supposedly a woman in Austin whose nighttime reputation was too delicate for discussion in polite company. The captain had taken a shine to her before he became an honest man and married the current Mrs. Fikes. Josiah was not sure, nor did he care, if the scuttlebutt were true. Fat Susie was a dependable horse, and that's all that mattered to him. He did imagine, though, that a horse as handsome as the chestnut mare was *did* mind the name.

Behind Josiah and Clipper were a couple of packhorses, loaded down with supplies. The ponies were Josiah's charge. Captain Fikes had told him that he wanted a good deal of distance kept between Josiah and Charlie Langdon once they were on the trail, even in camp.

A fly buzzed Josiah's nose as he watched the captain, and waited.

The captain was nodding, talking under his breath angrily, finishing up an obviously frustrating conversation with Sheriff Patterson.

Josiah swatted the fly, and scanned the crowd for a glimpse of Juan Carlos. Not surprisingly, the old Mexican was nowhere to be seen.

Josiah knew the captain and the sheriff were talking about the old man's fate for the killing of Burly Smith. It didn't sound like the captain was getting his way, and that didn't surprise Josiah in the least.

Juan Carlos had known he needed to sneak out of town, but from the sound of things, a posse was being formed to hunt down the Mexican, so he could be brought back for a trial. It didn't seem to matter to the sheriff that Burly Smith had been hired to kill Josiah, a Ranger at that, and had nearly succeeded. All that seemed to matter to the sheriff was that Juan Carlos was one more Mexican with Texan blood on his hands.

Josiah heard the words "fair trial" come from the sheriff's mouth. "And that's the final word, unless you want to take it up with the circuit court judge in the morning."

The captain spit on the ground, just missing Sheriff Patterson's mud-caked boot, and threw up his arms. "Let's move out of here before I shoot somebody and get myself thrown into that poor excuse for a jailhouse."

Sheriff J. T. Patterson shook his head, smirked, and watched his deputy lead Charlie Langdon to the waiting horse. The deputy unshackled Charlie's feet, then another deputy came and helped Charlie mount the horse.

Fikes watched, his arms folded. Josiah knew it was a stubborn move, not taking responsibility for Charlie until he had to, not ordering one of his Rangers to help Charlie mount the sad-looking mare the sheriff had provided. There'd be plenty of helping Charlie Langdon up and down off the horse on the trail—if the horse made it to Tyler alive. It was the most haggard, swaybacked creature Josiah had ever seen.

Charlie settled in on the saddle as best he could, and cast a sidelong glance back to Josiah. "Surprised to see you here, Wolfe."

"Bet you are."

"Heard Burly met his maker at the hand of a Mexican. Why doesn't it surprise me one bit that you'd have a Mexican watching your back?"

Josiah glared at Charlie. His stomach was rustling about like there was a swarm of bees let loose inside him. He wasn't scared—maybe nervous, maybe anticipating whatever it was that was coming next, because it wasn't going to be pleasant.

It was, he knew instinctively, going to be a long ride north, and he couldn't let Charlie see one buzzing bee of discomfort in his stomach or he'd be a dead man . . . sooner rather than later.

"Shut up," Captain Fikes said, as he mounted Fat Susie in one swift blur of movement. The captain's spryness never ceased to amaze Josiah, as did his directness.

Not one minute into the ride, and Josiah had already broken one of the captain's rules. He wasn't quite sure what had caused it . . . other than that Charlie always threw him off center when he was in his company. Always.

"Both of you just shut up," the captain continued to rant. "Don't make me regret my decision bringing you down here, Wolfe."

"Yes, sir. It was the right decision, sir."

Sheriff Patterson walked up to the captain and offered him the key to the metal bracelets that bound Charlie Langdon's wrists. Fikes snatched the key from the man's hand and stuffed it in his vest pocket.

"Stop in the office the next time you ride into town, Fikes. I want to know you're here."

The captain squinted his eyes, rolled his tongue in his mouth, and spit again. This time he hit his target dead-on. The sheriff's boot dripped with spit. At some point the captain had stuffed a fresh plug of tobacco in his check, and he'd been working up a mouthful of stringy brown juice to release at just the right moment.

Scrap had to restrain himself from laughing out loud.

Without saying another word, Captain Fikes let out a yell that sounded like a whoop, then waited for Sam Willis and Vi McClure to get the escort party moving.

Sheriff Patterson started cursing the captain and the Rangers as they began to move forward. Fikes ignored the sheriff, stared straight ahead like the man had never existed.

Out of the corner of his eye, Josiah was certain he saw a quick smile pass across Captain Hiram Fikes's weathered face as they rode out of shouting distance, but he couldn't be quite sure. The captain always celebrated his victories in subtle ways.

Now that they were on the way, Fikes was focused on his prisoner, and there was no mistaking the tension that came from escorting a man as dangerous and loathsome as Charlie Langdon. The tussle with the sheriff was the last thing the captain would be worried about.

Though Josiah was sure that Juan Carlos's well-being wasn't too far out of Fikes's mind.

CHAPTER 7

San Antonio disappeared quickly behind Josiah and the other Rangers. It did not take the horses long to find a comfortable rhythm. Even the supply ponies and the heavy breather that Charlie was riding offered no restraint or stubbornness as they eased up a slight ridge on the trail.

Josiah stared at the back of Charlie Langdon's head for the longest time, trying to force himself not to remember all of the times he had ridden with the man in the past. Obviously, the bees were still buzzing in his stomach, and the last thing he wanted to do was show Charlie, or the captain, any fear . . . so he began whistling.

Lily played the piano, and the only songs Josiah knew were a few waltzes and some church songs. He avoided the church songs, and as he whistled a waltz, a song of happier days, he could almost smell Lily's skin, her neck resting on his shoulder at a social dance when they were courting. He would rather ride away the hours wrapped in the memory of the music Lily loved than the memories of the war as he rode behind a killer like Charlie Langdon. He was desperate to rid himself of all the wartime memories that had come surging back to him since seeing Charlie. He hadn't expected that to happen.

Captain Fikes looked at Josiah in surprise once he began whistling, then nodded, giving silent permission for him to continue on. It was nearly afternoon. The sun was already high in the sky, and even though it was still spring, mid-May, the air was hot and dry. There was hardly any breeze at all. The wind was silent and the sky vacant of clouds. Josiah's whistling echoed off the boulders and cliff faces.

All of the Rangers had sweat on their brows.

The trail was reasonably wide, and the rocky landscape was mostly brown and dull, in comparison to the lushness around Tyler. East Texas and its vast pine forests, where everything was as green as green could be, seemed like it was a world away. There were splashes of color, though, like a spattering of bluebonnets along the trail, spring wildflowers that were starting to bloom into their prime.

Farther off the trail, the bluebonnets gave way to a few yellow flowers—primroses, buttercups—with some verbena mixed in. The early season had to have been wet considering that some of the flowers were almost thriving—though struggling by comparison to the lush wildflowers around Josiah's cabin and in the forests that surrounded his barn and pasture.

Josiah decided that life in and around San Antonio must have been far more difficult than he'd realized, or cared to think about.

He had never had the wanderlust, and he was thankful for that. Having a home to return to at the end of a long ride had always meant the world to him. Even now, he looked forward to returning to what was familiar. Pine trees. The smell of Ofelia's menudo simmering in the pot—honeycomb tripe, chilies, calf's foot, and some hominy, all joining together to warm a home that was once alive and throbbing with the giggles of three little girls. He really missed the familiar, but mostly Josiah was stricken with how much he longed to see his son.

He gazed upward, whistling softly, and studied the stiff oak trees that reached to the sky with grizzled fingers and towered over the trail.

The trees looked a hundred years old to Josiah. Just the sight of them made him a little melancholy. The big old trees had survived the sun, storms, rain, and probably fire, too. A few of them bore scars from lightning strikes, black wounds that looked like they would never heal. Josiah felt an odd kinship with the old trees.

High in one of them, a cuckoo clucked away at the sun, or called for a mate, Josiah wasn't sure. Most every other creature had taken refuge from the heat of the day.

Hunting was done in the early morning, late evening, or at night. Killing in the bright heat of the day was either out of necessity or for pleasure. Anything with any sense, or knowledge of the natural way of things, was fast asleep under a rock or some well-sought-out shade.

More than a few times, out of the corner of his eye Josiah thought he saw shadows moving. But, when he focused his sight, there was nothing to be seen in the thickets or on the hilltops except a stand of trees or the occasional hawk soaring high in the sky, casting a shadow downward—like a harbinger of some foreboding darkness to come, his cry carrying effortlessly in the dry air for miles.

Josiah's imagination was playing tricks on him again. He thought his awareness was reasonably keen, but he still felt uncertain of most everything he saw or thought about doing. His senses weren't as sharp as they had been on the battlefield, where day after day living and dying hinged on killing and not being killed.

It would take a long time to get back to that place, that process of consideration where physical survival was the only thing that mattered. Even with all that had happened in San Antonio, especially at the Menger with Burly Smith, he still didn't feel threatened, or fully awake to what was happening around him.

Josiah wasn't sure if he could ever regain the skill he'd possessed as a young soldier. Maybe that was something to consider about becoming a Ranger at this age, he thought to himself. Maybe he could never recapture the enthusiasm that was so apparent in Scrap Elliot's every word and deed.

Either way, now was not the time to judge himself as inept. He was far from that—he just wasn't as sharp as he used to be. Time had taken his thoughts and skills prisoner, and he had to figure out how to release them, free them from the past.

He knew one thing to be true if nothing else, though: Charlie Langdon was being too quiet, too compliant.

Something was up, he was sure of it.

Leaving the jail had been too easy.

The crowds had parted and watched solemnly. Not once did anyone try to stop the escort from leaving town. It seemed like the entire population of San Antonio was glad to see Charlie and the Rangers go.

Captain Fikes brought the party to a stop about three hours after leaving San Antonio.

Josiah stopped whistling.

They had come down an easy sloped hill and gathered in

a clearing, their formation around Charlie still reasonably tight.

There were hills on all sides of them—but the hills were distant, too distant for some unseen shooter, outlaw or Indian, to attack from and take cover in.

The trail was wide, and in the mud there were wheel ruts that ran into and out of a slow-running stream. At some point in history, the spot had sported a population of settlers. There were a few foundations alongside the trail, cracked slabs of stone lying about haphazardly and crumbling remnants of buildings or houses that looked like giant footprints. It had not been a big town, only three or four buildings at the most, probably a stagecoach stop at some point, but now all of the buildings were gone—the wood rotted, stolen, or burned by travelers in need of a nighttime fire.

Josiah listened and looked around, trying to figure out if there was a railroad anywhere close, trying to solidify his bearings. That's what had happened to his town, Seerville—the railroad hadn't come close enough to keep it alive—but that didn't appear to be the case here. There was no railroad in San Antonio or this part of South Texas yet, and from what Josiah understood, it would be a few more years, or longer, before that life-changing event occurred.

Whatever the cause, the town was gone, just a memory. And the place made Josiah uneasy, because there were plenty of places for cover close-up.

Across the stream, through a healthy grove of pecan trees, sat a cemetery. The weeds around the grave markers were already tall. A few yucca plant spikes reached to the sun, not yet in bloom. It was no surprise that the cemetery was in disrepair, a neglected garden of crosses and broken-down picket fencing used to keep the animals and any other unwelcome creatures out. The fencing had been trampled. Some of the grave markers had toppled over a long time ago.

"Let's water the horses, men," the captain said, as he dismounted from Fat Susie.

"Man ought to be able to relieve himself," Charlie Langdon muttered.

Captain Fikes stalked over to Charlie's horse and glared up at the man, shaking a finger as he yelled, "You obviously don't understand the rules here, mister. You speak when you're spoken to. You piss when I say you can piss. I don't want to hear another word from you until I tell you to dismount—and when that happens, there will be six guns pointed at that empty head of yours. So don't go thinking we're a bunch of idiots. Do I make myself clear?"

Scrap Elliot, who had been holding the rope on Charlie's horse throughout the trip from San Antonio, jumped off his own horse, placing himself directly between Charlie and the captain.

Josiah watched Charlie closely, and saw his lip twitch just slightly at the left corner of his hard, pursed mouth. Josiah started to warn the captain, because he knew something was coming, but it was too late.

Charlie kicked his right foot up as hard as he could and caught Scrap Elliot just under the chin.

"Son of a bitch!" Scrap yelled as he flipped backward, nearly knocking Captain Fikes to the ground.

Charlie Langdon laughed, but stopped suddenly midway through his guffaw.

In one swift motion, Pete Feders had pulled the hammer on his Colt and stuck the barrel in Charlie's ear. "You'd do best to shut up and be apologetic to the captain and Ranger Elliot, Mr. Langdon. I'd hate for your ride to end before you got a chance to relieve yourself."

The smile fell from Charlie's face like a curtain falling on a fancy theater show. "I ain't apologizing to no one. I've been sitting here mindin' my own business for miles. Seems to me this young feller wasn't paying attention."

Peter Feders pushed the gun harder against Charlie's ear. "I said apologize."

"That'll be enough, Sergeant Feders." The captain pulled Scrap to his feet, and the young Ranger rubbed his jaw furiously.

Josiah had jumped off Clipper, and in a matter of seconds had the Sharps carbine aimed squarely at Charlie's head.

Willis and McClure had their guns drawn on the prisoner, as well. One false move, and Charlie Langdon would meet his maker, without the pleasure of a trial or a crowd at the hanging. He'd be riddled with enough bullet holes for plenty of daylight to shine though on a gloomy day.

There was still a twitch in Charlie's lip that Josiah could see. No one else seemed to notice.

"I'd stand away from the coward, Scrap. And Pete, watch his hands," Josiah said, coming up alongside the captain.

"Do as he says, Sergeant," Fikes ordered.

There had not been any rank mentioned among the six Rangers until that moment. Josiah wasn't surprised—the Rangers worked in a loose fashion, not as defined militarily as the Brigade—but there was definitely rank among the members.

Pete Feders carried himself like a soldier, so it came as no surprise to Josiah that he had been deemed a leader.

It did surprise him, though, that the captain had not made them all aware of the chain of command. So Josiah was glad to see the captain wasn't offended by his observations about Charlie's possible actions.

"Wolfe knows this man better than any of us. You'd do well to heed his advice," the captain said.

"Josiah Wolfe doesn't know a damn thing about me," Charlie said.

"Do I need to strap you to a tree and whip you with a pistol, Langdon?" the captain snapped. "You don't speak until you are spoken to. I'm not going to repeat myself again."

Charlie Langdon drew in a deep breath and glared at Josiah. His eyes were black and cold. A look Josiah had seen more than once.

"Get him down," Fikes said to Willis and McClure. Then he turned to Scrap. "You all right, boy?"

Scrap nodded his head yes. "Fine, Captain. I'm just fine." He wiped a stream of blood from the corner of his mouth.

Pete Feders pulled his Colt back as Charlie slid off his horse into the confined custody of Willis and McClure. Neither man looked too happy about the prospect of leading Charlie off the trail to relieve himself, but Josiah wasn't going to volunteer for that duty. He was going to be ready with the Sharps, and not take his eyes off Charlie Langdon for a second.

Scrap Elliot had wandered over to the stream and started rinsing out his mouth, muttering curse words under his breath.

"I'll need you to be a sergeant as well, Wolfe, but Feders has a little more recent time by my side. He was with me when he caught up with Charlie there. He's my first sergeant, but I need you to fall into step right behind him."

"I understand."

"McClure and Willis know how to do their jobs. Once we get this prisoner delivered, then move on to the Red

River camp, I'm hoping the rest of the company'll be mustered. Be plenty of room for a man with your fighting experience to advance if you so desire. I think the future is bright for the Rangers now that Governor Coke has taken office. And I can't imagine a better man than Jones to lead us all. We'll all be better off serving under a man like him."

"I appreciate your confidence, Captain." Josiah did not look the captain in the eye as was his normal manner. His gaze was fixed on Charlie and the two Rangers. They were about ten yards off the trail. A hawk screeched overhead, and a chill ran down Josiah's spine. "I sure don't trust him," he added, almost in a whisper.

"Just keep your head about you. Holler if you see something we don't. You seem to have an eye for his trickery."

"I've seen Charlie Langdon kill more men than I can rightly count, Captain. And most of them didn't see a thing coming their way until it was too late."

Pete Feders had remained mounted on his horse. His attention was drawn behind them—something the captain and Josiah noticed right away.

The sound of horses running full-out reached their ears, a low thunder growing louder, and a plume of dust became visible on the horizon, heading directly toward them.

Charlie Langdon had noticed, too. A slow smile crossed his face, then disappeared as quickly as it had appeared.

CHAPTER 8

By the time the first rider became fully visible, Willis and McClure had secured Charlie Langdon back up on his horse.

All six Rangers surrounded their charge, guns at the ready.

Josiah and the captain had agreed that the coming horsemen were most likely members of a gang sent to set Charlie free. There was no way that was going to happen—not without a fight, anyway. There was not a man among them, as far as Josiah could tell, who would not lay down his life to protect the people of Texas, and save them from one more vengeful ride of a criminal who should have been jailed, or hanged, a long time ago.

Josiah wasn't thrilled at the idea of taking a bullet because of Charlie Langdon, but he'd damn well take a bullet for Captain Hiram Fikes. The last man who'd given him a second chance, who'd shown any sign of faith or belief in Josiah like the captain had, was his father—and that was so long ago, just after his return from the war, he had nearly forgotten the simple act of encouragement. It was the day his father signed over the deed to the small farm just outside Seerville.

The approaching horses were louder now, a storm trying to gain its strength. It was surprising to Josiah that the gang would approach in such a brash manner—in broad daylight, without the aid of any cover. Though it was a tactic that seemed much in line with Charlie Langdon's talent in planning attacks.

Scrap Elliot seemed to be the only one who was outwardly nervous about the visit from the unknown riders.

He couldn't quite keep his horse from fidgeting back and forth like she was getting ready to run a race. The horse was a young blue roan mare Scrap called Missy, and she looked like she was about three hands too tall for the kid.

That's what Josiah considered Scrap, a kid, and there had been moments when he wanted to ask the captain why he'd brought Elliot on as a Ranger, but he never got around to it, never really figured it was any of his business. He was just curious, because so far the only quality that Scrap Elliot exhibited was an unyielding enthusiasm for clumsiness and the trouble that always seemed to follow.

Captain Fikes was getting annoyed at Scrap, casting angry glances his way. But he didn't say anything—he just spit tobacco juice at the ground more frequently than normal, trying to stay focused on the riders.

Scrap's horse, Missy, continued to struggle at the bit like she had seen a rattler.

There were no snakes on the ground that Josiah could see—just a nervous owner who lacked the horsemanship to quiet his beast. The thought made Josiah uneasy about Scrap's shooting skills. He hoped he would never have to rely on the kid to cover his back.

Charlie Langdon's face was expressionless. He just stared off in the distance like he was biding his time. If he had smiled at first sight of the riders, he wasn't showing his hand now.

The first rider was followed by three more men.

As they got closer, Josiah was certain he recognized the rider in the lead—he was sure it was Sheriff J. T. Patterson. Even so, he didn't relax his finger on the Peacemaker's trigger.

"Feders, stay here with the rest of the men. Wolfe, come with me," the captain ordered. There was a scowl on his face that convinced Josiah he'd recognized the lead rider as J. T. Patterson, too.

Fikes spurred Fat Susie and tore away from the cool spot in the road, kicking up a cloud of dust of his own, in a huff.

Josiah followed close behind, holding the reins with one hand and balancing his carbine with the other.

The four riders did not slow as they were approached by the captain.

They had their guns drawn as well, and bandannas covering half their faces, which didn't make too much sense to Josiah. The sheriff had most certainly figured out who they were approaching. One of the men was a black man, most of his face shielded by a red bandanna. He was a big man, and stood out from the rest, not only because of his skin color, but because of his sheer size—if Burly Smith was a boulder, this man was a mountain. Josiah was surprised Sheriff Patterson was riding with a Negro.

Finally about twenty feet away, the four men brought their horses to a stop. The captain and Josiah did the same, kicking up another round of dust as they circled the sheriff and his men. Their horses exhaled heavily. Clipper kicked at the ground with his right front leg once Josiah got him settled down.

"That's a fine way to get shot," Fikes said, holstering his Colt.

"Be a fine way for you to get hanged, too, Fikes." The sheriff followed suit, putting away his weapon, pulling the loosely knotted bandanna down so he could speak. None of his men joined in—they kept their guns handy, though pointed away from the captain and Josiah.

Josiah held on to the carbine, and made sure he wasn't threatening anyone with it. He didn't want to be the spark that lit the fire. There was an obvious nervousness and tension in the air, and one false move could have prompted a full-blown shoot-out.

"Not going to be my day to be hanged today," the captain said.

"Day's not over with yet."

"So what's your hurry? You come up on us like you're running a posse."

"I told you we were going to bring in that Mexican. My man, O'Reilly here, tracked him close behind you right out of town. You harboring a criminal, Captain Fikes?"

Patterson had motioned to the man on a horse right behind him wearing a long red beard, dirty white hat, and a fringed buckskin coat that looked like it was more suited for winter than a South Texas spring day. O'Reilly wasn't one of the deputies Josiah had seen in all the commotion in San Antonio.

Now that he looked closer, he saw that neither were the other two riders—at least, he didn't think so. They were strangers just like O'Reilly. And neither wore a badge. Only the sheriff had a star pinned to his chest. The two men kept the bandannas on their faces even though the dust had cleared. O'Reilly pulled his ratty bandanna down and breathed heavily.

The tracker stared at Josiah and the captain with blue eyes as hard as a gun barrel, but said nothing to defend what the sheriff had said about Juan Carlos skirting the Rangers' ride. There was not a bead of sweat to be seen on the man's sunburned face. He had a wise look about him, like some of the other trackers Josiah had encountered over the years. There was no reason to doubt that what Sheriff Patterson had said was true . . . but Josiah *did* doubt that Juan Carlos was careless enough to lead a posse straight to Captain Fikes. At least, he hoped he could doubt Juan Carlos in that way. It made no sense to him otherwise.

O'Reilly squinted, narrowing his eyes into an even harder glare at Josiah. It was like he was trying to start something, provoke Josiah into challenging him.

Some people hated the Irish about as much as they hated Mexicans, Josiah thought to himself. But he didn't say anything. It would take more than a glare to provoke him.

The other two riders remained quiet, their shaded eyes darting at every movement.

Josiah turned away from O'Reilly and kept his own eyes on the other riders, specifically their gun hands.

He would have preferred to have a new model Winchester in his possession, instead of the carbine, since he could fire off the rounds quicker, but the carbine would have to do . . . for now.

The two riders did not look like typical lawmen any more than O'Reilly, the tracker, did.

"I am harboring a criminal, yes," the captain said.

"Figured as much."

"You should have—you watched me ride out of town with him."

"Not Langdon, you damned old fool."

"He's the only criminal I've seen all day. Though I'm starting to wonder what side of the law you truly stand on."

"The side that sees the necessity for one man to stand trial for killing another."

Josiah started to bite his tongue. He wanted to have his say about Juan Carlos, but he wasn't sure what the captain's reaction would be if he jumped into the fray, so he continued to restrain himself. Though he didn't know how much longer he could keep quiet.

"There won't be a fair trial for that Mexican, and you know it," Captain Fikes said. "No Mexican's ever got a trial that wasn't tainted in some way or the other."

Sheriff Patterson did not offer any sign that would suggest he disagreed with the captain. Nor did he indicate that he cared in the least about the welfare of a Mexican. He just stared past Josiah to the other Rangers and Charlie Langdon.

"You wouldn't mind if we look over yonder for a sign of the Mexican. I sure don't mean to imply that a revered captain in the Rangers would lie. You still call yourself that don't you, Fikes? A Ranger? Last I heard you were conducting raids on innocents with the State Police."

"There is no such organization called the State Police these days."

"A change of name doesn't stop a man's memory of the misdeeds carried out in the past."

"I suppose what matters is the man determining what the misdeeds are. What side of the law he stands on."

"Governor Davis seemed none too impressed with some of the misdeeds committed by his past emissaries."

"Did you ride all the way out here to bicker about the politics in Austin, Patterson? Maybe you should protest where it matters. It's a three-day ride last time I made the trip."

"I believe I have better things to do with my time these days. Nothing will be the same under Coke. Davis should have never gave in, and surrendered the office. Now, are you going to allow us to take a look around?"

Josiah determined that the captain and the sheriff stood on opposite political sides. Most any two men in Texas did these days, but that didn't fully explain the contention that weighed heavily between these two.

Patterson had implied that the captain had carried out a misdeed . . . in the name of the State Police. Which seemed odd. The captain had always been a Ranger, and never worked in the capacity of the State Police as far as Josiah knew. But the last couple of years had been difficult for Josiah, left him out of touch. Maybe the captain had ridden with the State Police in some capacity, but it would have only been because the Rangers were poorly funded under Governor Davis.

Any notion of a misdeed having occurred would depend on whose moral code that deed, or misdeed, was siphoned through, who was doing the judging. Josiah didn't trust a man like J. T. Patterson. The sheriff seemed bitter, angry about having to let go of the ways of the past. Being an expert in that quality himself allowed Josiah to recognize with certainty the man's character. The man craved power, and for some reason he had chosen to challenge the captain to prove his own worth.

Whatever the cause of the dislike that existed between the two men, all Josiah could hope for at the moment was that his new Mexican friend was safe—and smarter than an Irish tracker. He scanned the horizon as quickly as he could, hoping to see a sign of Juan Carlos's presence, a shadow that assured him the man was at a safe distance, watching . . . but he saw nothing.

Captain Fikes stroked his chin. “You don’t need my permission to ride past my men, Sheriff. Not if you’re to be on your way.”

“Well, that I am. I’ve wasted enough time tussling with you for one day—a year for that matter, but our business is unfinished for now. Your man could be miles away.”

“For his sake, I hope so.”

“Just as I thought,” Patterson said.

Fikes nodded. “Just as you thought—you’re right this time, Patterson. But I have no criminal in my custody other than Charlie Langdon. And the sooner I am free of that low-life pearl, the better off my life will be.”

Sheriff Patterson swung his horse around with a nod and a glare, ordered his men to follow him, then headed slowly up the trail toward the waiting Rangers.

Fikes and Josiah held back, waiting a good minute or two before trotting slowly after the posse. “Shoot first and ask questions later if it comes to that,” the captain said, barely in a whisper.

Josiah nodded.

Patterson and O’Reilly split and each paired up with one of the other two men, then they all circled Charlie Langdon like a kettle of buzzards, black-winged birds swirling in the air like a mountain-sized stew pot.

Pete Feders sat erect on his horse, unwavering and quiet, not looking to Captain Fikes for any orders. He already knew what to do. There was no question about that.

The wind had kicked up a bit, and a few dirt devils swirled to life in the broad dry patches beyond the towering oaks, between the hills and the cemetery. Other than the sound of the wind and the steady gait of horse hooves hitting the ground, the air was quiet. Not one bird bothered to sing or shriek in warning. It was easy to guess that they were all watching, though, with a heightened fear of humans.

Charlie Langdon snickered, then started calling the sheriff every name he could probably think of . . . trying to light a fire, trying to create an opportunity for escape.

Josiah had seen him do it before.

Once in Suffolk, three Union soldiers had made the mistake of capturing Charlie and not taking their captive as seriously as they should have. Before it was all said and done, each man was dead, or lay dying, from wounds inflicted by his own weapon.

There were other times, but that was just the first one to come to Josiah's mind. And the lesson was clear: Never leave a knife open to a man like Charlie Langdon, or it would be the last regret a man had before he died a slow, painful death.

Luckily for all of their sakes, no one was riled by Charlie's onslaught of insults. O'Reilly's face reddened when he was called a Mick, but beyond that, the trick did not take.

The posse gathered up, and the sheriff commanded them to go forward, north on the trail, away from San Antonio.

They took off like they had set a house on fire and were afraid of getting caught.

Captain Fikes didn't say a word until the sheriff and his riders were out of sight. "I sure don't understand how a damn fool like J. T. Patterson got himself elected as sheriff of San Antonio—and come to think it, I probably don't want to know." He spit a load of tobacco juice to the ground and shook his head in disgust. "We haven't seen the last of that bunch."

For once, Josiah hoped the captain was wrong. But he doubted that he was.

CHAPTER 9

The air dramatically cooled as night fell. Two jackrabbits roasted over a healthy fire. The cooking meat was a welcome smell to Josiah, overtaking the stink of trail sweat; his own, as well as the other Rangers'.

Charlie Langdon seemed to revel in his own filth. Anyone within three feet of the criminal could tell he had not been afforded a bath since his capture . . . and he didn't seem to mind. Josiah knew the last thing on Charlie Langdon's mind would be the cleanliness of his own person. What mattered to Charlie Langdon more than anything else would be surviving first, and being free second. He was as patient as a heron stalking a minnow—he would wait to strike at the most appropriate moment, when there was no doubt his attack would result in the highest amount of intended success. Given the opportunity to escape, he would surely be ready.

Josiah was surprised Charlie hadn't tried anything before now, beyond kicking Scrap Elliot when he got down off his horse. That was just a message for the greenhorn to keep his distance—but it was a message to everyone else as well: Give Charlie Langdon as much space as possible. Josiah hoped everyone in the escort party had paid attention.

All things considered, it had been a harder ride from San Antonio than he'd thought it would be. In a way he was glad to be riding with a group of men for once, but rarely was there a moment when it was possible for Josiah to let down his guard. Now he was tired, and glad for a moment's rest once the camp had been set. But he continued to keep a close eye on Charlie, who sat, wrists still bound by the metal bracelets, across the fire from Josiah.

Willis and McClure had bound the prisoner's feet together with a strong piece of rope once they'd hoisted him off the horse and led him to his resting place for the night—every gun in the camp trained on Charlie's egg-shaped head. One false move and he'd be full of holes, and nobody knew that better than Charlie himself. He didn't speak a word, hadn't since he'd been placed in front of the fire glaring at Josiah.

Scrap Elliot had first watch, and Josiah was thankful for the quietness in the camp.

Elliot never seemed to shut up. It was like silence scared him. Josiah figured Scrap was sitting on a boulder just at the crest of the hill they had settled on, muttering all kinds of nonsense to himself. Didn't matter, as long as he didn't have to hear it . . . but the kid sure was starting to grate on his nerves.

The horses had been corralled, watered, and fed, and were resting comfortably under a spindly oak. They had left the stream several hours ago. The landscape was almost barren, quiet and lifeless now.

Captain Fikes, Pete Feders, and Sam Willis were huddled together just off to Josiah's left. They sat in a semicircle about ten feet from the fire, among their bedrolls, backs to everyone else, participating in a hushed conversation. Josiah didn't know Willis very well and didn't think too much of the threesome holding a private talk. But other concerns were on his mind.

He hoped he would have time in between delivering Charlie and leaving for the Red River camp to spend a little time with his son, Lyle. It was something he would have to talk to the captain about. But now was not the time. Josiah had enough sense about him not to interrupt the meeting.

Instead, his gaze shifted to Vi McClure, who was steadily tending to the rabbits.

McClure was a big man with black shoulder-length hair that curled up over his collar. Josiah guessed the Scot to be a few years younger than himself, probably a little too young to have any wartime experience—it was hard to tell.

McClure's eyes were dark and a bit brooding, and he wore a serious look on his face most of the time. There was a slight hint of a Scottish brogue when he spoke, but it was distant, like he had been born in the States but lived among people who spoke in the tongue and language of his home country from the time he was a child.

Josiah had never heard pure Scottish spoken before. There were plenty of German immigrants in Texas; Chinese, too, and plenty of Mexicans—so he had heard a lot of different languages over the years, just not Scottish—or Irish, now that he thought about it. He wondered what it sounded like. The idea of languages had always fascinated him, but not enough to learn any more than he had to understand and communicate with Ofelia in some basic sort of way, and with some of the help he had around the farm.

McClure and Willis appeared to have an easy relationship, a bond that seemed to be as strong as the captain and Pete Feders's. Josiah thought the two men were probably friends off the trail, and there wasn't an apparent rank between the two of them. Neither seemed in charge of the other.

There were few men in the world Josiah really considered true friends, though he didn't feel envy, or regret for that matter, when he saw it. He had always been more comfortable on his own. But watching McClure hustle around the fire, tending to a pot of boiling vegetables, all the while baking a round of biscuits and warming a fresh pot of coffee, was comforting to Josiah. The smells made his stomach growl.

The grumbling noise brought a quick smile to McClure's face. "You got a wee bit of hunger in you there, Wolfe?"

Josiah smiled. "A bit, yes."

"Won't be long now."

"You sure seem to know your way around the fire. It's good to have a cook among us. If I was on my own, it'd be a jerky supper."

"My sweet mother, bless her heart, taught me to cook. Said a man needed to know how to fend for himself out on the land. Not too many womenfolk are likely to stick around a wandering oaf like myself, and I suppose she knew that. Course I'd be a lot more comfortable with a pile of sheep innards than the cow beef, but I've learned to make do."

Josiah grimaced at the thought of innards, but said nothing. "Is she in Scotland?"

McClure looked at Josiah questioningly. "My ma?"

Josiah nodded.

"No. Heaven." McClure made a cross from his forehead

to his chest and across. "She came to this country with me in her belly. I spent the years of my boyhood in Kentucky. The war was a hard time for us. Both my parents are dead and gone now. My poor ole dad was a soldier, killed at Gettysburg. I think my ma died of a broken heart after that. I was nearly grown, but not old enough to go off and fight . . . though I wanted to. I ran away as many times as I could. Darn near got myself killed a few times. When I saw how that affected my ma, I just planted my feet and waited to leave when it was the right time. Guess a man can't run into nature. Nature has to run into him. Just wasn't my time to fight. I left three days after she journeyed to Heaven. I've never been back to Kentucky since. It was a land of death and destruction as far as I was concerned, and I wanted to be as far away from the memories of war as possible."

Josiah nodded again. The war had been a hard time for most everyone he knew or met. It was hard to believe that the fighting had ended nine years prior. It seemed like yesterday that he was in Suffolk. And some men still carried the fire of the war with them. It wasn't over for everyone. Not even Josiah on some days.

McClure continued to fuss around the fire.

"There's going to be hell to pay if my biscuits burn," Charlie said.

The big Scot stopped and glared at Charlie. "If I was you, Mr. Langdon, I wouldn't be so certain on getting a bit of supper." He paused and cast a glance over to the captain, and then added, "Especially if you're going to continue to be such a disagreeable man."

Josiah ignored Charlie, who seemed surprised that he might be deprived of food.

"So, you're a Ranger now?" Josiah asked McClure.

"I am. I met Sam in my travels, and he hails from near

Austin. This is the most beautiful country I ever saw. I hope to never leave. We were working the cattle lands for a while, but the Comanche were always causing us grief. We figured joining up with the Rangers would be a good thing for us both. I never plan on leaving Texas."

"It's good to have a home. A place where it feels like you belong."

"'Tis. Most certainly 'tis. I plan on buyin' a piece of land outside of Austin. Start a family of my own someday."

"You should have joined up with the Travis Rifles. You wouldn't have to travel so much."

The Rifles, a small but formidable militia in Austin, was getting a lot of press in the newspapers lately. They had physically escorted Governor Davis out of the capitol, making way for Coke to take his duly elected seat. If Josiah had been a betting man, he'd have put down a week's wages that a lot of the men in the Rifles would become Rangers sooner or later.

"Well, you see, Sam is my best mate, and he has known the captain for a long time. There's no other man I'd rather be ridin' with. If this is where I'm meant to be, then that's that. 'Tis a better day at the side of my friend than on the trail alone. Rangering is going to be an adventure, and the Rifles aren't Indian fighters. I'm anxious for my first trip into Indian Territory with a group of like-minded men."

Josiah nodded that he understood.

McClure was not the first Ranger he had met who did not originally come from Texas, but he sure seemed like one of the most interesting. The Scot was confident in his movements, his voice was musical, and he really took pleasure in cooking. Josiah was enjoying being in camp with Vi McClure.

It was a good way to end the day, he thought, as the big

man handed him a plate of steaming food that looked fit enough for a king to feast on.

"That ought to take the bite out of your stomach," Vi McClure said with a huge a smile crossing his face.

"I believe it will," Josiah said. "I believe it will."

Scrap Elliot nudged Josiah's boot cautiously with the butt of his rifle. Being a light sleeper had always been a dependable trait for Josiah, but he was as much out of the habit of sleeping on the ground as Clipper. The trip had taken more out of him than he'd anticipated.

He barely roused at the nudge.

Scrap had to put a little more persuasion against his boot the second time around.

Josiah sat straight up, reaching for the carbine at his side. "What?" He had been in a dreamless state. At least he thought so. There was no memory of anything other than a full, satisfied belly as he quickly fell asleep. Vi McClure's supper was about the best food he'd ever tasted on the trail.

"It's your watch," Scrap said.

Josiah wiped open his eyes, caught a whiff of lingering smoke from the coals in the fire pit. The embers glowed orange. The sky was black and cloudless. Stars with pulsing silver tips filled Josiah's gaze—they did not give enough light to navigate away from the bedroll, so he sat for a moment gathering his bearings.

It was clear it was the middle of the night. The moon was nowhere to be seen.

"Been pretty quiet, with the exception of a few coyotes yipping about," Scrap whispered.

Charlie Langdon snored loudly, capturing their attention for a second. Satisfied the outlaw was still sound asleep, and was no threat, Josiah slipped on his boots. "Good," he said. "Didn't figure you'd have any trouble."

"I'm worried that Langdon's gang is laying in wait."

"Did you hear something?"

Scrap hesitated. "It was probably a critter, but I thought I heard a horse at the bottom of the hill. I only heard it once."

"How long ago?'

"'Bout an hour ago. Might have been a stray."

Josiah stood and wiped the chill off his arms. "I doubt there's any chance of that." There hadn't been any sign of a ranch or farm since they left the torn-down old town by the stream . . . and even there there'd been nothing living or even any sign of anything recently.

With that thought in mind, he headed off to the bushes.

Scrap kept whispering, keeping a good amount of distance but talking in a low tone nonetheless. Josiah couldn't hear a word the kid was saying, nor did he care. He finished up his business and came back to grab up his carbine. "You better get some shut-eye. Captain will want to ride as soon as he can in the morning."

"But . . . ," Scrap said.

Josiah stopped. "No buts. Get some shut-eye. If there's a gang out there, we'd know it by now." Without waiting, he headed up the hill to take his post. The last thing he was in the mood for was a long, drawn-out conversation with a greenhorn about things that might or might not happen.

The spot Captain Fikes had chosen as a lookout took about five minutes to get to. It didn't take long for his eyes to fully adjust to the darkness and to see that the trail around here was lined with rocks all about as big as cow heads.

Josiah was careful with his steps. He'd kicked up a

snake more than once at night, and the last thing he wanted to do was draw any undue attention to himself . . . especially if they were being tracked.

He settled in on top of the hill, propping himself against an old fallen tree. The view, given the limitations of the darkness on the moonless night, was more than he'd anticipated.

A valley swept out below him, and if he turned all the way around in a circle, he could see hills reaching to the mountains in front of and behind him. There were shadows of trees—limbs with tender new leaves that were so soft they made little noise in the slight breeze—spattered about, but not thick enough to even be considered a stand. He couldn't make out much detail in the distance. The trail was not visible, nor was any water source, which he had hoped to find for the morning ahead.

The smoke from the dying campfire touched at his nose, but it was far enough away to just be sweet, not pungent.

Dew had formed on the tree he was leaning against, and it was dampening his shirt. He had not lost the chill from sleeping.

Oddly, he found that he was still tired—sleep had not refreshed him at all.

It was at times like this that Josiah wished he had taken up the habit of tobacco—either chewing or smoking. But neither habit had ever agreed with him. Letting his mind wander would only take him on a journey into the past, and that was the last place he wanted to visit in the middle of the night. So he got as comfortable as he could, satisfied himself that Scrap had been hearing things, and began to whistle again—so softly he could hardly tell the difference from the song in his head to the song that was twittering out of his lips.

Minutes turned to hours. The stars twinkled. A coyote yipped a good distance away. How many miles away was hard to tell. And the sky started to fade to gray on the eastern horizon.

Josiah stood up when he heard some movement down in the camp, glad that his shift at watch was nearly over.

He was certain the captain was waking up the men—until he heard the first gunshot shatter the calmness and promise of the rising dawn.

CHAPTER 10

Josiah didn't take the time to consider that Scrap Elliot, in all of his eagerness and insistence, might have been right about Charlie's gang lying in wait. There would be time enough for second-guessing himself later.

After the first gunshot, a sudden volley of shots erupted almost simultaneously, accompanied by a thundering of horse hooves.

A rush of wind delivered the whinnies and neighs, the shouts and commands, to Josiah's ear quicker than he would have liked. Even though it was still dark, the quiet world of only a minute before had exploded into a storm, a sneak attack born in the early dawn hour. There was just enough light coming from the camp that Josiah could see shadows dancing on the cliff face—though he couldn't make out any faces.

Any sense of fear or physical discomfort from the morning cold left Josiah as quickly as his feet would move.

The flashes of gunfire in the camp continued rampantly.

He could hear more yelling—and his own heartbeat raced rapidly, adrenaline pumping into his veins like a dam had been unleashed, adding to the sudden bursts of sound. He was numbed, felt nothing, couldn't even hear himself think.

Josiah wanted to stand with his fellow Rangers and fight off the attackers, whoever they were. His wartime senses had come home without any begging. He scuttled down the trail, crouching as low to the rocks as he could, hoping that no one had been sent to kill the lookout.

But anyone planning a surprise attack would know where the lookout was, and somehow, they had got past him, sneaked into camp from another way—under the cover of darkness, or in the shadows.

Josiah had been able to see every way in and every way out of the camp. How had he failed? The questions came unbidden, rising over the shouts and gunfire. Surviving meant pushing away every doubt. There was too much on the line to fall victim to doubt.

A bullet glanced off a rock just at his knees. The spark briefly lit the trail, made him blink and stop to gather his breath and thoughts, then he dove to the right, off the trail, to gain some cover. It was barely light, so he knew he was taking a chance, gambling with his own life that he would be safe since the shot came from the opposite direction.

As he rolled, balancing the carbine as best he could, he fired off two rounds from the Peacemaker.

The unseen shooter returned fire.

Josiah's shots had missed. He pulled the trigger three more times, wishing he trusted the new weapon enough to load it fully.

The need to reload the Peacemaker came a second sooner than it should have—he wasn't sure if he'd hit his unseen target. No shots were immediately returned, so he took another deep breath, half-cocked the gun, and opened the loading gate.

He popped in a bullet, skipped the next chamber, loaded the rest, closed the gate, drew the hammer to full cock, and waited for a noise, a shot, anything that would give him a clue about where to shoot.

Nothing came. At least nothing close. Camp was another story.

There was more yelling, still plenty of shots being peppered about.

Josiah was pinned in, at least for the moment.

He heard Sam Willis call out to Vi McClure. More shots followed, bright sunny orange blasts of light that looked like fireflies in the gray dawn, the noise deafening, overtaking Vi McClure's response. If he had one.

The carbine already had a cartridge chambered home. It had been in the ready position since Josiah took watch. He was glad he wouldn't have to load the Sharps, glad that the loud lever action wouldn't give up his spot off the trail. A repeater sure would have been preferable at the moment.

He couldn't wait there forever, not knowing what had happened to the shooter or who it was who had spotted him. Slowly, he began to ease down the trail again, slinking on crouched knees behind the rocks and boulders toward the camp, the carbine in one hand, the Peacemaker in the other.

His ankle slid down a hole.

He was surprised he didn't pull out a dangling rattlesnake as he moved on, trying not to overreact. It would be his luck to get snakebit while there was an attack on his fellow Rangers.

Morning was coming on fast.

The horizon was now fully lit with the rising sun. Gray

had burned white. Soon the white would bloom a fragile blue, filling the sky with color and cotton-ball clouds, and there would be no hiding in the dark—either for himself or the attackers. Josiah figured the shooting would be over by then.

The smell of gunpowder mixed with the waning campfire smoke, a blend of carbons that burned Josiah's nose and throat. The coming day had arrived in the blink of an eye, and change had arrived at the pull of a trigger, and like so many days in the past, it was likely to be stained with blood and death.

He could see the trail in front of him, and every few feet he would stop, peer around a corner, or over the top of a rock, to see if he could see who had had him in his sights.

It wasn't until he was nearly to the entrance of the camp that he discovered one of his own shots had found its target . . . and there was one less shooter to concern himself about.

A man Josiah had never seen before lay propped back against a huge rock, a carbine on both sides of him. He had been outgunned and felt extremely lucky to be alive at the moment.

It looked like the man was not much older than Scrap Elliot. A patch of soft stubble was hardly visible on his chin, and his hands looked like they had never seen a bit of farm work. A kid. He had shot a kid. Albeit unknown to him. He could feel a load of bile rising in his throat.

Josiah knew he had only been protecting himself. But killing never came easy to him.

This kid's eyes were glazed, vacant, and his shirt soaked with fresh blood.

Mixed with the shooting and smoke, the air now held the familiar smell of blood. The flies that feasted on the bounty of man's madness would not be far behind. Josiah shivered at the thought. Pushed away ghost images that were not welcome, but were persistent and uncontrollable, regardless of his effort.

It looked like the bullet had caught the shooter in the throat just right. Depending on how he looked at it, Josiah's aim was a lucky shot or a ricochet. Regardless, the kid was dead.

He hesitated for a second, stared at the dead man, and realized there was nothing he could do—and he wasn't sure that the man would have deserved it even if he could—then he made a beeline to the camp, still skirting the trail, not taking any more undue chances but a little more confident in his movements.

He had no idea how many more men were among the attackers . . . or what their motive was. Though it wasn't hard to figure out that the men were after Charlie Langdon's freedom.

Josiah glanced back over his shoulder and thought the dead kid had gotten the short end of the stick.

A devil like Charlie Langdon wasn't worth losing your life over as far as Josiah was concerned. No man was worth that, but it never ceased to amaze Josiah what one outlaw would do for another.

The shouting and shooting calmed. Then stopped suddenly. There were a few muffled voices, nothing that he could decipher, but any urgency seemed to be gone—vanished like a tornado rising back into the smoky sky.

Josiah froze in his tracks as he came to the largest of all the boulders at the entrance to the camp, the spot Captain Fikes had chosen to spend the night at.

Josiah was about fifty feet from the fire Vi McClure had cooked supper over.

There was no one to be seen. He was shielded but could see nearly everything. Charlie was gone from his bed on the ground, the blankets left behind in a bundle that looked more like a rat's nest than a bedroll. And no one was in the camp.

A quick glance upward told him Clipper and the other Rangers' horses were still corralled. Josiah was glad of that.

When he looked back to the camp, Scrap Elliot appeared, edging around the cliff face, his head down, his gun pointed to the ground, barely in his grasp. The kid was in a stupor it seemed. Not quite staggering, but listless, like he was lost.

Josiah knew the look. It was a good bet that the kid had killed, or at least shot, his first man. He edged out from his hiding place.

Scrap jerked and started, and looked up quickly, aimlessly raising his gun at Josiah.

"Oh," he said. "Wolfe, it's just you." He hesitated, then let the gun fall back to his side. "They're gone."

For some reason Josiah wasn't entirely relieved. The expression on Scrap's face gave him no reason to be glad of anything. The kid's skin was ashen, and he was damn near in tears once he realized it was Josiah coming at him and not an outlaw.

"What about Charlie?"

Scrap nodded. "Gone."

"Damn it."

"It's the captain, Wolfe. He's been shot pretty bad."

"Where?"

Scrap pointed from where he'd come. "Up near the horses. Feders told me I was no help there, to get the hell out. That's what I'm doing. Getting the hell out." He reached out, propped his hand on the cliff face to steady himself, then slid down to his knees.

Josiah glanced up the trail, then hurried over to Scrap. There was a dribble of blood on his sleeve, growing larger. "You've been shot, too."

"It's a graze. I'll be all right."

Sure, Josiah thought. Sure you will. He tore open the sleeve to see the wound for himself. Scrap offered no resistance. The kid was right. It was a graze, but the bleeding needed to be stopped.

The closest cloth was a shirt next to the bedroll Charlie Langdon had been using. Josiah jumped up to grab the shirt, but stopped when he saw the metal bracelets that had bound Charlie's wrists, lying on the ground, popped open like they had never been locked in the first place.

Josiah left Scrap to tend to himself and pressure the wound.

Captain Fikes was sprawled out on the ground about ten feet from where the horses were corralled. Someone, probably Feders, had covered Fikes with a blanket. His eyes were closed, but his chest rose and fell rapidly, like he was battling for each and every precious breath.

The wheeze coming out of the captain's mouth was unmistakable . . . Death was approaching, growing closer with each attempt, even though the captain's body was putting up a fight against the inevitable coming of darkness.

It was a hard thing for Josiah to see. Hiram Fikes was a man cast of iron, a warrior with more lives than any cat, and his death in the middle of nowhere, at the hands of unseen attackers, seemed so unlikely and surreal that Josiah could hardly believe what he was witnessing.

The sun had peaked over the horizon.

The gray dawn was just another bad memory, the quiet night before suspect, and accordingly, every action and word would be pored over, tossed and turned, in search of apparent failures, answers about what had occurred from shortly before the shooting began in the camp.

But as far as Josiah was concerned, now was not the time to go looking for blame.

A small cloud of rolling dust in the distance caught his attention.

Riders heading back toward San Antonio.

The dust was too thick, too small, too far in the distance, to make out any detail, how many horses, who they were—impossible to tell. But one thing was certain: Charlie Langdon was nowhere to be seen. He had escaped.

The small cloud quickly joined up with a larger cloud—a group that had been waiting, which struck Josiah as strange.

Pete Feders stared up at Josiah. He was crouched at the captain's side, dabbing the wounded man's dry lips with a wet handkerchief. In Feders's eyes there was anger that bordered on rage. "No one heard your warning, Wolfe."

"That's because there wasn't one. They came in around the cliff face, in the shadows. There's no way I could have seen them. We needed two posts."

"So you're saying it's the captain's own fault he's laying here dying?"

"I am not assigning blame, only answering your question. If the captain dies, we'll all bear the burden of being present at his last breath," Josiah said, averting his attention from Feders back to the captain.

Fikes looked like he was shrinking, the life vanishing from him before Josiah's very eyes. Lily had withered away just like that—all too fast. One minute she was there, and the next gone.

"I'm going after them."

Feders shook his head. "Willis is on their trail."

"What about McClure?"

"He was the one that let Charlie loose."

Josiah lowered his head and took a deep breath. "What the hell?" he whispered. "Are you sure? McClure seemed like a gentle man, one of us."

"Elliot saw it with his own two eyes, probably saved us all from having our throats slit while we slept. Kid's lucky to be alive."

"The wound is little more than a knick, but he is a lucky one. I'm glad for that," Josiah said, casting a glance down the trail at the camp. He could see Scrap, still propped against the rock, his eyes frozen into an angry, confused stare at McClure's empty stack of dishes next to the fire.

"Him and Charlie must've had it all figured out." Feders paused, chewed the corner of his lip in thought for a second before continuing. "Waited until his gang was on us. They came from the inside out. Guess that's why you didn't see anything moving around until it was too late."

"How many of them where there?" Josiah's question was flat. He was angry that he had been duped by Vi McClure. But it wasn't only him. All of them had believed in the man.

"Hard to say. At least three."

Josiah kicked the dirt with his boot, looked out over the valley, and saw Sam Willis riding full-out toward San Antonio. He was certain that Willis was no match for Charlie Langdon and his gang, but at least he'd keep on their trail. "Four. I shot one on my side of the camp."

Feders wet the captain's lips again. "I owe you an apology then."

"No need for that now. We need to back up Willis."

Feders nodded, and stared out at the lone rider in the valley. "Sam Willis has got a score to settle. We'll catch up with him soon enough."

"He trusted McClure," Josiah said. "The Scot told me they'd known each other for a long time. Whatever made him turn on his friend must have been pretty powerful."

"Turned on us, too. Called himself a Ranger. Rangers don't kill Rangers."

"How do we know Willis is telling the truth? That he's not one of them, too?"

"He wounded McClure. Shot him in the back of the leg as he and Charlie jumped on their horses to flee." Feders paused, gritted his teeth. "Like low-down cowards. Low-down damn cowards."

Before Josiah could say anything else, Captain Fikes opened his eyes suddenly, but wasn't able to focus them on anything in particular. His fingers curled under and he gasped again, this time more deeply than ever. His chest rose high up off the ground—his back was a perfect arch, holding for a long, long moment. The wheeze was loud and hard, like a heavy scratch at the door. And then there was silence, as the captain's body heaved even harder and fell still on the ground.

Pete Feders waited a minute, leaned in to detect breathing, then closed the captain's eyes when he was certain of death. "I'm going after them, Captain. You can count on that. Charlie Langdon and Vi McClure aren't going to get away with this. If I have to track them to my own last day, I will. I promise you that," he said, through clenched teeth.

"So do I," Josiah added. "So do I."

CHAPTER 11

Pete Feders climbed up on his horse. "I think this is the best thing to do."

Josiah was more than upset at the orders he knew were coming, but Captain Fikes had made it clear to him that Feders was higher in rank, so there was nothing he could do but quit the Rangers right then and there if he was going to object strongly. That wasn't going to happen. He would be a good soldier . . . even though he was nothing of the kind anymore . . . but he would serve the captain, regardless of what he thought ought to happen next.

"I'm hoping to catch up with Willis," Feders continued. "Then I'll put the word out to the other companies of Rangers that Charlie Langdon is on the loose and the captain's been killed. You and Elliot need to get the captain home for a proper burial."

"But that's a three-day ride," Scrap protested. "He'll be drawing all sorts of critters with his stink."

"Captain Hiram Fikes is a son of Texas, a hero to our

beloved state and country, and he will not be laid to rest in some hole by the edge of the trail where he was shot down while upholding the law. He has a family who deserves to pay their respects. And, besides, he's a Ranger, and that's not how we do things, Elliot. Do I make myself clear?"

Scrap Elliot looked like he had just been scolded by his father—even though Feders wasn't old enough for such a thing to be considered, his being Scrap's father, that is. But the captain's death had squared the sergeant's shoulders. There was no doubt Feders was in charge now.

Josiah watched Scrap cast his forlorn eyes to the ground, bite his lip, and then kick his right boot back and forth, stirring up a cloud of dust at his feet. He was certain the kid was going to say something that would provoke Feders even further.

Josiah didn't think that would be a good idea at the moment.

"I'd just hoped to bring those outlaws to swift justice," Scrap said.

Josiah stayed out of the argument even though he pretty much agreed with Scrap.

"I would think you would find it an honor to ensure the captain's return home, Private Elliot," Feders said, adjusting the reins to his horse in his hands and stiffening his back for a long ride.

"I do. I most certainly do. It's just that . . ."

"Don't be so anxious to get into a fight. Your alertness served us well, and I will make sure that Major Jones knows of your attentiveness and enthusiasm. But I will take up this fight, and round up the necessary men I need to see it through to the end. You two have an equally important task."

"Yes, sir," Scrap said.

"Wolfe?"

"Understood," Josiah answered. "We'll head to Austin."

"Once you get to Neu-Braunfels, go straight to the mayor's office. Kessler is an acquaintance of the captain's. He'll spare you some fresh horses and a night's rest on a soft mattress. The news of the captain's death will have reached the capital by the time you arrive there, but when you deliver the body to the family be as gentle as possible about it. The captain's wife has a history of hysterics."

Josiah nodded. "I can do that."

"And then await further orders from me before doing anything else. You will be at the beck and command of the captain's family until we meet up again. Anything they ask. Do you have any questions about what I expect? Am I clear?"

Josiah nodded his head yes. He restrained himself from calling Feders sir—even though Feders had picked up Captain Fikes's habit of asking if he had made himself clear.

Feders had, no question, viewed the captain as a role model, but at the moment, the man was a sergeant, not an officer. He worked for a living just like Josiah did. Scrap didn't know how things like that worked. Feders hadn't earned the right to be called sir, and Josiah wasn't sure if such a title fit within the Texas Rangers in the first place. It wasn't a military organization. At least not yet!

"I'm serious, Wolfe. Elliot, do not even think about taking up the cause of bringing in Charlie Langdon or Vi McClure until we have had full communications. Understood?"

"Understood," Josiah said.

"Yes, sir," Scrap said.

"Good. I know I can count on you both to see the captain delivered to his final resting place." Pete Feders swung his horse around, flipped the reins, then tore out in the direction of San Antonio without saying another word.

All Josiah and Scrap could do was stand there and watch Feders's dust disappear over the horizon.

They rolled out three blankets to bundle Captain Fikes's body in. Josiah grabbed the captain by the shoulders and Scrap picked up his feet. It surprised Josiah how light Hiram Fikes really was. Even though it was obvious the captain was a small man, Josiah had really never seen him that way. Odd how a man's personality will make him seem bigger when he's breathing.

In death, the captain was light as a feather.

They laid him gently on the blanket, and Josiah reached inside captain's breast pocket. At first, Josiah thought he was mistaken, until he dug a little deeper. He pulled out the key to the metal bracelets that had bound Charlie Langdon's hands together. He remembered the captain taking the key from Sheriff J. T. Patterson right before they departed San Antonio.

He raised the key out in front of him and inspected it. "You're sure you saw Vi McClure shoot the captain, and then take the key out of his pocket?"

"I think so," Scrap said.

"You think so?"

"Yeah, it all happened so fast."

"But you told Feders that's what you saw. McClure shot the captain, grabbed the key, then freed Charlie. Willis shot McClure in the back of the leg. How could that be if I'm holding the key?"

"Maybe there was two keys."

"That doesn't make sense. I think that's what you wanted to see."

"I swear it, Wolfe. Vi McClure shot the captain."

"Maybe he was shooting at somebody behind the captain. It was still dark, right?"

Scrap took off his hat and scratched his head. "I 'spect it was still night, but nearing daybreak. Kind of murky at the moment, standing here over the captain's dead body. I don't like dead bodies. They make me nervous."

"And you're a Ranger?"

"Well, I suppose a dead Indian wouldn't bother me. I just can't help but thinking about all the bugs and such that'll chew on the captain before we get him home and they put him in the ground. It doesn't seem right, the captain being dead. It's a nightmare."

Josiah exhaled deeply. "Try and remember what you saw. If you're wrong about what you saw, then McClure might not be a traitor. He might be in trouble. He'll need our help. Feders and Willis might kill him before he has a chance to clear himself."

"I know what I saw, Wolfe. I just know it's true."

"McClure killed the captain?"

Scrap nodded.

"All right. But think it through."

"I will."

Josiah looked at the key closely again, then put it in his pocket. He wasn't convinced that Vi McClure had let Charlie Langdon loose. Especially now. But that didn't change things. Captain Hiram Fikes, war hero and Texas Ranger, was dead, and Charlie Langdon, legendary soldier and killer, was on the run again. Josiah exhaled deeply at the disturbing thought. "Come on, let's finish this."

They rolled the captain's body in the blanket, tied it up

as tight as possible, picked him up, and laid him headfirst across Fat Susie's saddle.

Fat Susie didn't take too kindly to having a dead body placed on her back—she instantly reared up and whinnied madly, but Scrap grabbed her loose reins and got her under control before she bucked off the captain's body.

Josiah was glad to see the kid had some horse sense about him, but he didn't say so.

Scrap grew quiet and distant as they finished readying up the trail horses and loading camp, and Josiah pretty much wanted to keep it that way. Not that he wanted to wallow in the somberness, just the opposite. He shared Scrap's desire to bring in Langdon—but the matter of McClure's guilt was weighing heavily on his mind.

The key really changed things.

If McClure didn't take the key from the captain's pocket, then somebody else had another key.

That somebody else was most likely the sheriff from San Antonio—or one of his deputies.

Patterson came immediately to mind because of the visit he'd paid to them yesterday . . . and the conflict in San Antonio. There had seemed to be some underlying amount of angst between the captain and the sheriff. Something about the State Police that Josiah knew nothing about.

The captain's recent history, over the last couple of years, was mostly a mystery to Josiah. Just as his own doings and losses were a mystery to the captain.

There was no way to know what had happened in the time Josiah was by Lily's side, while she was pregnant with Lyle, and the captain was out in the world, doing what the captain did best as far as Josiah was concerned—being a Ranger, a man of the law at the very least. He was going to have to keep his ear out on the subject of the captain's past once he arrived in Austin—that was a certainty.

Josiah knew, as he finished packing up camp, that something just wasn't right. There was more to what was going on than met the eye.

McClure had struck Josiah as an honest, earnest fellow. Maybe it was an act, a put-on. But Sam Willis didn't quite seem like the kind of man who could be easily tricked. It just didn't add up . . . that the two would ride together for months—or years, he wasn't sure—with McClure being a traitor the whole time. But he'd only heard McClure tell the story of their friendship.

Willis had not talked much about his past . . . if at all. In fact, Josiah couldn't remember any conversation that Willis had participated in since all of the Rangers joined up.

And, he couldn't quite bring himself to think that Scrap Elliot might have made up his story about McClure shooting the captain, but he was second-guessing the kid, and beginning to wonder if he could really trust him.

Time would tell.

He'd have to keep a closer eye on Scrap than he'd originally intended to. It was almost like he had landed square in the middle of a flock of mockingbirds, and he couldn't tell what was real and what wasn't.

It was nearing noon by the time they departed the camp.

The sun was high in a cloudless sky. Most creatures had already taken refuge from the heat, though a few vultures had appeared out of nowhere and started to circle overhead.

Josiah was tempted to shoot the birds out of the sky, but he decided not to.

Their presence was a signal, a sign, that he would have to remain alert all the way to Austin, protecting the captain from carrion lovers, flesh eaters—as well as keeping himself and Scrap Elliot safe from Indian parties or any other bad elements along the way.

He wondered about Juan Carlos, too. Wondered where the old Mexican was at, if he was safe. The thing Josiah most hoped was that the captain's friend had not been captured by Sheriff Patterson. That would be a tragedy. Rarely did he wager against a lawman, but Patterson confused him . . . and Josiah suspected that the sheriff was somehow involved in the murder of Captain Fikes.

He also did not let it leave his mind that Charlie Langdon now walked in the world again as a free man.

There was no telling what that man was capable of doing—and Josiah knew better than to rely on Willis and Feders to give him any peace of mind. He would have to be vigilant about every movement, every sound, on the trail.

He eased Clipper along, eyeing the trail as closely as possible.

The nearer they got to Neu-Braunfels the more the land opened up to broad fields carpeted with more bluebonnets than Josiah had ever seen in his life.

From a distance, the fields looked like large bodies of water, the wind rippling over the top, blossoms rolling like waves on a shallow ocean.

The air was sweet, and a subtle taste of honey settled on Josiah's tongue.

A few clouds had puffed up in the sky as they rode through the hot afternoon. The vultures followed the three of them, disappearing now and again, but when visible the ugly red-faced birds kept a respectful distance, soaring just above the rising green hills and gray limestone outcroppings.

Everywhere Josiah looked the vegetation was healthy, thriving, and vigorous. Spanish daggers dotted the rocky slopes on both sides of the trail, sharp spikes rising above prickly pear, neither offering a welcome climb into the hills.

Some trees bore flowers—fruit trees the identity of which Josiah had no clue. Other trees, like the honey mesquite, were yet to bloom, their autumn beans little more than coyote food, yet to prosper. It didn't matter. For a brief moment, Josiah allowed himself to enjoy the spring day, all the while missing the piney woods of home.

It took his mind off the multitude of deaths and despair he'd encountered since leaving home.

CHAPTER 12

The sign on the stagecoach stop said "Wilkommen," so Josiah knew they were getting close to Neu-Braunfels.

The little settlement around the stop was called Stringtown and wasn't on a whole lot of maps Josiah had ever seen. Mostly, the town was just a spot in the road. It could hardly even be called a town, since there was only a small mercantile, a few hand-hewn log cabins, and the stagecoach stop, which was located in yet another small cabin.

Josiah was uncertain about a lot of things too far outside of Tyler and Seerville, but he knew a little German because his grandfather spoke the language, so he knew the sign on the stagecoach stop meant welcome.

His heritage never seemed important, though he imagined there were traditions, and certain foods, that appealed to him because of how he was raised. But as far as Josiah's father had been concerned, they were Texan, not German. He never knew why that was.

The stagecoach stop rose up out of a blooming wildflower field as the limestone outcroppings subsided, and the freshly painted welcome sign was posted on the main cabin. Stringtown was small, but it did not look desperate or run-down.

"See if you can get the horses watered," Josiah said to Scrap, dismounting from Clipper. The horses had held up pretty well, but flies were buzzing over the captain's body, and Fat Susie was swishing her tail madly. She looked like she could use more than a moment's rest.

Scrap started to say something, then just nodded, turning his attention quickly to the trough on the north side of the cabin. He had offered little in the way of conversation since Josiah had questioned him about Vi McClure's involvement in the captain's death. Maybe the kid was thinking things through . . . replaying the events over in his mind. Josiah hoped so. He'd like to believe McClure was innocent.

After the dismount, Josiah settled his feet on firm ground and took stock of the area. It was late afternoon. Evening was approaching quickly, and any stagecoaches would have been well on their way by now.

The mercantile door was still open, and probably would be until late into dusk.

A lone horse, a big gray gelding, was tied up outside the store, looking unconcerned about anything. Somewhere in the distance Josiah could hear the keys of a piano tinkling clumsily, like a child practicing an unfamiliar set of scales. Music always reminded him of Lily, of his girls . . . and he wondered how he could give Lyle Lily's gift of music, and worried that there would be no songs in his son's life.

Morning doves cooed back and forth, and crickets chirped. There was nothing unsettling, nothing to set him on edge, but for some reason Josiah felt the need to constantly look over his shoulder, scour the rooftops of Stringtown, and search the shadows for anything out of place, before going inside the stop.

Cedar beams stretched out overhead, and the small interior of the cabin was filled with a pleasant aroma. The cabin also served as a home—a linen curtain behind the counter hid the living quarters of the stage master.

On the far wall there was a window, just to the left of the solid oak counter. A breeze blew in, making its way out the door behind Josiah.

An older woman stood behind the counter, stocky, a little taller and bigger around than Ofelia, gray hair tied tight on top of her head. Her bright blue eyes flickered, almost like she was startled, scared of something, when Josiah entered the room.

It was an odd reaction, and it didn't go unnoticed. Josiah thought the woman would be happy to see a potential customer, if she, indeed, made her living selling passage on stagecoaches.

The woman looked up and took in all of Josiah, running her eyes head to toe, sizing him up, for a long second before saying anything.

"The stage haz already gone for dis day. If it'z a ride you seek, you vill have to wait until dah morn." Her German accent was thick, and her inflection was sharp and precise at the end of each word.

"We just need to rest a bit, water our horses, and get on to Neu-Braunfels before dark, I hope."

"It iz just directions you need, then?"

"Yes, ma'am."

The woman nodded. "It vill be close. There are many farms along the way. Gruene is about three-and-a-half miles down the road. The *Schlitterbahn*, um, the Comal

River, is about three miles past that. You vill cross dat river and find Neu-Braunfels easy enough, heading north."

"Good. Thank you. You don't mind if we water our horses?"

The woman looked Josiah over again, then said, "*Hilfe sich.*" Still eyeing him carefully, she waited a second, and added, "Help yourself."

"Thank you."

"You're not *Unruhestifter*, are you?"

"Ma'am?"

"Um, troublemakers. You're not troublemakers, are you?"

Josiah smiled slightly, realizing that he must look a little less than presentable. Most lawmen had the requirement of a badge to make them stand out, identify themselves. Rangers didn't wear badges. Never had, and he hoped they never would.

"My apologies for concerning you, ma'am. No, we're not troublemakers, we're Rangers."

The woman nodded. "Rangers. *Gute, gute.*" She hesitated again before asking, "The new governor's Rangers?"

"Yes," Josiah said. "The new governor's Rangers." He wondered why the woman seemed so on edge, why she was so worried about troublemakers. He wondered if Charlie and his gang had been through here recently.

"*Gute, gute.*" A smile grew on the woman's face.

Josiah returned the smile. "Is there trouble here, ma'am? We really need to make Neu-Braunfels by dark, but if you are in need of help?"

"No, no trouble. Not now. People come and go here every day. We have been, um, robbed, in the past. I am always just *vorsichtig*. . . . wary, these days. You are *gute*, yes? My husband was killed less than a year ago. Robbed.

We vere never able to have children. So now I am alone. It iz easy to be afraid. But I have nothing else I can do. So I pass my days here, at the stagecoach stop."

"I'm sorry to hear your troubles. Were the men caught that killed your husband?"

"No. They run with the wolves now."

"Indians? Here?"

"No, no, no. Evil men ashamed to show their true faces. Justice will come to them, though. As there is, um, *ein Gott im himmel*, a God in heaven."

"There is nothing I can do for you then?"

The woman shook her head no.

"All right, we'll be on our way. Thank you, again, ma'am." Josiah forced a smile, then walked out of the cabin, the woman's heavy German accent and words ringing in his ears. *Ein Gott im himmel.* A God in heaven.

Josiah wished her belief in the delivery of justice were more easily justified. He felt bad for the woman.

Scrap looked up when Josiah walked outside the cabin. "Well?"

"We're about six miles from Neu-Braunfels. There's another town before then, Gruene. So we'll have somewhere to spend the night if we don't reach the mayor before nightfall."

Before Scrap could say anything, the German woman bustled out of the door, a fresh-baked loaf of bread cradled in her arms. She stopped just outside the cabin, the smile falling from her face when she saw the captain's dead body slung over Fat Susie's back. "*Meine Gott.*"

"We're not troublemakers, ma'am, I promise. Our captain was killed in an ambush. We're carrying him home to be buried proper," Josiah said, once the woman caught her breath.

"Veer iz home?" she asked.

"Austin. The captain hails from Austin, ma'am. We still have some traveling ahead of us."

"Yah," she said. "Vat iz your captain's name?" The woman's eyes narrowed curiously as she perused the horse head to tail.

"Hiram Fikes. Captain Hiram Fikes."

Scrap stood by Fat Susie, his head down, saying nothing, leaving the talking to Josiah.

"Oh," the woman said, again. "You vill hav to find Mayor Kessler, and make him avare of dis tragedy."

Josiah and Scrap exchanged a glance that was curious at the least. "Why is that, ma'am?" Josiah asked.

"The mayor iz a couzin to the captain'z wife. They are family. Captain Fikes iz a legend in dis part of da world."

The woman's bread came in handy, providing something to chew on as they made their way out of Stringtown toward Neu-Braunfels.

The mayor being the captain's wife's cousin had come as a slight surprise to Josiah, but it didn't concern him much that he hadn't known about the relative.

There was quite a bit about Hiram Fikes's personal life that he did not know. But he hoped locating a member of the family this early on in the journey would make the rest of the trip, and ultimately the delivery of the body, easier.

It had never occurred to Josiah that Fikes might be a German.

He'd really never thought much about the captain's ancestry. His own bloodline, other than being Texan, mattered little to him. Maybe when he returned home he would have to reconsider his lack of interest in his family's past.

Lyle had a right to know where he came from. What his blood was. There would be little or nothing of Lily to pass on . . . What family of hers remained was out east, detached and unheard from for ages.

The boy deserved to know something . . . if he was interested.

Josiah chewed on the bread as he and Scrap headed out of Stringtown, and chewed on the thought of giving Lyle a full life. Lyle was weighing on his mind heavily—and Josiah knew why. This trip had been dangerous, and it would be a long time before it was all said and done. Longer than he'd ever been away since Lyle had come into the world and Lily had left it. He was surprised to find himself so homesick.

Pushing forward, Josiah started to pay closer attention to his surroundings.

He had never been in this part of Texas before, and found it different from anyplace he had ever been. It was almost like he and Scrap had ridden straight into a foreign country.

There was an unmistakable German influence on all of the buildings and land once they left the stagecoach stop. Every cabin they passed was neat and well cared for. Some had lattices carved on the eaves, and there was an equality to the freshly planted and abundant vegetable and flower gardens that looked measured, more perfect than Josiah had ever seen before.

Hay mounds were rounded, perfect, too, so their arches matched the curve of the sun—it was as if the mounds had been molded like candles, for each looked the same.

Even the milk cows looked scrubbed and brushed. Everything was clean and shiny . . . where the shine was demanded and even in some places where it was not.

But one thing was unmistakable: Josiah and Scrap were viewed as men to be leery of by all they encountered on the trail into Neu-Braunfels. No one approached them, or even waved to them in the distance, not once the onlookers realized the bundle on Fat Susie's back was a dead body. It was as if the stench of the captain's body preceded them more and more the farther away from San Antonio they got.

"Where do you think we'll find the mayor?" Scrap asked, bringing his horse head-to-head with Clipper. The trail horses traipsed after Josiah at a steady pace, and Fat Susie was tied to Scrap's horse. The flies were still annoying her.

"This time of night? Hopefully at home."

"Do you know where he lives?"

"How would I know that?"

"I don't know."

"I would imagine the sheriff will be in his office. Or at least one of his deputies will be. They'll know where the mayor lives."

"I hope they ain't like the lawmen in San Antonio."

Josiah didn't respond, realizing that he didn't know anything about Scrap Elliot's life before they'd met in San Antonio. He had taken it on good faith, on the captain's judgment, that Scrap had what it took to become a Ranger.

It was not the first time in his life that he had left home and joined a group of strangers and put his life in their hands, but for some reason this time felt different to Josiah.

Not only was Josiah's youthful enthusiasm for adventure lacking, but his emotions, his heart, were being pulled in too many different directions. Upholding his duties felt as difficult as crossing the Guadalupe River.

"I'm sure this town is different."

"Hope so."

Josiah hesitated. "How long had you been in San Antonio?"

"Got there a few days before the captain went out after Charlie. I heard he was looking for Rangers, and I signed up right away."

"Where you from, then?"

"Cooke County. A little ranch in the middle of nowhere."

"But nowhere near a hanging tree?"

"No, sir. Nowhere near that tree. My pa saw that day come and pass. Says it was one of the ugliest days in his life. It was a long time ago—more than ten years since a hanging has been held at the tree."

"I know," Josiah said flatly.

The Great Hanging of 1862 had occurred just outside of Gainesville. Forty Unionists were hanged, considered traitors . . . even though there was little to no proof the men had conspired against the Confederacy.

Some folks thought the hangings were a crime, mostly abolitionists. Josiah was fighting in the Deep South at the time, but news of the mass hanging got back to the Brigade. Charlie Langdon celebrated the hangings with a rash of whiskey drinking and a whole lot of whooping and hollering. Then again, Charlie was always looking for a reason to celebrate, rile the troops, and death was usually his way.

As far as Josiah was concerned, there was nothing to celebrate . . . especially when he returned home and found out it was suspected that most of the men hanged in Cooke County were innocent.

The judgment had been a matter of single-minded violence, a taste for blood because of the times, the hate in the air, nothing else but urges pushed by war. The thought of the hangings, and the cause, saddened Josiah. He didn't ask any more questions, and Scrap became unsettlingly quiet again.

It was nearly two hours later when Josiah stopped Clipper a few feet from the bank of the river. Josiah stared across it at the town rising up on the other side. Clean, pristine, whitewashed clapboard buildings seemed to glow in the late dusk.

It was not quite dark, the stars overhead dim, too far away to twinkle and burn silver-hot holes in the solid black fabric of night.

Neu-Braunfels was quiet and peaceful, candles and lamps flickering in a few windows, no saloon noise competing with the insects, birds, and other critters welcoming the coolness of night.

"I sure do hate to be the bearer of bad news, but I 'spect that's the way it's got to be," Josiah said out loud, but not necessarily to Scrap. Then he eased Clipper into the river, toward the waiting town.

CHAPTER 13

A. L. Kessler did not look too happy to have a stranger knock on his door at so late an hour. The man's face was narrow, wrinkled with deep crevices, covered in day-old gray stubble, and his eyes were weary, bloodshot. Kessler wore a mustache as well, and it was in need of a trim. He had thrown his pants on, and his day shirt was only half-buttoned. Disruption looked to be an irritant that occurred on a regular basis—the mayor eyed Josiah angrily; he was almost seething as he gripped the door, which was only open a crack.

"There had better be a good reason for this." Like the woman at the stagecoach stop, Kessler's words bore a German accent, but it was not quite as thick, and easier to understand.

"I apologize for the late night call, sir," Josiah said, standing back off the stoop. "But I have some bad news that I did not think could wait until a proper time."

"Who are you?" Kessler demanded, running his hand

through his hair trying to straighten it, all the while looking over Josiah's shoulder, as if to see what lay in wait outside the iron fence that surrounded the tall two-story house that the mayor called home.

Darkness had completely fallen by the time Josiah and Scrap had found the mayor. It had been difficult for them to see two feet in front of themselves. There was no moon, hardly any light at all to guide their way. Even in the town of Neu-Braunfels, the victory of night had been won yet again, and darkness was nearly total.

Josiah had not been entirely sure he could find the correct house in the first place, but the woman in Stringtown had told him it was the biggest house on Main Street, just south of the town square—and it couldn't be missed. There were other houses. But the woman was right. This was a grand house, one that looked to be of Yankee design. Josiah had seen houses of the type, with turrets and cantilevers, in Virginia.

"I beg your pardon. I'm Josiah Wolfe. I'm a Ranger."

A freshly lit lamp burned on a table behind Kessler, flickering, casting shadows on a wall adorned with pink, red, and white flowered wallpaper. A clock ticked loudly in the distance, probably in the parlor. There was no question that the house was filled with finery that Josiah could hardly imagine.

"I have news about Captain Fikes," Josiah continued. "Hiram Fikes. I am told you are an acquaintance, and a cousin of the captain's wife."

The mayor made direct eye contact with Josiah, giving up his curiosity about what lay beyond him immediately upon hearing the captain's name.

All of the anger disappeared from Kessler's narrow face. "Bad news, did you say?"

"Yes, sir. The captain is dead. He was killed in a gun battle, fighting valiantly, trying to keep the people of Texas safe from the despicable outlaw Charlie Langdon."

What color there was in Kessler's face drained quickly away, leaving him ashen, his pale blue eyes paler. Tears did not come to the man's eyes, but they looked glassier than before.

"I always feared it would come to this. When did this happen?"

"Early this morning. We were transporting Langdon from San Antonio to Tyler for trial," Josiah said.

Kessler began shaking his head. "It's an exciting time for the Rangers. Was for Hiram, too. Such poor timing. And the body?"

"I was instructed to stop here to make the announcement of the captain's death by my fellow Ranger, Pete Feders, and then see the captain home to Austin for a proper burial. Feders said his kin would appreciate that. It would be expected."

"Ah, Feders. He is a good man." There was a hint of the stagecoach woman's pronunciation, *gute*, in the mayor's way of speaking. "He is correct. Hiram deserves to be given every opportunity at the entrance of heaven. A man like him will most definitely be in need of a proper church burial. Where *is* Feders?"

"He went after Langdon and those other scoundrels that freed him. I expect to meet up with him in Austin. We lost another Ranger, Vi McClure. Do you know of him?"

"Never heard of him. Another Ranger killed, too." Kessler shook his head no.

Scrap cleared his throat at the mention of McClure.

Josiah was sure he heard the word "traitor" in Elliot's grumble, but he ignored it. There was no need to spread curiosity about McClure's guilt or innocence at the moment, as far as Josiah was concerned.

"McClure's fate, and involvement in the incident, is uncertain at the moment. The only proof that lies before us is a vague bit of witnessing. Divining the truth will take some time . . . if it is possible at all. None of which will bring the captain back to us. The sad truth is that Texas has lost one of her greatest sons," Josiah said.

"All right, so it is," Kessler said, almost exasperated. His breathing had quickened slightly after Josiah told him of the captain's fate. "This is bad news, indeed. Go to the livery and wait there. After I stir the telegraph operator at the Western Union office and have him make the proper notifications, I will wake the undertaker and have him get a coffin ready for Hiram's body. We'll get you a buckboard to make the rest of the trip. It will be ready to go first thing in the morning. That should be easier than wearing poor Fat Susie thin to the bone with Hiram thrown deadweighted over the saddle."

Josiah tipped his hat. "My condolences, sir. This is a hard loss for us all. The captain was a hero . . . and a true friend, of which I have had very few."

"To some, that is true," A. L. Kessler said, easing his front door to a close. He stopped just before the door latched, peering through the crack, and said, "But there will be others who will happily celebrate when they hear the news of Hiram Fikes's untimely death. Mark my words. There will be a grand celebration in some corners of this state. Grand celebrations, indeed."

Morning broke, and Josiah awoke in the livery, where he had stowed away comfortably on a bed of straw in the corner of Clipper's stall.

The promise of an unknown soft mattress never came from Kessler, and all things considered, Josiah preferred to sleep in a barn.

A night's sleep had done him good, and his rest had been void of dreams or nightmares. But he could not help but think of the night he spent in the livery in San Antonio, and he wondered if Juan Carlos knew Captain Fikes was dead. The old Mexican had saved his life, and Josiah felt indebted to the man. He hoped he would see the day when the opportunity arose to repay that debt.

Clipper was standing steadily in the opposite corner of the stall, comfortable and at ease. Outside the sun had barely peaked over the horizon, and the blue sky did not look like it was going to last very long.

Thick gray clouds were marching in from the west quickly, hungrily gnawing away at the clear sky in the east. A spring storm was brewing. The only question remaining was whether it was going to be a quick downpour or an all-day event, making the trail from Neu-Braunfels to Austin a challenging course of muddy ruts and further delay.

Navigating a buckboard with a coffin tied on the bed was going to be a feat of its own on dry ground, but Josiah was not particularly looking forward to the coming day now that he saw the clouds, heard the thunder rumble low, and smelled the promise of rain in the air.

Scrap had spent the night in the next stall.

Josiah could hear low murmurs of conversation and quickly learned, when he stood and dusted the night off himself, that Scrap was talking with the liveryman.

"I saw it sure as day. McClure aimed square at the captain and pulled the trigger without a blink or a warning. It was cold-blooded is what it was. One shot to the chest, just above the heart. Then he set Charlie Langdon free and the two of them just about got away without a scratch, but Sam Willis got a shot off, hitting McClure in the leg. I sure as heck hope the gang dumped him and the traitor is dead by now," Scrap said with a bit of glee in his voice.

The liveryman, a fair-haired and smooth-faced kid who was probably a few years younger than Scrap and hardly a man at all, was completely enamored by the tale. His eyes were glued to Scrap. He was listening intently to an account by a Ranger about another Ranger's death that he thought just *had* to be true.

This is how legends and lies get started, Josiah thought to himself. The truth wasn't entirely known to anyone, but the spinning of vicious perception had already begun. He was disappointed in Scrap, but not surprised in the least.

"I woulda jumped the scoundrel and dry-gulched him. Killed him with a single punch to the throat," the liveryman said. "Then I'd be a hero, like one of those new dime novels I just got myself."

"If you could have gotten close enough. They was fast, and it was dark, just the glow of the embers from the fire to light your vision," Scrap answered.

Josiah had eased up behind the two. "Which means you could be mistaken, Ranger Elliot, am I not right in that thought?"

Scrap stiffened. The two were sitting on a bale of straw, just inside the open barn doors that faced Main Street. The town of Neu-Braunfels was quick to wake up. A few delivery wagons were already on their rounds, and the mercantile stood open, ready for business.

A breeze snaked inside the livery, bringing further proof of the coming storm, blowing up straw and the stink of manure with it.

Scrap remained sitting, but the liveryman jumped up and

faced Josiah. He looked like a little boy who had just been caught stealing a piece of candy.

"I've got to tend to my chores. Don't tell Mr. Hickam that I wasn't doin' what I'm supposed to."

Hickam's Livery was one of the most well-kept liveries that Josiah had ever seen. It did not look to him like idleness was well tolerated, and judging by the reaction of Scrap's sole audience member, he was probably right. The boy tripped over a bucket of oats—but managed not to spill any—and recovered, then turned back and grabbed the bucket, and hurried off like he was half scared silly.

"You shouldn't be doing that," Josiah said.

"What?" Scrap's jaw was tight. "Talking to you is like talking to a big ol' rock. I'm just wonderin' out loud if what I saw was really what I saw, since you made me question it. I was telling my story, that's all."

"The captain has family here. Word will get back to them how he was killed soon enough. But let it come from Feders if you will. No sense in contributing to a lie if that's the case."

Scrap bolted up and turned to face Josiah. "What did I ever do to you?"

The outburst took Josiah by surprise. "Nothing."

"I ain't a liar."

"I didn't say you were. But once your story gets into somebody else's head, it becomes their story, and soon enough, there isn't any truth to it at all. It's a lie."

"Well, you sure ain't very friendly. We're Rangers. You're supposed to have my back and I'm supposed to have yours."

"You don't need to worry about your back."

"Don't feel that way."

"You've been a Ranger for what, two days?"

"Nearly three weeks. I was with the captain when he caught up with Charlie Langdon. I was there—you know that. I helped."

Josiah looked away and in a low voice said, "I was riding with Captain Fikes before your head breached your momma's waistband."

"Yeah, so? You're older than I am. I bet I'm a better shot than you are."

Josiah took a deep breath. He wasn't going to be goaded into a shooting match with a storm brewing and a dead body to cart to Austin. He had nothing to prove to Scrap Elliot. "It doesn't matter. It's been a hard ride, Elliot, that's all. We've still got a ways to go. The last thing I want to be doing with my time is arguing with you."

"It sure doesn't feel that way."

"It *is* that way. Now gather up your things, and let's get ourselves over to the undertaker's, and get on with this before the storm forces us to stay back another day. I'd like to get to Austin as soon as possible." So I can rid myself of you and find some older, more reliable Rangers, Josiah thought to himself.

Scrap Elliot was really getting under his skin.

Scrap nodded. "I'm not a liar," he muttered, repeating himself, as he walked past Josiah, toward the stall he'd spent the night in. "I know what I saw."

Josiah just let him babble. There was no use trying to make a point with the hardheaded kid.

Even if Vi McClure did turn out to be an outlaw, Josiah didn't want the world passing judgment before justice got its own chance to make the truth known. But he doubted that what he wanted would matter in the end.

The story of Captain Hiram Fikes's death had already been set loose.

The wind was really riled up, and small drops of rain had started to pepper down from the roiling clouds overhead.

The morning had turned a little cooler than it had been in the previous days, so Josiah prepared for the worst and put on his slicker. Back in the war, the slickers were called gum blankets—regardless, he was glad to have it in his possession, now that the clouds were bursting open. The coat would go a long way toward keeping him dry.

For outerwear Scrap wore a regular duster and nothing else other than his well-worn hat. He grumbled something unintelligible when he saw Josiah don his waterproof long coat. The air between the two had not recovered since they left the livery. Neither had made an attempt, and Josiah was in no mood to make nice in the rain. He had a job to do, a completely different one than he'd originally started out with, and he wanted to do it—and nothing else. Including breaking in a greenhorn Ranger.

They eased both their horses to a stop at the undertaker's.

Josiah tied up Clipper to the post and looked to the sky. "This is not going be enjoyable."

Scrap glared at him. "No, sirree, it sure ain't."

The undertaker had a small shop just across the street from the civic square. A few finished coffins lined the outside wall. A separate entrance to the office stood off the boardwalk, and a lamp burned brightly inside.

Across the street, a gazebo with a dome top painted gold sat directly opposite the door of the undertaker's. It sat next to a whitewashed church, with a tall steeple rising, and almost disappearing, into the low clouds.

The gazebo caught Josiah's attention, not only because it was ornate, hand-carved, and darn near fancier than any other gazebo he had ever seen . . . but also because there was a man standing under the domed roof, staring back at him.

It was too far to make out any of the man's facial features, and the light was too gray and murky to assume the man was interested in Josiah or Scrap. The stranger was prepared for the coming storm, too, protected by a long black duster, a wide-brimmed black hat, and a hood. He was smoking a cigar, and turned away when he saw he had captured Josiah's gaze.

Probably a curiosity seeker, Josiah thought, casting a look back at Scrap.

Scrap was off his horse, tying up his mare next to Clipper.

"Stay out here, and keep an eye on that fella," Josiah said, tipping his head toward the gazebo.

Scrap looked across the square. "Why do I have to be the one to get drenched?"

"You want to deal with the undertaker? I thought you didn't like being around anything that was dead or of the like?"

"I don't."

"Well?"

Scrap exhaled. "All right. He's probably just watching . . . or a reporter from the newspaper."

"They have a newspaper here?"

Scrap nodded. "The *Zeitung*. It's all in German. Hickam's boy warned me about the reporters. Says they're relentless. The captain's death will be a big headline."

"All the more reason for you to keep an eye on him. Stand under the eave here, and you won't get so wet."

Scrap stepped up onto the boardwalk that edged the undertaker's shop, and Josiah stopped before he went inside. "And don't say a word to that man, if he comes this way. Just in case he is a reporter, you've had enough to say about the captain's death."

"Do I look that stupid?"

Josiah just shook his head and walked inside the shop. It smelled of fresh-cut wood. A thin coat of sawdust covered the floor. The mayor and the undertaker were having a discussion, and stopped talking as soon as Josiah was fully inside.

The undertaker looked to be about Josiah's age—a little young for an undertaker. He had carpenter's hands, rough and callused. His face was free of a beard or mustache, and he was dressed like he was ready to leave for a funeral. He wore a knee-length black frock coat, a top hat, and boots that were shined to a high degree—the reflection of the lamp on the man's desk glared in the boots like they were a mirror.

"Ah, Ranger Wolfe, we are just waiting delivery of the buckboard. The undertaker here has the coffin readied, and the captain's body loaded inside," A. L. Kessler said.

The undertaker offered his hand to shake, and Josiah obliged. The man didn't offer an introduction of himself, and Josiah didn't think knowing his name mattered in the least. In fact, the less he knew about the undertaker the better. The man's hands were as cold as ice.

A clap of thunder rumbled overhead, shaking the inside of the shop. Rain began to pelt the door, and from outside, Josiah heard Scrap's voice rise in a greeting and muffled discussion. He assumed the buckboard had arrived.

The door was pushed open, and they all turned to see who was coming inside.

Josiah eased his hand inside the slicker and grasped the Peacemaker. As far as he knew, Kessler and the undertaker weren't aware of the man standing in the gazebo. He wasn't taking any chances.

Scrap entered first, rain draining off his hat in streams. There was an odd look on his face, and to Josiah's relief, he did not look distressed, but he did look a little confused.

A man followed Scrap inside. It was the man in the gazebo. A man Josiah recognized immediately.

Juan Carlos smiled, and said, "Hello, Señor Wolfe, it is good to see you again."

CHAPTER 14

Josiah was glad to see Juan Carlos, though he worried about the man's safety. The old Mexican must have read Josiah's concern, because he immediately went to the mayor and shook his hand. "It is good to see you again, too, Señor Kessler."

"It has been too many years, Juan Carlos," the mayor said, his voice soft and mournful, clasping Juan Carlos's hand firmly in both of his own hands.

"*Sí.* I only wish our meeting was under kinder circumstances."

Kessler nodded and said to Josiah, "Juan has told me of the events in San Antonio. The posse who sought to take him to trial has given up, returned to the city. There is a reward out for his capture. I have wired Sheriff Patterson and Major Jones, making them aware that you have Juan Carlos in custody, and you are escorting him to Austin, where he will be turned over to the local authorities." He paused and took a deep breath. "I have known Juan Carlos almost as long as I have known Hiram Fikes, and have vouched for his honor . . . A fair trial is never a guarantee, but I am assuming that you are willing to recount the events that took place at the Menger and brought the trouble into Juan Carlos's life?"

"Of course," Josiah said. "He saved my life."

"I wasn't worried," Kessler answered. "I assume you know Juan Carlos and the captain have been friends since boyhood?"

Josiah sighed, was relieved. He hadn't known how long the captain and Juan Carlos had been friends—had known little of their relationship—but he was still concerned about the Mexican's welfare. The old man was taking a big chance showing himself in public, considering that he was wanted.

"I wouldn't trust Patterson. I think he may have been involved in the shooting of the captain and the release of Charlie Langdon," Josiah said.

Juan Carlos shook his head no. "I do not think so, señor. Only one man broke off from the posse. The rest returned to San Antonio before the captain was killed. If the sheriff is involved, it is from a distance. The man acted on his own as far as I could tell. But I was only following them, skirting the side of their camp. I was not able to get close enough to listen to them."

"Who was the man that broke off on his own?" Josiah asked.

"I do not know. He was with the captain at the Silver Dollar the night Burly Smith attacked you. But I do not know anything of him . . . other than the captain seemed to know him reasonably well. That means nothing of course. The captain knew a lot of *hombres malvados*, evil men . . . on both sides of the law."

Josiah tried to remember back to that night, to walking into the Silver Dollar. The captain was at a table with three other men. Two of them turned out to be Willis and McClure. The other man, the stranger, was never named. If he was, Josiah couldn't remember—any more than he could remember anything about the man's features. The man was a shadow in his memory, and Josiah had to wonder now if that had been the man's intent.

At the time, Josiah had just assumed the stranger was another new Ranger the captain had enlisted to take Charlie Langdon back to Tyler—and then to offer up training and indoctrination at the Red River camp, like the rest of them. That obviously was not the case.

Josiah turned to Scrap. "Do you know who that man was? Was he riding with the captain when they brought in Charlie?"

"Don't know anything about that man. I wasn't in the saloon. I was outside, keeping an eye on the jail with Pete Feders. Sam Willis and that traitor Vi McClure were inside the saloon losing their wages to the captain if I am to believe what I heard."

Josiah cast an annoyed glance at Scrap when he called McClure a traitor.

"So you don't know who this man was, Juan Carlos?" the mayor asked.

"No, señor, I lost him, then tracked him back to the captain's camp south of here. By the time I was upon him, the shooting had started. I was too late to save the captain. *Fallé a mi mejor amigo*. I failed my best friend," Juan Carlos said softly. He looked away with a hint of a tear in his eye. "And now he is dead."

"I still don't trust Patterson," Josiah interjected, trying to turn the subject away from Juan Carlos and his familiar and painful emotion. To Josiah, seeing someone else's loss was like throwing lye on an open wound.

The undertaker kept his head down during the entire conversation. Acting like he wasn't listening looked to be a skill one would acquire among the mourners of the dead. Though he did look up when Juan Carlos made mention of being in the camp when the shooting started. Josiah noticed that Juan Carlos's words had caught the undertaker's attention, and he made eye contact with the man with cold hands.

The undertaker said nothing, but looked away quickly.

Outside, another loud clap of thunder boomed overhead.

"You really should be on your way," Kessler said. "It will be a treacherous trip to Austin, without the annoyance of bad weather. This doesn't sound like it is going to let up anytime soon."

Josiah agreed.

"I would like it very much if you would allow me to cart the captain home," Juan Carlos said to Josiah.

"He's a prisoner," Scrap said abruptly. "And a Mexican at that!"

"He's the captain's best friend," Josiah said to Scrap sternly, then made an approving nod to the Mexican and headed for the door.

Neu-Braunfels disappeared slowly behind the three men.

Rain fell hard from the dark, gray sky. The light was dim and looked closer to evening than mid-morning. Thunder boomed almost constantly, making all of the horses nervous . . . and lightning flickered and jabbed down from the angry sky almost at every breath, making all three of the men wary of being struck.

If delivering the captain's body to Austin as soon as possible wasn't so important, the journey could have easily been considered an escapade fit only for a trio of fools.

Josiah and Clipper led the way, followed by Juan Carlos, easily handling the duty of driving the buckboard.

The captain's coffin—a fresh pine box that had darkened, aging almost before their very eyes, from the unrelenting rain—was bound, and centered, in the bed.

Before leaving Neu-Braunfels, Josiah had expressed a desire for another gum blanket to cover the coffin, but there wasn't one to be found. A black wool blanket from the captain's own bedroll had to make do, even though its effectiveness was questionable.

Fat Susie and the two trail horses were tied to the back of the buckboard. The trail horses had been refreshed and restocked with food to take to the captain's family. Bread, strudel, cakes, and some cheeses—all of which Josiah could smell, and had to force himself not to break into.

Scrap Elliot, begrudgingly, brought up the rear of the pack. He had wanted to bind Juan Carlos's wrists and ankles, treat him like a true killer. The kid had not expressed it vocally, but all of his actions seemed to suggest that judgment had already been passed on the captain's childhood friend.

To most Anglos, the only good Mexican was a dead Mexican, regardless of the Mexican's capacity for courage and heart. Scrap was obviously in the majority . . . and Josiah didn't think that type of thought bode well for a man who had enlisted himself to become a Ranger. But then again, questioning Scrap Elliot's capacity to be anything other than an annoyance was quickly becoming a pastime. Though not a favorite one.

Mayor Kessler had also entrusted to Josiah a letter for the

captain's wife and daughter. The mayor planned on attending the funeral, but had some business to attend to before he could depart Neu-Braunfels for Austin—and he expressed a desire to wait out the rain . . . if that was possible.

The undertaker did not express any interest in traveling to Austin, which suited Josiah just fine. Something about the man . . . something more than his being an undertaker, bothered Josiah—he just couldn't put his finger on what that was.

The storm seemed to be tracking northeast. After they'd been on the trail to Austin for about two hours, the clouds started to break up and slices of blue sky started to appear overhead.

They were able to pick up the pace of their travels as the wet ground began to dry out in front of them. It had been a struggle getting the buckboard through some of the deep mud.

The trail was reasonably well worn, and was cut through the rise and fall of the hills at the most navigable points. There were times, though, when Juan Carlos barely had enough room to get the wagon between opposing limestone outcroppings. The wagon nearly tipped, testing the ropes that held the captain's coffin—which held fast, thankfully.

Once they were on flatter ground, and the rain had completely ceased, Josiah eased Clipper over to the buckboard so he could talk with Juan Carlos.

"It is good to see you again. I was not able to thank you properly for saving my life. I know you did not intend to kill Burly Smith. I am sorry for the trouble my lack of awareness has caused you."

"Ah, *sí*, it is good to see you again, too, Señor Wolfe. Anytime you take a knife to a man's throat, you are taking fate into your hands. I promised the captain I would look after you. I did not want to fail him, Señor Wolfe. Or you for that matter. I am the one who has caused trouble. Not you."

"Josiah. Please, call me Josiah."

Juan Carlos smiled, exposing a mouth that had as many teeth missing as were there. A cigar stuck out of the top of his shirt pocket, and the Mexican adjusted his ragged black hat with an air of satisfaction. "We must be careful, though, señor, as we make our way into Austin."

"Why is that?"

"There are as many storms brewing on the ground as in the sky."

"Indians?"

"*Sí*. Isa-tai, the Comanche warrior and medicine man, has, um," Juan Carlos stopped mid-sentence, and cast his eyes to the clearing sky, searching for the right word, it seemed, "*organizó una danza* . . . organized a dance. A powerful dance they call the sun dance."

Josiah shrugged his shoulders. He knew little of the ways of the Comanche, and had never heard of the sun dance.

"Isa-tai is a prophet. He has made a comet disappear and commands great respect. The dance is said to give the power to the dancers to be able to spit out bullets . . . *la inmotalidad es su promesa*. Immortality is their promise."

"Sounds like a tale to me," Josiah said. "Nothing can stop a bullet."

"I would not question the power of a man like Isa-tai. He has brought Lone Wolf and Quanah Parker together. It was not hard to feed on the hate Lone Wolf bears toward the white man since they killed his son."

"Or toward the Rangers."

"*Sí*. The captain was aware of Lone Wolf's rage, and

feared the consequences—which seem about to come to pass. The tribes are gathering together. The Comanche, Kiowa, Cheyenne, and Arapaho—heading north in great numbers to save what remains of the great buffalo hunting grounds. So it is said. Isa-tai has done this—um, knitting together of tribes with his gift of tales. No other man has ever done such a thing. It will be a storm not soon forgotten if he is successful."

"You believe the gathering is about something else?"

"He wants war, and has no concern for the hunting grounds. Of that I am certain. I do not trust a man such as Isa-tai. His name means coyote's ass. I never trust a coyote. Especially the dirty end of one."

"How do you know this, Juan Carlos?" Josiah asked.

"The land speaks to me, Josiah Wolfe. And the shadows and wind, too. There is the scent of blood in the air. If you lick your lips, you can taste it." The Mexican licked his lips in a large, exaggerated way, then nodded to Josiah for him to copy his actions.

Josiah did as he was told. He couldn't taste anything but dust and mud. He shook his head no as Juan Carlos looked on expectantly.

"Nothing."

Juan Carlos chuckled. "Someday, Josiah Wolfe. Keep practicing. I believe there is much more to you than what you show on the outside. You have powers that are untouched."

"I don't know about that."

"Trust me."

Clipper's ears perked up, and both Josiah and the Mexican took notice. They stopped almost in unison.

"Whoa," Josiah said.

The clouds had parted, the slices of blue giving way to

full patches of calm and peaceful weather to the west of them. The angry cloud bank was east of them now, and could do no more harm.

A red-tailed hawk soared in the distance, riding an unseen spiral of hot air higher into the sky. The bird was either playing after the weather had broken, or was gaining height to see its prey better because it was hungry, in need of food. Somewhere a jackrabbit was about to step out into the sun at the wrong time.

The hawk called out, and the cry echoed eerily across the limestone rocks.

The talk of Indians gathering into one large tribe, a fierce fighting force, bothered Josiah, but Adobe Walls was north of them. Far north. If there was a gathering, then there shouldn't be any trouble near them. Still, if Juan Carlos was right and there were four tribes combining, who knew whose path they lay in?

Juan Carlos scanned the shadows and fixed his gaze on an open crevice about thirty yards ahead of them.

The Mexican was intent, searching for anything that moved.

For the moment, Josiah could see nothing—but something told him to be ready, to take whatever cue the old man gave him and not question it.

Scrap pulled up alongside them, and Josiah put up his hand to silence the kid before he said, or did, anything stupid.

Josiah eased his hand inside his slicker. Even though the weather had broken, he'd left the coat on, but unbuttoned, wide open so he could reach the Peacemaker without any effort at all.

The red-tailed hawk cried out again, the call rolling across the jagged limestone. Almost on command, another hawk appeared, a mate. It was still early enough in the spring for them to have chicks in the nest. They were most definitely on the hunt after the storm had passed.

A smile suddenly crossed Juan Carlos's face. "It is only a *tejón*, a badger."

Josiah relaxed his grip on the Peacemaker.

Without hesitating, Scrap Elliot raised his rifle and fired a shot off in the direction of the badger.

The shot missed the unsuspecting creature, but only by a few inches. The badger jumped straight up, landed on its feet, turned, and growled, which sounded almost like a bark, then hurried off into the shadows of the limestone crevice.

The report from the shot rose into the air, drowning out any call from the hawks, and alerting anything—or anyone—of their presence in the shallow, unprotected, canyon.

"Damn it, Elliot, are you a fool or what?" Josiah demanded. "Your idiocy might just lead an Indian raid right to us."

"Good," Scrap answered.

"You won't think 'good' if they outnumber us ten to one. Then what will you have to say for yourself?"

"I ain't apologizin' to you for nothin'." Scrap dug his heels into Missy and sped off in a cloud of dust and anger.

Josiah secretly hoped the kid would never come back, but he knew better. Scrap Elliot was going to be a burr in his butt all the way to Austin and beyond.

CHAPTER 15

After the storm passed, and Scrap shot at the badger, there were no other events of the day that brought any immediate concern to Josiah. The well-worn trail transformed into a wider road, known to everyone as El Camino Real, and it would take them a good way toward their destination.

Josiah's mind *was* on edge because of the old Mexican's warning of Indians and Scrap's constant disconcerting actions—but finally, the rhythm of the ride had calmed them all into a silent drive northward. There was nothing he could do about outlaws, renegade Indians, or trigger-happy boys but keep an eye out and proceed on with his duty to deliver the captain to his final resting place in the capital of Austin.

Night came and went with Josiah and Scrap trading off watch duties. Juan Carlos filled in as cook, and did a fine job, though his rabbit was a little tougher than Vi McClure's. It probably had more to do with the age of the rabbit and nothing to do with the old Mexican's cooking method. But still, Josiah noticed, and he wondered about the big Scot, wondered if he were dead or alive . . . and silently hoped the latter was true.

Coyotes yipped. Owls hooted. Josiah passed the time by whistling. And a cloudless sky stretched overhead.

On previous nights, the moon could not be seen, but on this night, a sliver rose in the sky, a waxing crescent that barely lit the ground. But the dim moonlight succeeded in creating a forest of shadows in the valleys and canyons that could be seen from the top of the hill the camp had been set on, forcing Josiah to second-guess everything he heard or thought he saw moving.

Once an owl flew over his head and he nearly shot at it, nearly acted as impulsively as Scrap Elliot. It was probably that thought that kept him from pulling the carbine's trigger.

The captain's body lay undisturbed in the coffin on the back of the buckboard, close enough to the fire to ward off any seekers of carrion, but far enough away not to encourage the further quickening of rot and decay.

Juan Carlos did not stray far from the buckboard, and he and Josiah were both well aware that the smell of death attracted all kinds of creatures—seen and unseen—but so far they had not had to run any such creatures off.

There was nothing they could do about the swarms of flies that constantly hovered during the warm day, but at least at night the flies tended to disappear to somewhere unknown.

Josiah was glad he would not have to lay eyes on the captain's mortal body again. Now, like all of those who had passed on, the only form the captain would be able to take was in his memory, a flickering image that, as Josiah knew all too well, would fade quickly with time.

Some days he could not remember what Lily's voice sounded like, and would give anything to hear her whisper in his ear, swear her true love to his heart—and he to her.

He knew that with time he would have to strain to hear the captain's voice—the commands, the duties, and the lessons—he would need to learn how to be a new kind of Ranger, riding with a new, unknown captain. That is if he chose to remain a Ranger, now that the captain was dead.

He hadn't thought much about his future, since there were unfulfilled tasks at hand, but there was a nagging pull in his stomach, something he knew he would have to examine once he was free of his duties in Austin and facing Pete Feders again, awaiting his next set of orders.

He wasn't sure if Feders would be made a captain, but he guessed that would happen. But that sure didn't mean he would be riding with the man who was always Captain Hiram Fikes's second in command.

There was only one order that Josiah was interested in taking from Feders, or whoever his new captain would be, and that order was to track down and bring in Charlie Langdon. Beyond that Josiah was not certain what he would do.

As the days ticked by, he knew that the pull to return home would become stronger and stronger, especially now that Captain Fikes was dead. Just as he had to strain to hear the captain and Lily speak or sing, he also had to strain to hear the coos and giggles of his son. At times, it was almost as if Lyle were dead, too.

"We are not far from the Rio Blanco," Juan Carlos said, bringing the wagon to a stop.

The brake creaked, and Josiah feared the axle might be

about to give out. It had been hard going since leaving Neu-Braunfels.

"How hard is this river to cross?" Scrap asked.

Josiah had pulled Clipper ahead of the wagon, looked out in the distance, then circled back. "Looks like some spots of the river run underground, so there is nothing but boulders and shrubs up ahead, as far I can tell," he said.

Morning light dappled on a rise of more limestone outcroppings that then gave way to rolling green-topped hills in the distance. Austin was still a long way off, another day at least, probably a day and a half.

"*Sí*. We are not too near the narrows, a deep ravine with treacherous rapids. It will not be a problem here where the river falls beneath the earth."

Josiah nodded, urged Clipper on, and headed north again.

He could hear the river running the closer they got to it, but the sound was muffled, since it dropped under the earth where they were crossing. The ground rumbled, vibrated from the power underneath his horse's hooves. He had never felt anything so strange in his life.

The spring rains had swollen the streambeds, and rushing, muddy water gushed up out of a well-worn hole in the ground not too far ahead of Josiah.

The roiling water hadn't crested the banks of the streambed, but it was close to flooding over into a well-defined floodplain. It would have been impossible to navigate the buckboard across the Blanco River if the rushing water had broken out of its banks and not been contained in an underground riverbed.

Their timing was just right.

The limestone ledges stair-stepped upward to about fifty feet at the pinnacle, then flattened out. Grasses and bushes grew happily on the rocky shelves, while the top of the outcropping was dotted with various types of trees: elm, mesquite, juniper, and oak. The trail edged along the river, in between the bank and the limestone stairs.

Josiah thought about doing some hunting on top of the limestone, but decided that it was too late in the day.

There would be plenty of creatures that lived near the water. Swallows were already swarming, diving, and soaring widely over the water, eating as many flies as they could gather in their open mouths. And he'd seen signs of plenty of rabbit, deer, and coyote—their paw prints pressed in the fresh mud.

He'd probably have more luck hunting closer to evening, if they found themselves near a watering hole.

The last bit of fresh meat was stowed away on the wagon, and all that was left of the dry goods, beans, and jerky—as well as the food sent along from Mayor Kessler, but there was no way they were breaking into mourning food, food meant to save the captain's family some trouble and give them a bit of comfort.

A cedar tree stood in the middle of the streambed that grew quickly into a river, and there was a large nest in the top of the tree, which, at the moment, appeared to be vacant.

Knowing little about hawks or eagles and their mating times, Josiah wasn't sure if there would be eggs in the nest or not. He hadn't seen any big birds in the sky recently, but then he hadn't been looking, either.

The tree looked a little spindly to try and climb anyway, but for some reason, food was solidly on Josiah's mind.

He was almost tempted to challenge Scrap to climb the tree, taking advantage of the kid's eagerness to prove himself. But he couldn't bring himself to indulge in that kind of behavior. It just wasn't his way. Besides, it was probably past time for fresh eggs anyway. Chicks were probably hunkered down inside the nest, eyeing him with fright and uncertainty. There was no way Josiah could bring himself to kill a chick, a youngster of any kind. Not now.

His life would have to depend on killing and eating something tough and old, like the rabbit Juan Carlos had cooked the night before.

There were moments when he wondered what the hell he was doing, riding the trail as a Ranger, when he had most certainly lost his nerve, his gut instinct to kill.

Men with Soldier's Heart talked of the same thing, all the while battling for their own measures of sanity. He wasn't crazy. He was sure of that. And if he had the opportunity to shoot Charlie Langdon square in the forehead, then he wouldn't hesitate, not for one second. He longed to be the one to face Charlie down, and that in itself reassured him that he wasn't crazy, or useless, or, worse, a coward who'd lost his trigger finger.

There was no question in Josiah's mind that if it came down to killing or being killed, his instincts were ready to awaken.

Juan Carlos brought the wagon to a stop again, this time more suddenly, a loud "Whoa" accompanying his hard pull on the reins.

Uncertain why Juan had stopped, Josiah swung Clipper back around, just in time to see Scrap Elliot reaching to pull his rifle out of its saddle sheath and aim upward, at the top of a rocky cliff.

An Indian sat on a pale white stallion, staring down at them.

"Don't shoot," Josiah yelled at Scrap.

Scrap settled his rifle against his cheek and sighted the Indian, ignoring Josiah's command.

"I'm serious, Elliot, don't shoot."

Josiah quickly unholstered the Peacemaker and brought the gun straight up so the barrel was even with his face, pointing straight into the sky.

"You're serious?" Scrap smirked.

"Yes."

Juan Carlos sat impatiently on the seat of the buckboard. He had no firearm that Josiah knew of. It had been taken into small account by everyone but Scrap that the Mexican was harmless, more a hero than a killer, but since there was a warrant out for him . . . Josiah had insisted that he hand over his weapon, a small-caliber derringer that looked more like a woman's gun.

Both men, Josiah and the Mexican, knew, of course, that Juan Carlos had a knife stuffed inside his right boot. Josiah had been blessed at the Menger by that very same blade . . . his life saved because of his weariness and lack of scouting. Scrap wasn't aware of the knife, and that was just fine with Josiah.

The Indian appeared to be alone. He sat on the pale white horse, looking down on the three men.

He wore a deerskin breechclout and no shirt, which showed, even at a distance, black lines drawn permanently onto the Indian's sun-bronzed skin. Buckskin leggings covered his legs, and bison-hide moccasins protected his feet. A small white feather hung on a braid of black hair that glistened in the sun. There was no sign of any garb, no headdress or war bonnet, that suggested he was a warrior or intent on attack. He looked more like a scout.

"He is Tonkawa," Juan Carlos said.

"He is a not threat, Elliot. Put the gun down," Josiah ordered. He knew the Tonkawa didn't wear war bonnets; they were nothing like the Comanche.

"Ain't no such thing as a redskin who's not a savage killer. They are a threat to every living, breathing Anglo in Texas and beyond, and I mean to make certain the threat is extinguished." Spit spewed out of Scrap's mouth, and his finger trembled on the trigger.

Josiah pointed the Peacemaker at Scrap's head. "I'm not asking, Elliot."

Tears welled up in Scrap's eyes. "Comanches killed my ma and pa, Wolfe," he said through gritted teeth. "Butchered them like they were animals."

"This Indian is a friend, not a Comanche. They have scouted for the Rangers for years. Now remove your aim." Josiah cocked the hammer in position, knowing full well he was on the Colt's empty chamber.

Scrap let out a yell that was as painful as it was startling, then let the barrel of his rifle drop.

Josiah breathed a secret sigh of relief. The last thing he wanted to account for to Pete Feders or Major John B. Jones was a dead Tonkawa. When he looked back up to the top of the rock, the Indian was gone.

"We have not seen the last of that one," Juan Carlos said.

"I hope you're wrong," Josiah answered.

"They are probably aware of the captain's death. They have been following us for many miles, and will more than likely see us into Austin."

Josiah was annoyed at Juan Carlos. "Why didn't you tell me?"

"I thought you would see for yourself. But I was wrong."

"Yes, you were."

Juan Carlos nodded. "My apologies, Señor Wolfe."

"No need. I know what to look for. I just missed the signs for some reason."

"Indians don't protect no one," Scrap interjected, wiping a tear away from his eye with his sleeve.

Josiah lowered the Peacemaker's hammer back into position, holstered the gun, then eased Clipper over next to Scrap.

"You've got a little learning to do about Indians and the like. This isn't Cooke County. There is such a thing as friendlys." He paused, saw the pain of loss twisted across Scrap's face, and recognized a bit of himself in the hard, frightened glare that stared back at him. "How long have your ma and pa been dead?"

"Little over a year. Only family I got left is a little sister, Myra Lynn. She's with a friend of my ma's, a church lady that will raise Myra Lynn right. I couldn't do it. Don't know nothing about being a pa to a half-growed little girl. I send money when I can. Get home even less. Some days I hope I never see Myra Lynn again 'cause she looks just like my ma, and it brings all those bad memories right to the top of my head. Other days, that's all I want to do, ride home as straightaway as I can 'cause my heart is longing to see my mama's eyes."

Josiah nodded. He'd give the kid a bit of a break. Had to now that they had something in common. But that didn't mean he liked Scrap Elliot. Maybe he just understood him a little bit more. "All right, then. But you have to follow my lead on the Indians hereabouts. Not every rock has a rattlesnake lying underneath it."

"Well," Scrap said. "I 'spect we're about to find out." He nodded, and Josiah followed his gaze.

The Indian that had stared down at them from the ridge was heading their way, across the river, followed by three other men—two more Tonkawa on horses and one Anglo on foot, who looked an awful lot like Vi McClure.

CHAPTER 16

Juan Carlos leaned forward, slid his hand down to his boot, and pulled up his pant leg.

There was no question now that the white man with the Tonkawa was Vi McClure, but even from where Josiah sat, he could see that the Scot was a prisoner, his hands bound behind his back and his waist tied in heavy hemp rope that connected to the last rider.

The big Scot looked weary and pale. He was staggering, his face dirtied and covered in scratches, like he had been pulled through a thicket of blackberry bushes. A bloodied cloth was loosely wrapped below the knee of his right leg, an obvious sign of the gunshot wound deposited by Willis, and each time McClure put his foot down to move forward—given little choice by the Tonkawa who had him bound to his horse—it looked to cause him a great deal of pain. A grimace was plastered on his face that made him barely recognizable.

Anything that put the old Mexican on alert made Josiah

a little more than nervous, but he wasn't sure why Juan Carlos was pulling the knife into a moment's grasp—whether he was concerned about McClure, who looked like he was of little threat being as weak as he appeared, or the Tonkawa, which also didn't make much sense, but then, Josiah thought, he really didn't know how the Indians looked on a Mexican . . . or a Mexican on a Tonkawa. He was pretty sure Juan Carlos held the Tonkawa in a respectable regard . . . but he wasn't entirely sure.

He didn't want to move for his gun, didn't want to encourage Scrap or startle the Tonkawa into an unnecessary shooting match . . . but the air had changed quickly, and now it was full of uncertainty and nervousness, even though the sky was blue and it was a perfect spring day.

Josiah had his doubts about what he was seeing, even though he had tried not to hold Vi McClure to account for the captain's death.

At the moment, it looked like he had been wrong—and Scrap had been right. McClure was a killer and, worse, a traitor, a Charlie Langdon sympathizer, a member of the killer's gang since he had run along with them. Josiah had to wonder how he could have been so stupid not to have seen through McClure's act, but he would have never considered a Ranger to be a traitor. Especially one that had Captain Fikes's approval.

The lead Indian stopped a few feet from the three men. "Josiah Wolfe?"

Curious, and surprised to hear his name come from an Indian's mouth, Josiah nodded. "Yes."

"I am Little Spots. I have a letter for you from Sergeant Feders." The Indian pulled a neatly folded piece of parchment out of a small buffalo-hide satchel and offered it to Josiah.

Josiah nudged Clipper over to the Indian, took the letter, then backed away slowly, never taking his eyes off Little Spots, his two trail mates, or Vi McClure . . . who had offered nothing to say and would not look Josiah in the face. He hung his head down and massaged his leg with a low, aggravated, groan.

The letter was sealed with a bit of candle wax, and Josiah was mildly surprised that Feders had the utensils and the capability to send a proper letter—but once he thought about it, he realized he shouldn't have been surprised at all. Captain Fikes had been a prolific letter writer, a top-notch communicator. Josiah had received a letter of the same sort ordering him to come to San Antonio to escort Charlie Langdon back to Tyler. Feders, more than anything else as far as Josiah could tell, was a student of the captain's ways. It was, after a number of hard-battled days, a hopeful thought.

He broke the seal and read the letter:

Wolfe,

If you are reading this letter, then Little Spots has been successful in finding you. Ranger McClure was left for dead, tied to a tree. He claims innocence. But that is neither your decision or mine to make. Retain him in close custody and see him to Austin, where he may make his own case to the proper authorities.

I am continuing in pursuit of Charlie Langdon. We are heading north at the moment and a half day behind him. Please pass this communiqué on to Major Jones, or the nearest ranking Ranger, on your arrival, and unless the major has specific orders for you, await word from me about your next assignment.

Please pass on the other letter, I have entrusted to Little Spots, to the captain's wife and daughter. I fear I will miss the captain's funeral while performing my duties, and it is my desire to convey my condolences personally.

With regards,
Sergeant Peter L. Feders

Josiah took a deep breath, nodded slightly, then looked up and made direct eye contact with Vi McClure.

"'Tis not true, what the sergeant says, Wolfe. I am innocent."

"Feders made no judgment about your crimes, or lack of, and neither will I. You will have a chance to speak for yourself." Josiah turned his attention to Little Spots. "I appreciate this. Is there anything we can offer you?"

Little Spots shook his head no. "Be wary. There is a battle coming on the northern plains. Though it may be far from here, those that were once enemies are gathering together against the buffalo hunters, against the white man. It will not matter to them that you are carrying the dead. The smell may draw them to you."

"Thank you. I am aware of this coming together. We feared you were Comanche upon first sight of you."

"There is nothing to fear from us," Little Spots said. He handed another letter to Josiah, then pulled his horse back to the Indian who had custody of McClure and said, "Turn him over to them. We are glad to be rid of this darkness."

The Indian, who looked a lot like Little Spots, so much so that they were probably brothers, agreed, and dismounted from his horse.

"Tie him to the back of the wagon, Elliot," Josiah said, glaring at McClure.

"But 'tis a long walk to Austin, and my leg is more than a wee bit infected," McClure protested.

"Then Juan Carlos will drag you."

Scrap took the rope from the Indian, grabbing it away as quickly as possible, saying nothing to the Indian, and did as he was told, looking at Josiah with a shade of approval that had not been apparent before then.

Josiah noticed, but didn't think much of the look. He felt as betrayed by McClure as the rest of them . . . now that it looked like he had been wrong. But he still favored the opportunity for a man to prove himself innocent if it were possible.

Once Scrap secured McClure to the back of the buckboard, Little Spots and the other two Indians rode off slowly at first, then broke into a full gallop, heading northeast, probably to catch up with Feders. At least that was the assumption Josiah was left to make on his own.

Juan Carlos relaxed, let his pant leg fall back over his boot, and urged on the horse that was pulling the wagon.

"'Tis not right, Wolfe, pullin' me along like a low-life criminal. An injured one at that. I could die out here."

A hawk screeched overhead, drawing Josiah's attention momentarily away from McClure and the trail ahead.

San Marcos was over the next hill, and Austin wasn't too far beyond that. The journey with the Scot wouldn't last too long, and for that, Josiah was grateful.

The Tonkawa probably had little desire to ride into the capital city. Not with every Indian, friend and foe alike, under the cloud of suspicion that they were gathering for another battle. Some men, like Scrap, didn't trust anyone whose skin was not white . . . while others, like Josiah, didn't trust any man white or red, and if he did, it seemed he always came to regret it, sooner rather than later. Like now. With Vi McClure.

"There's a few critters who'd be happy for that, McClure," Josiah said. "It sure would save a lot of people a lot of grief if you'd oblige them by departing this world before we reached Austin. But something tells me that won't happen. Not if I have anything to do with it."

It did not take long before El Camino Real crossed the San Marcos River.

The town of San Marcos had only been settled by Anglos for about thirty years or so, and as in San Antonio, there was no railroad that serviced the town . . . yet. But with all of the ginning and milling that sustained the coffers of the town bank, it was only a question of time before the railroaders took notice and started laying track to connect San Marcos, and all of South Texas, with the rest of the state.

Josiah was not bitter about the railroad; he had just seen how it changed people's lives for better and for worse. If the tracks had come through Seerville, he'd probably still be the marshal, still following in his father's footsteps, still questioning himself about why he had ever trusted Charlie Langdon enough to appoint him as his deputy in the first place.

Still, after all these years, Josiah didn't have an answer for that, for why he had trusted Charlie.

His mind was foggy for more than a few years after the war. Charlie had come home a hero, a survivor, a teller of tales, and Josiah had seen him commit acts of courage more than once. What was missing were acts of honor. Now that he thought about it, honor had always been hard to find among Charlie's actions. The only thing that was consistent, the one thing that always accompanied Charlie Langdon, was blood—and death. Always. If honor was present, it was left on the battlefield, and the dead told no tales . . . at least that anyone cared to hear.

Nevertheless, questioning himself as they made their way through San Marcos was not the thing to do, and Josiah knew it. Doubt had been a constant companion in the last few days, and honestly, he was about as tired of its company as he was of Scrap Elliot's.

The lack of a railroad had prompted him to think of home, and he pushed thoughts of Charlie Langdon away—for the moment, always for the moment—and allowed his mind to return to Lyle, to Ofelia, to home.

Josiah had not seen a post office in the small river town, so he halted Clipper and the rest of the ragged crew: Scrap, a new recruit, hungry for revenge, anxious to kill an Indian, any Indian, for the crimes committed against his family; Juan Carlos, a Mexican wanted by the sheriff of San Antonio for an act that was not a crime, but an act of bravery—the type of honor that Charlie Langdon lacked; and Vi McClure, a Ranger suspected of murdering Captain Hiram Fikes—who claimed innocence but had witnesses and actions piling up against his version of the truth. This band of men was surely a curious sight to most onlookers . . . though McClure, for all intents and purposes, was the only one of them that looked like a prisoner.

A man passed by, who looked more like a banker than anything else, stopping only when Josiah bid him a good day and asked for directions to the nearest place to post a letter.

"Onion Creek, just before you get to Austin," the man said, then hurried off, looking over his shoulder as if the crew of men were inflicted with consumption, or a contagious disease of some other type.

Sometime between San Marcos and Onion Creek, Josiah needed to draft a letter to Ofelia, to Lyle, who would not understand a word of it, but perhaps would have it in his possession later in life—if something happened to Josiah on the trail. Josiah had a strong desire to tell Lyle how much he meant to him. How much Josiah missed him—all the while knowing that what he was doing was the only thing in life he knew how to do. Someday, he hoped, his son would come to understand that fact.

"Wolfe," Vi McClure said, almost screamed, while they were sitting there. "I can't make it any farther. Me legs are about to fall off. The infection is tearing my heart out with pain. A wee bit of whiskey, and a ride on the back of the wagon, would be appreciated."

Josiah stared at McClure, then turned to Scrap Elliot. "Give him a swig of water, Elliot. Then help him up on the buckboard."

"You sure have been acting a lot like a captain lately," Scrap said, sliding off his saddle. He started to share his own water with McClure, then stopped, looked around, and saw a bucket and a ladle just outside the mercantile across the street. Scrap walked over to the store with an intentionally slow swagger, filled the ladle, then brought it back to McClure. "That's all you get."

"You're a wee wet behind the ears to start acting like a real Ranger." McClure downed the water, but saved a bit and blew a spray of it out of his mouth at Scrap.

"Dang it! I ought to let the horses trample you right

here," Scrap shouted, raising his fist and wiping his face with his other hand.

"Elliot," Josiah yelled. "Stop it. McClure. Get up on the back of the wagon, and keep your mouth shut. If I hear another word from you, I'll let Ranger Elliot drag you into Austin behind his horse . . . and I doubt there'll be one bit of sympathy for your wounds."

McClure slowly climbed up on the back of the wagon without saying anything—but it was obvious he was less than pleased, even though Josiah had done him a great favor by allowing him to ride into Austin, instead of forcing him to limp up and down all the hills in between.

CHAPTER 17

Reading and writing didn't come easy to Josiah.

He could remember struggling to make each letter of the alphabet legible under his mother's constant tutelage—she was a firm believer that a child should be educated, as well as learn to work the land, feed himself, hunt, and prepare the animals that were there to be killed. Josiah preferred spending time with his father hunting, killing, and standing in the shadows, listening to tales about the Cherokee War and the Battle of Plum Creek, but over time, he'd become a competent writer of sorts and could read nearly anything. Maps were his favorite.

He corresponded back home as often as he could when he was away as a young man, fighting with the Brigade. Courting Lily came at the tip of a pen in his absence. Those letters were bound with a white satin hair ribbon and tucked away in a hatbox under their bed.

Even though he had been tempted to burn the letters, in the end death could not force him to part with the words he'd written so long ago—it would have been like cutting out part of himself.

He could not bring himself to rid the cabin of anything that had belonged to Lily, even now, two years after her passing. He wasn't sure if he'd ever be able to part with the dresses, the blankets they'd slept on. It was all he had of his old life, all he had to remember when he was once happy and optimistic about the future, no matter how brief that time really was.

As he handed Lyle's letter to the postmaster in Onion Creek, it occurred to Josiah that he did not know if Ofelia could read English. And then he realized it didn't matter. What would a two-year-old boy remember of his father if the unthinkable should occur? The words he had written by a tiny candle flame on his watch were for later. Not for now.

There had been little drama as they all made their way out of San Marcos and on to Austin. The stop in Onion Creek was brief, just long enough to post the letter to Lyle and Ofelia.

The captain's coffin garnered immediate attention as they made their way north, and it was becoming widely known that Captain Fikes had been killed, cut down at the most inappropriate time imaginable in the history of the Texas Rangers.

The reemergence of the Rangers was more and more welcome, the closer to the capital city they got. Governor Coke's decision, and passage of the new legislation, was on nearly everyone's mind . . . the long awaited return of a force of men that could be trusted to protect all of Texas. But when people realized it was Captain Fikes's body the coffin bore, his demise, at the start of something so important, made everyone a little melancholy and thoughtful about what might have been.

Josiah knew the murmurs and whispers would grow in the coming days, as the funeral march became a reality, through the streets of Austin. He wasn't sure if he could bear it himself, but orders were orders, and he knew he had no choice but to push on. It was what he always did—push on. It was all he knew to do.

Night passed, came and went peacefully, and they were well within reach of Austin by midday. After leaving Onion Creek, Josiah had avoided Vi McClure as much as possible. He had fallen into the trap of the man's musical tongue outside of San Antonio, fooled like the rest of them by the big man's affability and obvious talent with rabbits, carrots, and a bit of water from the stream. He wasn't going to make that mistake again.

Feders was right in the letter. McClure's guilt or innocence was not for him to decide, and he did not want to place himself in that position . . . even though he had defended the Scot early on. Now he just wanted to be in the heart of the capital and free of responsibility for the captive.

Which, of course, meant his next duty would be delivering the captain's body and facing his family for the first time. No matter how he looked at it, Josiah was not looking forward to the coming day.

But there were a few things he wanted to settle in his mind before turning Vi McClure over to the local authorities.

Bearing the physical proof of the bad news, preceded by a telegraph from Mayor Kessler to the captain's grieving, waiting family, would come much easier if he was certain of what had really happened the night the captain was killed.

If there was the slightest chance that Vi McClure was

innocent, then it was Josiah's duty to find out, his duty to bring the truth to the surface, no matter how much he disliked participating in the effort.

He had been riding steadily alongside the wagon, alongside Juan Carlos, allowing the landscape to unfold, keeping his mind as occupied as possible. Then, without warning, he slowed and eased Clipper back so he was at pace with the rear of the wagon . . . within a reasonable talking distance of McClure.

The trail horses and Fat Susie followed between the wagon and Scrap, who was about fifteen feet behind the last horse.

Vi McClure was resting on the farthest side of the wagon, leaning against the sideboard, his left arm slung over the side, his right arm shading his eyes. His face was pale, a stricken look twisting almost permanently down across his mouth. The Scot's stark white skin almost glowed bright against his coal black shoulder-length hair—a sickness had set in deeper than Josiah had suspected it might. Now there was no question that a bad infection had taken hold in the man's leg.

The wound might not have been a threat to his life at first, but as Josiah had seen in the war, there were unseen entities waiting anxiously for the advantage of a cut or wound.

In his memory, gangrene was a common sight to Josiah, mostly in the aftermath of battle. Almost every injury he'd witnessed once he returned home after the War Between the States would take him right back to the battlefield, where the surgeon's saw always remained sharp, and piles of legs and arms grew like firewood in autumn. Old war veterans hobbled on one leg or wore an empty sleeve pinned to the side of their shirts. Seeing them always brought memories of the war flooding back. It was amazing how many amputees had survived such surgery.

"It won't be long now, McClure," Josiah said. He meant the ride into Austin, though he might have meant that death was waiting in the shadows of the trail. It sure looked that way.

"Why don't you just shoot me now? Put me out of the misery of living," McClure said.

"I suppose I could let Elliot have a go at you. He's more than willing."

"Makes no difference to me. I just want the pain to cease."

"That bad?"

"You've never been shot, have you?"

"I've got my wounds, thank you."

McClure took a long, deep breath, narrowed his eyes, and glared at Josiah. "I've not the strength for your taunting, Wolfe. What is it that you want?"

Josiah looked over his shoulder. Scrap was eyeing him closely, but keeping his original pace and distance.

"I have some questions I want to ask of you before I turn you over, before we reach Austin."

"Why should I tell you anything? You've made up your mind, just like me friend Sam, Sergeant Feders, and that greenhorn trailin' after us. I'm a cold-blooded killer. You tell me, what can change that? Three Rangers saying you're guilty of killing one of the greatest heroes of Texas?"

"Austin's on the horizon. You'll not likely have another chance to tell another Ranger your version of the truth."

"'Tis true."

"If you have proof that you're innocent, then now's the

time to convince me." Josiah hesitated and lowered his voice, realizing that Scrap was trying to listen to every word spoken. "I didn't want to believe that you shot the captain, that you were riding with us just to set Charlie Langdon free. I didn't want to believe that you really weren't one of us, a Ranger through and through. That's how you seemed to me. But I was wrong if I am to believe Feders's and Elliot's account."

Vi McClure shook his head no. "Me leg is really hurtin', Wolfe."

"There's nothing I can do for you but get you to Austin and let the sheriff take over from there. He'll either call in the doctor or make you suffer. I don't know what kind of a man he is."

"Quick to remember, or slow to forgive like the rest of you?"

"Could go either way. Tell me what happened," Josiah insisted.

"All right. It's not all that clear."

"It's not for any of us that were there." Josiah edged Clipper a little closer to the buckboard.

Juan Carlos plodded ahead, keeping his eyes forward, acting like he was a fly on the wall, or at the very least unseen, uninterested, even though that was doubtful. The Mexican had not been shy about his feelings concerning McClure.

Josiah was careful not to leave the two alone, for fear Juan Carlos would put his knife to use, avenging the captain's death and granting McClure's request in one full, bloody swoop.

Scrap pushed as far forward as he could come, but the trail horses and Fat Susie were in the way, a measurable distance, so he was only allowed a bit closer. Not close enough to hear everything that was being said.

Both Josiah and McClure were aware that they were being regarded in ways they probably wouldn't appreciate or even want to know about—either as a traitor or an interrogator, neither of which was an appealing title. But Josiah didn't care. He wanted to hear McClure's side of the story.

McClure cleared his throat and looked back at Scrap, then to Josiah. "The night was fair, and I was glad to be tending to supper. Always did wonder why I got cook's duty, but after servin' up my stew, I seen a lot of content faces. The captain included."

"You'll get no argument from me on that note."

A brief smile flashed across McClure's face, then disappeared just as quickly as it came. "I cleaned up the pots and dishes as everyone settled in for the night. Elliot had first watch if I remember right."

"He did." Josiah looked over his shoulder again.

Scrap glared at him, assuming they were talking about him.

"Is there anything to worry about here, Elliot?" Josiah asked.

"I'm just bringing up the rear."

"Sure you are."

"The captain," McClure continued, ignoring Scrap's intrusion, "seemed ready for a rest. He took his place next to the fire. And Feders wasn't that far off. The two of them talked in low voices for a while, had a smoke, then called it a night. I had my spot on the other side of the fire. Sam was a bit down the hill, stretched out under a tree, about thirty feet from me. He always did that, never slept close, always wanted to be out a bit, so he could hear anything coming along outside of watch. He's always been a distrustful sort."

"I could pretty much see everything up and around the camp once I took over watch," Josiah said.

"But there were shadows." Vi McClure winced with pain; he grabbed his leg and groaned softly. "Damn it, you sure there's not a spot of whiskey to share with a hurtin' man?"

Josiah shook his head no.

"You're a hard man, Wolfe."

"You were saying there were shadows."

"Ah," McClure said, still exasperated by the pain. "There were, always were. After you relieved Elliot, he came back to camp searching for a bit of jerky to chew on before he went to sleep. I've never been a deep sleeper. Thought I saw something off behind the captain. Something lurkin' around that shouldn't be. I watched for a bit, saw nothing more, then decided I was wrong. I fell back to sleep, kind of."

Josiah nodded. "I shot a man on the trail, hard to say if it was the same one, but that's my guess. He held me back, kept me pinned in, or I would have been right in the thick of things. Maybe seen a little more, instead of finding the captain in his dying moments. You were gone by the time I reached camp."

"You're certain about shooting that man?" McClure asked.

"Well," Josiah said. "I didn't see the shot hit him—it was too dark, too much going on—but I was shooting in that direction."

"I'm getting ahead of myself. I didn't think much of the shadow then . . . just enough to think it might be a critter of some sort. Elliot was up and hovering by Charlie Langdon, who was wide awake, sittin' up against a rock, his hands secure in the metal bracelets, settled in his lap. They were talking in low voices. Once they saw I was awake, Elliot took his bedroll and settled in about twenty feet away from

Langdon—about noon on the circle around the fire. He was square in between me and the captain. I stayed awake for a little while after that. It seemed like I had just fallen asleep when the captain yelled . . . and Charlie Langdon's hands were free."

Scrap had eased closer, and now he yelled, "He's a liar. I wasn't talkin' to that weasel Charlie Langdon. He was goading me. Saying I was scared of my own shadow. I told him I'd stood up to Comanche and he was the last thing I was afraid of."

Josiah stared at Scrap and gritted his teeth. "You need to hush and let this man tell his story. You've been spouting your side of things to every man who would listen. Now it's McClure's turn."

"Ain't nothing but lies."

"Might be," Josiah said. "You've got Feders and Willis backing your side of things. Is there a reason for you to be worried?"

"I ain't no coward."

"Nobody said you were."

McClure stayed silent, grimacing in pain as Juan Carlos bounced the buckboard over a hole in the trail. The captain's coffin jostled but stayed centered in the middle of the wagon.

"Go on, McClure, finish it up," Josiah said.

The Scot took a deep breath and bit the corner of his lip. "I jumped up and Charlie Langdon was a free man. I saw the man you claim to have shot coming up behind the captain, so I didn't hesitate. I pulled me gun out and fired. At about the same time a shot came from behind me. There was another man . . . a man who made it past Sam Willis, and I swear on my sweet mother's grave he fired his gun about the same time I did, and hit the captain square in the chest. I took off after him, but Sam hollered at me to stop, screaming I'd shot the captain. He shot me in the leg. I kept running. I guess Charlie and the man who'd let him free figured I might be a bargaining chip. They took me up on a horse, and we rode off."

"Who was the man?" Josiah asked.

"Not sure of his name, but he was playing cards with the captain at the Silver Dollar the night before. Captain Fikes took every coin the man had."

Josiah nodded. "I saw you in the distance meet up with another group of riders. Who were they?"

McClure didn't hesitate. "Patterson. The sheriff from San Antonio. And his posse that was looking for the Mexican."

"You sure?"

"As sure as I didn't shoot Captain Fikes. That I am. Sure as I didn't kill the best Ranger I've ever had the pleasure of knowin'," McClure said sadly, then closed his eyes, signaling that he was finished telling his tale.

Josiah still wasn't sure of the truth. Some of what McClure said still didn't make sense to him, but he decided to let the man be. There'd be time later for more questions.

CHAPTER 18

Juan Carlos brought the buckboard to an easy stop on the crest of the hill. A valley stretched out in the distance, and Austin, cut by the mighty Colorado River, which was swollen from the spring rains, rose up on the side of a ravine like a long-lost city, basking in the golden evening light, glowing almost as if it were the promised land, Heaven itself.

Josiah halted Clipper and sighed as he took in the view.

Clipper, on the other hand, seemed to be in no mood for reflection or for celebrating the end of the journey from San Antonio. The Appaloosa was nervous, dancing back and forth and snorting harshly. Josiah quickly trained his attention back on the horse. The view could wait.

He tried his best to calm his trusted ride, a feat that was normally reasonably easy, due to Clipper's kind nature, but every trick Josiah knew was not working. He wondered if there was a rattlesnake nearby, even though he didn't hear anything but the rush of a northern breeze caressing the hill they were atop, showering his face with a preview of the coming, cool night. The beauty of spring in Texas was hot days and cold nights.

"Whoa, what's the matter, boy?" Josiah said, looking all about for a snake hole, mostly down at the hard, packed-down ground that made up El Camino Real.

It only took a matter of seconds to figure out what had spooked Clipper.

McClure shouted, then pointed at a boulder in the distance, nearly a hundred feet to the west of them, on a small rise. "Wolfe! Over there!"

Clipper scurried backward, defying Josiah's pull on the bit. Fear was stuck in the whites of the horse's eyes, like he had seen his own death.

A shot rang out, shattering the silence, proving that Clipper's sense of worry was warranted—once again.

Vi McClure had only a second to react to the pain, to try and raise his hand to his face, like he was flicking away an insect or something biting, before his cheek exploded into a wad of flesh, then splattered outward in a bloody shower of grain and flecks of bone.

His body bounced back against the captain's coffin. The force of the hit was nearly as loud as the shot—which boomed and echoed around them all like a .50-caliber, a buffalo gun.

The second shot came immediately behind the first one, and this one, perfectly aimed, hit McClure squarely in the throat. The direct hit nearly severed the Scot's head, shoving it back, hard, against the sideboard. A stunned, surprised look froze across what was left of McClure's pale white face, then he collapsed in a convulsing shake that only lasted a little longer than a blink of an eye.

In the matter of a breath, Vi McClure was dead,

sprawled out. He was pinned up against the coffin, the major artery in his throat severed. Blood ran like the river in the valley below, anxious, rushing everywhere it could. The big Scot was left soaking in a pool of blood that poured freely through the slats of the buckboard, a crimson red waterfall dancing in the dirt of El Camino Real.

Josiah's body had jerked like he was startled when the first shot erupted. It looked like the shot had scared him—but he wasn't scared; he was ignited.

He saw each shimmer of McClure's flesh, each droplet of blood shower south of the Scot's head, and reacted in kind. His war-enabled muscles suddenly remembered what to do. He was not in control of himself from that moment on, but more so; he was outside himself, an observer set on revenge and, most importantly, survival.

He pulled the Sharps out of its sheath in one seamless yank, slid off Clipper, momentarily using his horse, and loyal friend, as a shield. In another swift motion, he swatted the horse's rump, sending the Appaloosa running down the hill, out of harm's way.

Clipper was more than happy to oblige.

Josiah dove under the buckboard and rolled into a shooting position, aiming the Sharps toward the boulder from where the shots originated.

More shots rang out. Two different puffs of smoke rose up from behind the big granite rock—two different shooters with one objective.

Dirt exploded inches from Josiah's face. He steadied the Sharps against the wagon wheel and returned fire, all the while wishing with more than a curse for a new Winchester repeater.

Juan Carlos joined him under the buckboard. There was

a rip on the Mexican's shirtsleeve and a bit of blood from where a bullet had grazed him.

"You all right?" Josiah asked.

"*Sí*, just fine."

Josiah tossed the Peacemaker to Juan Carlos. "You have five shots."

The Mexican nodded, grabbed the pistol, and aimed toward the boulder.

Scrap had hustled himself and his own horse alongside the trail horses and Fat Susie. All of the horses were startled. They were jumping, pulling, whinnying, at every shot.

A heavy volley of shots erupted, both from behind the boulder and from Scrap, Josiah, and Juan Carlos. The air was quickly filled with clouds of smoke, with the smell of gunpowder, death, and blood.

The trail horse on the outside, the closest one to the unseen shooters, stumbled and then fell, three gaping bullet holes appearing in its body in a thump and explosion of blood, the crucial one right behind the ear. Death had come quick to the horse, just like it had with McClure.

Josiah had plenty of metal cartridges, plenty of ammunition, and was a quick reloader. Juan Carlos had shot off all five rounds. Josiah tossed him a handful of bullets, then returned fire.

The other trail horse and Fat Susie stood in between Scrap and his horse, Missy. But the horses, save Missy and Clipper, were tied to the buckboard.

If it weren't for the dead horse, the wagon would have started to roll. As it was, the wheels were lurching back and forth, making it hard for Josiah and Juan Carlos to judge their shots.

"Elliot, calm those damn horses," Josiah shouted.

"They ain't going to calm down until the shooting stops," Scrap yelled back.

And, just as if the shooters had heard them, the shooting did stop. Josiah and Juan Carlos froze, looked at each other, then began shooting again. Nothing was returned. Just the wind, and the smell of a battle, an ambush that left a sour taste in Josiah's mouth.

"Maybe you hit them, Senõr Wolfe," Juan Carlos said, reloading yet another chamber of bullets.

"Would have been a lucky shot. All I saw was the barrel of a rifle. How about you?"

"*Sí*, I saw nothing but smoke."

"Did you hit them, Elliot?" Josiah called out.

"Don't know," he answered. "Couldn't see a darn thing."

"Us, either."

"Damn."

The smoke started to clear, and the hooves of running horses echoed down the hill.

Scrap rose up and shot at the departing horses in the distance. "There's two of them," he shouted. "Damn it, I missed them."

Josiah jumped from underneath the buckboard, just in time to see the tail end of the last horse disappear over the rise on the hill. All he could see after that was the rising dust of a clean escape, heading east, away from Austin.

Juan Carlos joined him and handed the Peacemaker back to Josiah. "*Graçias. Aprecio tu confianza.* I appreciate your trust."

Josiah nodded. "You'll never have to worry about that with me."

Scrap spit on the ground and looked away. "Looks like McClure got hit more than once."

"Looks that way." Josiah walked over to the Scot. There

was no question the man was dead, but he wanted to make sure, so he felt for a pulse. There was nothing to feel, nothing to hear. Nothing but the drip, drip, drip of blood. "What'd you see, Elliot?"

"Just two men. Looked a little familiar now that I think about it. One was a Negro and the other was a redhead, an Irish, I think."

Josiah nodded again. "Patterson rode with a Negro and an Irish. Said the Irish was a tracker, called him O'Reilly if I remember right. I think they might have accomplished what they came after."

"What is that, señor?"

"To silence McClure."

"Well," Scrap said. "They sure as hell did that. But if he was one of them, why in tarnation would they want him dead?"

"Maybe he wasn't one of them, Elliot."

"I'll never believe that. I know what I saw."

Josiah shrugged this time. "Makes no difference now, does it? The man's dead. He can't defend himself, or tell anyone his side of the story."

"He told you, señor?"

"He did. Almost. Enough, I think, but there are still some things I don't understand. But that's the way it goes. I guess we'll just have to accept the truth whatever way we can. Can't bring back the captain, anyway. The trials of the living don't matter to the dead."

"Or *el Hombre Grande*. The Big Man."

Josiah forced a smile and nodded toward Juan Carlos. "You're right. But we'll make sure the captain gets a decent burial, instead of being dumped alongside the trail."

Scrap stalked off and started to untie the dead horse from the buckboard. But before he did, he kicked the horse as hard as he could, then glared at Josiah so severely that Josiah wasn't quite sure if the kid was going to pull his gun on him or not.

They were just south of Republic Square, their first destination, where the courthouse and jail block were, just beyond a crowded street of clapboard buildings. It surprised Josiah that most of the people along the street were Mexicans. The air smelled of horse shit and spicy food.

Austin was nothing like Josiah had expected it to be.

"We must be a little careful through here, señor. It would be best if I am not seen as a *preso*, a prisoner. The locals call this place 'Little Mexico.' It is a wilderness of sorts. Several bad men I have known have met their fates here. Plenty of fandangos, shootings, and unlawfulness happens after the fall of night. The Anglos stay wide, mostly, unless they are looking for trouble in the form of drink . . . or a woman."

"I'll take your advice." Josiah nodded, then brought them all to a stop with a raised hand. He quickly released the rope that bound Juan Carlos's legs to the buckboard.

They had rolled McClure's body in the blanket that had covered the captain's coffin, and laid him out in the buckboard as well.

The dead horse had been left for the coyotes and wolves. Luckily, Fat Susie and the other trail horse had survived the shooting unscathed, though both were jumpier than before the ambush.

Josiah and Juan Carlos had no problem navigating through the streets of "Little Mexico," as Juan Carlos had called this section of Austin.

The buckboard was given a wide berth. It was almost like their arrival had been announced ahead of time.

Some businesses were closed, shades drawn. Most everyone stopped as they passed, Anglo and Mexican alike—though there were far more Mexicans to be seen than Anglos. Hats were doffed, hearts covered, eyes lowered. A few Mexican women wept openly once they realized there was a coffin on the back of the wagon.

Someone shouted, "*Las vidas del capitán en nuestros corazones*."

Juan Carlos nodded and said to Josiah, "The captain lives in our hearts."

"He was a hero here?"

"*Por todas partes*. Everywhere. Captain Fikes was an amigo to most everyone. Mexicano or Anglo."

The clapboard buildings in "Little Mexico" gave way to the square, a vast open space dotted with towering trees, and people began to become sparse along the street that cut through the field to the courthouse and jail block.

"I trust you will be all right once I relieve myself of your custody," Josiah said quietly to Juan Carlos, making sure Scrap did not get a whiff of his plan to set Juan Carlos free instead of turning him over for trial.

McClure's death had solidified the idea, the thought, even though he had been struggling over the rights and wrongs of such a release since Juan Carlos had joined them in Neu-Braunfels.

Josiah owed the Mexican his life, and as much as he trusted the captain's reputation to proceed them into Austin and keep Juan Carlos safe, in the arms of justice, he also was not naïve. The level of hate most Anglos felt against any Mexican was worn openly—the captain was a rarity.

Juan Carlos could just as easily get ambushed in the jail—with no place to go—as they had been on the trail.

The tricky part would be keeping Scrap at bay, making

him believe the escape was not premeditated, that Josiah himself had not subjugated the law and in the end become a criminal himself.

"I will be fine. I have family here," Juan Carlos said with a knowing glance. "They will know of my situation soon enough, if they do not already. And Pearl, she will know, too. I will not be alone."

"Pearl?"

"The captain's daughter. She is like my own flesh and blood." A slight smile crossed Juan Carlos's weathered face. "Do not take her for a fool, or you will suffer greatly."

Josiah said nothing.

He had a duty to do—to both the captain and Juan Carlos, and as soon as he was finished, certain that he was successful, he hoped to return home, briefly, to see Lyle and tend to his needs if there were any, then head on to the Red River camp with the other Rangers.

He had no plans of taking anyone for a fool.

Especially a woman.

CHAPTER 19

Josiah had to fight off the flies that were swarming over McClure's body when he tied Clipper to the back of the buckboard alongside Fat Susie and the remaining trail horse. They were stopped outside the jail block, and much to Josiah's relief, a crowd had gathered around the buckboard, though they kept a respectful distance . . . at least out of range of the flies and the stink of death.

Scrap did not question Josiah's action.

Once they finished this leg of the journey, meant to be the successful turning over of Juan Carlos to the sheriff, Josiah would have to take over the duty of guiding the buckboard through the streets of Austin, and delivering the coffin to the Fikes's home.

The kid had dismounted his horse, Missy, and was standing on the boardwalk in front of the jail, his right hand resting on the butt of his pistol, a .36-caliber Paterson Colt.

Josiah knew Scrap carried the Paterson because of another Texas Ranger, John Coffee Hays.

Hays was an early Ranger whose campaign against the Comanche in the forties was legendary now. That campaign was considered one of the first fully landed punches in the long fight against the Comanche in Texas. A Lipan Apache chief called Hays, who was little more than a kid himself when he became a Ranger, "Bravo-Too-Much." It didn't surprise Josiah that Scrap envied Hays's stature and wanted to be like him as much as possible.

"Damn flies," Josiah said out loud, swatting the insects away from his face.

Scrap laughed. "That traitor sure did draw the biters."

"You should be a little more respectful of the dead," Josiah said. He crossed around behind Clipper, chiding Scrap all the way, then stopped face-to-face with the kid—whose back was now to Juan Carlos.

"McClure'll surely rot in hell," Scrap said with a smirk. "Already is as far as that goes. Not a second too soon, either, if you ask me."

"You seem pretty positive that McClure had something to pay a penance for."

"I am. I most certainly am."

"The man deserved a fair trial, not being shot in cold blood like he was."

Scrap looked down to his boots. Kicked his right one, then stared back at Josiah without saying anything else.

"He killed the captain. That's that. Any misery that came to McClure after that was misery he brought on himself."

Josiah squared his shoulders. "You're positive of that, aren't you?"

Scrap started to say something, casting a quick glance over his shoulder before a word escaped his mouth. It took him a moment to realize what he was seeing: an empty seat on the buckboard.

Juan Carlos was gone.

"Where's the Mexican?" Scrap demanded, turning and unholstering his Paterson at the same time.

"Well, now look what you've done, Elliot," Josiah scolded, scanning the crowd for a sight of Juan Carlos, glad to see nothing that resembled the old man.

A mass of Mexicans was swarming the street, and to Scrap they probably all looked alike. Josiah had to forcibly keep a smile from crossing his face.

"Me? Why is it my fault?" Scrap said, stretching his neck up and about, looking everywhere for Juan Carlos. "Damn it. I can't see nothing but Mexicans. He could be staring me in the face and I wouldn't know it."

"How am I supposed to keep an eye on somebody when I'm behind the wagon, then behind a horse?"

"You let him go, then."

"Why would I do that?"

"Why wouldn't you? You've been chummin' with him since he showed up in Neu-Braunfels."

Josiah stared at Scrap and could tell the kid wasn't quite sure of his accusation, was searching for a way out of the mess he'd seemingly found himself in. "You saw the bindings on his legs as clear as I did. His wrists were bound, too, only with enough give for him to navigate the wagon. How, exactly, did I let him go?"

"I don't know, but you did."

"Well, you better go after him. I'll let the sheriff know what happened."

Scrap hesitated, the look on his face showing that he was actively rethinking his immediate accusation. "Maybe the ropes came loose," he finally said.

"Yeah, maybe they did," Josiah said with a sigh, as Scrap took off and disappeared into the crowd himself.

I hope those ropes stay off, Josiah thought to himself. And, as sad as it was, he hoped he never saw Juan Carlos again. He hoped the old Mexican would live out his life safely, in secret, now that his protector and friend, Captain Hiram Fikes, was dead. But something told Josiah that his hope was a waste of effort. He would surely see Juan Carlos again, and the circumstances were bound to be unpleasant.

Before Josiah climbed back up on the wagon, the sheriff, a sprite younger man with a finely waxed mustache, approached him hesitantly.

"I would imagine you are going to deliver the body of Captain Fikes to his home?"

Josiah nodded. The sheriff's clothes smelled clean, and his coat hardly had a speck of dust on it. His name was Rory Farnsworth, and the stiff, tart lawman had made it quick business to let Josiah know that he had attended college out east before returning to Texas. After, of course, Josiah had informed the sheriff of Juan Carlos's "escape."

Sheriff Farnsworth sent out two deputies to aid Scrap in the search, but showed little excitement about the Mexican's whereabouts. He was more concerned with wagging Josiah's ear about his stature as a lawman.

Sheriffs must drink a special brand of whiskey, Josiah thought to himself. One that raises their opinion of themselves to a dangerously high level. It'd be like living on a cliff as far as Josiah was concerned. He was glad he'd never developed a taste for whiskey.

Then the sheriff had gone on and on, babbling about his family life as if it mattered to Josiah.

Farnsworth was more than pompously proud of himself—he was elated with himself. According to Farnsworth his bloodline had dictated a higher calling, but he had bucked his family's view of how he should live his life as a legislator back east. Instead, he had taken up the badge in the rough-and-tumble state of Texas, rebelling and finding his true calling, all at once. It was a serious, if underpaid, vocation, as far as Farnsworth was concerned, but he felt certain he was up to the daily challenge of maintaining peace, reeling in ruffians, and shooting an exact and deadly shot if it was required of him.

Educated men, especially educated lawmen, who were vocally concerned about their legacy, unsettled Josiah, made him more nervous than a shoot-out in a wide-open canyon.

He wanted to get away from the jail block as quickly as possible. Especially considering that his last encounter with a sheriff, specifically Sheriff J. T. Patterson, hadn't turned out too well as far as Josiah was concerned. He was convinced that the sheriff in San Antonio was responsible for the captain's death, since before dying McClure had named him as one of the men in the fleeing gang after the captain had been killed. A murderous lawman, indeed, even though it didn't make sense. Still, a lawman with a bad streak was not unprecedented.

He gave Farnsworth the information about Patterson that McClure had given him, but the sheriff did not seem inclined to take the accusation too seriously. He said he would pass on the information . . . as would Josiah.

At that moment, Josiah wondered how Sam Willis and Pete Feders had fared in their quest. He didn't know if they were still alive, in pursuit of Charlie Langdon, or had him in custody. Sheriff Farnsworth had no news for him on that front.

"I do plan on delivering the captain home. As quickly as I can," Josiah said to the sheriff, looking out into the crowd that was still gathered around the buckboard. "As soon as Ranger Elliot returns. I doubt he would be able to find the captain's home if you drew him a map."

"And the other dead man? What are your plans for him?"

"I'm hoping for directions to the undertaker."

"Be about two blocks up and on your right. Once you're there, you're not too far from the captain's house. You won't be able to miss it. Go about half a mile past the governor's mansion, turn right on the third alleyway, and the house sits about another half mile down the way on the right. Same man that was responsible for the governor's mansion also built the captain's house. Abner Cook, do you know of him?" the sheriff asked.

"Can't say that I do. My father built my cabin." With that, Josiah climbed up on the buckboard and took the reins into his hands. "I'll check back after I've settled in, and give the circuit court judge my testimony, if need be, about Juan Carlos."

"There's no need to worry, Ranger Wolfe. It is well known here in Austin that Captain Hiram Fikes and Juan Carlos were longtime friends. It does not surprise me that he made his way into the streets. He's probably down yonder in the place they call 'Little Mexico,' deep in the arms of a woman by now, and swilling tequila."

"Good," Josiah said. "I'll take you at your word."

"Most people do. Good day, Wolfe. I'm sure we'll meet again at the captain's funeral. The governor is planning on attending, you know. And I heard that Major Jones is returning quickly from the new camp of Rangers specifically to pay tribute to Captain Fikes. Important men from all over the state, even Indian Territory, are expected. It will be a sad day for all Texas to bid farewell to the captain."

Josiah stiffened at the thought of the company of politicians. He had not considered that the funeral would be a draw to men of great importance, or that it would cause Major Jones to return to Austin.

"If Ranger Elliot comes looking for me, tell him to meet up with me at the undertaker's. I'll wait for him there."

Sheriff Farnsworth agreed that he would, then bid Josiah a good day.

Josiah did not return the gesture.

A good day would come when he was sitting on Clipper, alone, on the trail, heading back to the cabin in the piney woods, and not before.

Josiah was visiting an undertaker for the second time in just as many days, and he was none too pleased with the streak. He hoped this was the end of it.

Once Vi McClure's body was deposited with the undertaker, a large fellow with buckteeth and an odd smell to his breath, Josiah waited outside for Scrap. There would be no funeral for McClure.

A notice would be put in the paper announcing his death, and the circumstances under which that questionable event occurred, and then, more than likely, the Scot would be deposited in a pauper's grave, and his story would come to an end there.

Josiah tried to remember if McClure had said he was originally from Kentucky or Tennessee, but he couldn't remember. Couldn't remember the town the Scot hailed from, either, or if McClure had even said where he was from. There'd be no way to get word to his place of birth without knowing for certain. For some reason, Josiah felt sad at the thought.

Luckily, he did not have too much time to consider the effects of Vi McClure's passing. Scrap rode up on Missy with a scowl on his face as broad as the whole state of Texas.

"Didn't find the Mexican, I take it?" Josiah asked.

"How'd you guess?"

"Got lucky, I suppose."

"I suppose."

"Well, enough of your bellyaching, let's get Captain Fikes home. We're almost there. Once we're free of that task, you can stand around and accuse me of dereliction of my duty all you want, but I assure you, it will fall on deaf ears."

"Feders and Willis will listen to me."

Josiah nodded. "They will listen to us both. And to the sheriff, too. Oh, and if you're lucky, perhaps Major Jones will lend an ear to your tales as well."

"Major Jones?"

"Yes. He's coming for the captain's funeral. The governor, too, from what I understand. There'll be a long line of dignitaries, all in their finery, anxious to hear how Captain Fikes came to meet his maker. I would suggest you have your story practiced by then."

"I know what I saw. I ain't got a need to practice anything," Scrap said, the scowl still on his face.

"I suppose not," Josiah answered, grabbing up the reins of the horse and putting the buckboard in motion with one quick flick of the leather.

CHAPTER 20

Josiah stopped the buckboard, suddenly, before turning onto the lane that led up to the captain's house. It was an impressive structure. Not nearly as big as the governor's mansion they had just ridden by, but every bit as grand. Four white columns held up the gabled roof of a two-story portico that looked out over a calm meadow with a pond nearly in the center of it.

An empty bench sat looking out over the still waters of the pond, and Josiah could imagine Captain Fikes sitting on the bench, smoking after an evening meal, pondering about Rangering, politics, or Texas in general; all of the things he loved. Maybe the captain came home to rejuvenate, rest before tackling another journey on the trail. Being away from home took a special man. Josiah was relearning those skills . . . but he wasn't sure if he had what it took anymore. He was certain if he had a home as grand as the captain's, he'd never want to leave it.

Wrought iron fronted the second story of the house,

making entry and exit safe from the doors and windows that led outside to twin balconies. The red tile roof shimmered in the full sun, and the whitewash on the stucco exterior looked newly applied, like the work had been done in the last day or so.

Spring flowers lined the lane leading up to the house, another sea of flittering bluebonnets, and there were pots with fernlike plants situated at both sides of the main entrance. The air smelled like a sweet mixture of subtle perfume and freshly cut grass that had been taken nearly to the ground with a sickle. Everything around the house was neat, trim, and clean.

Two large barns stood just past the house, just beyond a series of well-maintained servant quarters and a large carriage house. Tall, imposing trees, cottonwoods and elms, populated the rest of the grounds, offering a healthy dose of shade to the round circular drive at the front.

It was hard to believe they were so close to the heart of Austin, and yet the house and surrounding land seemed so tranquil. It was not too long ago that there was a battle for the state house—a battle that almost brought in federal troops, the cavalry.

Black buntings were neatly adorned across the front of the house, swags of heavy cloth whose only purpose was to give the notice of death's certain arrival. Sadness at the estate was now fully advertised, and decorated properly for the men of high office and stature expected to pay tribute to the fallen hero and resident, a true son of Texas, Captain Hiram Fikes, on the grounds of his own home and final resting place.

But it was not only the sight of the house that stopped Josiah in his tracks, it was the woman, standing on the first balcony, who had made his heart rise unexpectedly in his throat.

The lane ended at the house well over thirty yards from where he sat, but he could see her clearly . . . almost too clearly, for the sunlight was perfect, beaming down on the woman's shoulder-length blond hair, soft-featured face, and hourglass figure, adorned in the proper black, as she stood on the second floor, gazing out in the distance at nothing in particular.

Her face showed strains of worry, but there was a sweetness projecting from the woman that was unmistakable, though not to be confused with fragility. And she was more than a girl, which is what Josiah had expected once he had learned there was a daughter of the captain's still living in his home.

Then Josiah remembered Juan Carlos's warning, and even without proper introductions, he knew he had laid his eyes on the captain's daughter, Pearl, for the very first time.

She was nearly the most beautiful woman he had ever seen.

He had to catch his breath at the thought, and looked quickly over his shoulder to see if Scrap had noticed his confusion—and embarrassment.

"Ride ahead, Elliot," he ordered, wiping the sweat off his brow.

Scrap looked at Josiah curiously. "You all right, Wolfe?"

"Why?"

"Your face just turned red as a sugar beet. Something the matter?"

"No, just ride ahead. Mind your manners if anyone comes out to meet you."

Scrap smirked, shook his head, and guided Missy slowly

around the buckboard. "I never met a man as contrary as you, Wolfe. Anyone ever tell you that before?"

"Go. Just go."

The woman, Pearl, he was still assuming, turned her gaze to Josiah and Scrap, as Scrap rode up to the house as fast as he could.

Her head drooped momentarily as she saw the coffin on the back of the buckboard, the reality of her father's death now a certainty instead of a rumor that hopefully, possibly, was not true. She did not need to see the body to know that his death was real now.

Two strangers had come calling, carrying a wood box that contained her worst nightmare—at least, that's how Josiah supposed she felt; it was how he would feel, how he *had* felt when he had watched Lily's coffin being lowered into the grave.

When the woman looked up, after realizing what she was witnessing, a tear glistened down her cheek, and knowing she had been seen as well, she turned and walked inside—but before she disappeared off the balcony, she looked directly at Josiah, looked him in the eye, nodded as if to say thank you, forced a smile that couldn't have been more beautiful, then disappeared inside the double French doors.

Josiah's stomach fluttered and turned in circles, like he was a schoolboy seeing a pretty girl for the very first time.

He never thought he would feel that way again, experience any kind of attraction to another woman.

Now was not the time, he told himself. He felt guilty. Silly. Out of control. Ashamed that he had even let himself think of another woman, a woman in mourning at that. He had betrayed his entire life with Lily in one moment of unprecedented weakness and surprise. He wasn't sure how to live with that.

There was only one thing to do now: Deliver the captain's coffin, express his condolences, and be on his way as quickly as possible.

Perhaps he wouldn't have to see Pearl, or meet her. Perhaps she had a beau, or was married. He knew nothing of her—other than that she glowed, radiated life and a loveliness that he had never seen before. Ever.

If he were not the bearer of a dead body, stuck smack-dab in the middle of a nightmare, then Josiah Wolfe would have thought that he had dozed off and woken up in the middle of a dream he'd never considered himself capable of having.

Maybe it was the season, spring, and the wildflowers, their fragrance making him drunk and lost to himself. Maybe, he thought . . . that was it. Even though he knew better.

He had forgotten the part of him that was weak to desire, the part of him that hungered for the softness of a touch and enjoyed the sweaty whispers of love in the middle of the night. He had willed that part of himself away, thought he had buried desire and need in a grave in East Texas, in a small cemetery that also held his three daughters, their life cut short, his emotional life ended as well.

Josiah knew that leaving quickly after depositing Captain Fikes's body would betray his orders.

Not only had Feders insisted that he stay in Austin, but Josiah was to be of service to the captain's family, in any way they needed, until he received his next set of orders.

Josiah took a deep breath at the thought of disobeying orders, knowing full well that he wouldn't. Then he chided himself once more for being inappropriate and headed to the captain's grand house once and for all.

Scrap was standing next to Missy, his head bowed to the ground. Four Mexicans had appeared out of nowhere and immediately moved to the back of the buckboard once Josiah came to a stop.

The front door of the house swung open, and Josiah held his breath.

To his relief, a tall Mexican man dressed in a formal black suit—frock coat, white gloves, and all—stepped outside, holding the door open.

Josiah knew little about the hierarchy of servants. His family had certainly never had the kind of money to employ any, with the exception of the help Ofelia gave him, but that was on a different scale, an emotional transaction as much as it was a monetary arrangement—Ofelia felt responsible for Lyle, and Josiah accepted that fully and was grateful for her help. He never felt ownership over the midwife. Never even considered it.

But this servant, this man, who looked quite a lot like Juan Carlos, enough to be his brother, was most definitely in charge, the hierarchy certain.

The four men behind the buckboard looked expectantly to the formally dressed man for orders, for what was to come next. The servant nodded, then flipped the palm of his hand subtly at the four, an obvious signal for them to wait.

Who came next was the lady of the house.

The captain's wife—or so Josiah assumed . . . again—spewing orders, directing each man to remove the coffin from the wagon immediately. There was no emotion. At least no hysterics like he had been led to believe might occur when he was first instructed to meet the captain's wife. Just the opposite. The woman was on a mission.

"Take that out of my sight," the woman said, pointing at the blanket that had covered the coffin all the way from Neu-Braunfels. "Burn it."

"*Sí*," the manservant said, nodding, backing away, sweeping up the blanket and stowing it behind him.

The woman ignored Josiah and Scrap as the four Mexicans pulled the coffin off the wagon, then hefted it on their shoulders.

"Take him to the parlor and put him in the new coffin there. Then burn that one along with that sorry blanket. And for God's sake, don't let Pearl see the mortal remains of her father when you put him in the new coffin. She is nearly at her breaking point the way it is."

No one said anything; all four men stiffened, then marched past the woman, carrying the coffin inside like they were instructed.

The woman, who was dressed head to toe in black widow's weeds, stood back and watched the coffin pass by closely—without showing any emotion at all. She looked like she was judging the quality of craftsmanship applied to the hand-crafted box and wholeheartedly disapproved.

If the captain were alive and standing next to the woman, she would have towered over him by a good head and a half. She was tall and bony and had wiry gray hair pulled up on top of her head, bound in the back, and topped with a small black hat, the suitable veil of which was pulled up out of her face. Her cheeks were a little sunken, and her blue eyes were pale, the color of a robin's egg.

Unlike her daughter, at least from a distance, the woman who Josiah assumed was the captain's wife did look fragile, as if a touch to her face would cause her to shatter like the thinnest glass vase Josiah had ever seen.

He'd expected the woman to resemble Mayor Kessler in a recognizable way, since they were related, but she looked nothing like the earnest man who'd seen them out of Neu-Braunfels.

"You, sir, what is your function?" the woman asked Josiah.

"I am a Ranger who served under Captain Fikes. My name is Josiah Wolfe, ma'am."

A quizzical look crossed the woman's face, deep crevices furrowing her brow. "I do not know any Wolfes in Austin."

"I hail from near Tyler. Seerville, actually. I have only come to Austin for the first time on this day."

"I see."

"I have a letter from Sergeant Feders." Josiah pulled out of his pocket the letter that Feders had entrusted to him, and offered it to the woman.

She stared at him coldly. "For me?"

"If you are the wife of Captain Hiram Fikes."

"I am."

"Then I am very sorry for your loss."

"Thank you," she snapped, taking the letter and shoving it into a hidden pocket of the black brocade garb she wore. "And you're a Ranger, too, I suspect?" She directed the question to Scrap.

"I am, Mrs. Fikes. It was an honor to know the captain and serve under him, even though it was for just a short time. I just joined up with him a few weeks ago. I hope you will accept my sincerest sympathy."

"Why, thank you, young man. Hank always did have a good eye for picking the right sort for his adventures."

"Hank, ma'am?" Scrap asked.

"No one here ever called your captain Hiram. It was an offense to the ears and likely to get you taken out behind the woodshed for a set of lashings you'd soon not forget."

Scrap smiled. "I am glad I never made that mistake."

Josiah had never seen a more charming, warm side of Scrap Elliot. He wasn't sure he recognized the well-mannered boy who was speaking. Scrap stood up straight, looked Mrs. Fikes in the eye, and actually acted like he had some sense. Wonders never ceased. Maybe there was hope for Scrap Elliot after all.

"And what shall I call you, young man?"

Scrap laughed. "Robert Earl Elliot. But folks all my life tagged me as Scrap if they were my friends. Scrap Elliot, ma'am, that's what you can call me if it wouldn't be too presumptuous to assume that we might become friends."

"Lord knows I could use all the friends I can get at the moment." Mrs. Fikes returned Scrap's smile, then looked to Josiah. "You will need to rest your horses and clean yourselves up before getting on your way, I assume?"

"Sergeant Feders ordered us to be of service to you and your family, ma'am," Josiah said. "We will stay here, unless you object, until we receive new orders."

The woman studied Josiah and flashed another smile at Scrap. "Yes, Pearl might like the company. There is extra room for you both in the carriage house. Pedro will see to it that you are comfortable."

The Mexican manservant nodded at Josiah, implying that he was Pedro.

"Thank you, ma'am," Josiah said. "Again, I am very

sorry for your loss. If there is anything I can do to ease your suffering, please don't hesitate to ask."

Mrs. Fikes looked past Josiah at the group of horses tied to the back of the buckboard. "Is Hank's horse there?"

"Yes, ma'am," Josiah said. "That's Fat Susie in the middle."

"Good," Mrs. Fikes answered over her shoulder as she made a quick turn toward the house. "Shoot her."

CHAPTER 21

The carriage house was well appointed, and large enough for plenty of storage and repairs. It was bigger inside than most barns, and cleaner, too. A four-passenger surrey sat next to a calash with a leather folding top. Beyond the calash sat a platform spring wagon, similar to what Josiah called a buckboard.

Every inch of every buggy and wagon was without a speck of dust. A fella could have eaten off the freshly swept floor. It must have been a difficult, and surely a constant, feat keeping such a place so tidy, but there was no question that on the captain's estate everything was kept in its place . . . even dirt.

Mrs. Fikes obviously ruled over the daily chores with an iron hand, had high expectations, and did not relent in her pursuit of those expectations. There were some similarities to the homes in Neu-Braunfels, now that Josiah thought about it. The captain's wife sure seemed like a demanding sort.

Josiah hoped his stay in Austin would be short, hoped Feders would show up soon. It still amazed him that the captain's home was so . . . grand. He had never taken Hiram Fikes for a wealthy man.

From the look of things, the captain had had no need to ride hard on the trail like he did—unless he just wanted to. How the money had been made to sustain a piece of property that was just shy of being considered a plantation was not immediately apparent . . . or really any of Josiah's business . . . but it did make him wonder.

There were no crops or harvesting equipment to be seen. And the captain had never, in all of the time they spent together, even hinted at any means of making a living other than being a soldier and then a Ranger.

Josiah had only been on the estate less than an hour, and he'd already experienced far more discomfort than he'd ever expected to. There was no place he would fit in on the land Captain Fikes called home. The captain's wife had looked at him like he belonged with the dirt. His place was as far away from Austin, and the estate, as possible.

Josiah stopped the buckboard just inside the double doors of the carriage house, and jumped down, glad to stand on two legs for more than a minute, glad to finally be free of the coffin, swarms of flies, and the ever-present smell of death.

"There are rooms in the back with fresh bedding, señor," Pedro said, appearing out of the shadows from behind the buggy. "There is also a place to bathe out behind the barn. Hot water will be waiting for you."

"Thank you," Josiah said, setting about to release the trail horse from the buckboard's harness.

"There is no need, señor, I have plenty of stable help here."

Josiah looked at Pedro oddly. He may have looked a little like Juan Carlos, but his speech was more Anglo, his Mexican accent less defined, almost impossible to detect. "I was hoping to avoid having Fat Susie shot. She's a good horse."

Pedro lowered his amber brown eyes. "The captain made some choices that were not always welcome here. He chose poorly to pay reverence to an ill-reputed woman his wife despises."

"I understand that, but she's a good horse."

"The madam has made her wishes known. I will have the horse taken care of, you need not worry about it."

Footsteps came up behind Josiah—he whirled around and came face-to-face with Scrap.

"Am I interruptin' something?"

Josiah shook his head no. "I'm just trying to save the captain's horse."

"I'll shoot her," Scrap offered happily.

Pedro turned his attention to Scrap, looked him up and down, kind of like Mrs. Fikes judging the coffin her husband had been brought home in. The result was the same. Pedro obviously wasn't impressed with what he saw. His lip curled up, and his eyes hardened. "Ranger Wolfe and I will see that task through, señor. You should concern yourself with a bath. There's a tub waiting behind the barn."

Scrap glared at Pedro, then turned to Josiah. "Did a Mexican just tell me I stink?"

Josiah couldn't contain the smile that rose to his face, or the laughter rising deep in his chest. "I think he did."

"That's not funny, Wolfe."

"Damn, if it's not."

Pedro had stiffened. He had far more control of himself than Josiah did.

Scrap started to say something, then obviously thought better of it, and stomped off in the direction of the bath.

Josiah just shook his head, a smile still on his face. "I'm sorry about that, Pedro."

"It is of no consequence, Ranger Wolfe. I have dealt with that all of my life, even though I was born and raised far from here. I was never a Mexican loyalist."

"I am sorry about that, too."

"Don't be. I have had a very satisfying life serving the captain and his family."

Josiah cocked his eyebrow, curious. "What do you know of Juan Carlos?"

Pedro sighed. "Juan Carlos, you know him?"

"He saved my life. They wanted to charge him with the killing of a man in San Antonio . . . the man he saved me from, so he had to disappear."

"Disappearing is one of Juan Carlos's many talents. It is a skill he had to develop a long time ago." Pedro stepped in closer, lowered his voice. "You do not know about him and the captain?"

"Nothing, other than they were good friends."

"Good friends." Pedro chuckled, then stopped, looking over his shoulder to make sure they were still alone in the carriage house. "They were brothers. Same father. Different mother."

"Brothers. I would have never guessed," Josiah said. "I would have figured you and Juan Carlos were brothers, not Juan Carlos and the captain."

Pedro chuckled again. "We are united only by our country of origin. I have long envied Juan Carlos, the errant brother, always in the captain's shadow, protecting him, doing his bidding. He must be heartbroken that he was not there to save the captain in his hour of need."

"I think he is," Josiah said.

"Do you know where he is?"

Josiah shook his head no. "It was a good secret, their being brothers."

"Only out of necessity, señor. The captain had ambitions. You must be aware of that. Having a half-breed brother reflects poorly on one's position."

"That explains a lot."

"I expect you will not betray my trust? There are not many who know that truth."

Josiah stroked his chin. "No, you have nothing to worry about from me." He paused, then said, "I don't mean anything by this, but you sure don't talk like you look."

Pedro nodded, and bestowed a genuine smile in Josiah's direction. His white teeth, against his bronze skin, gleamed in the sunlight.

"The madam sent me east for schooling, once she determined I had an inclination for it. I spent six years in Dartmouth. It has been many years ago, and I have been loyal and thankful to the madam ever since. I still maintain my native tongue, though it is looked down upon. It is imperative to know the language here. But I, too, have to be aware of how my actions reflect on the madam and the captain."

"Sounds like the captain's wife has plenty of ambition of her own."

"*Sí, señor, sí.*"

"That's good to know," Josiah said, staring up at the house, glad to be relegated as far from it as possible.

"Once you get your bath, Ranger Wolfe, you will be expected in the main house for a meal," Pedro said, almost like he could read Josiah's mind and mood. "The other one, as well."

Josiah looked at Pedro curiously. "The other one?"

"The one you call Scrap."

Josiah dropped his head, looking forward even less to the event now that he was expected to share it with Scrap. But his disappointment only lasted for a second. He jerked his head straight up. "I almost forgot." He went to the back of the buckboard and began unloading from the surviving trail horse's leather cargo bags the bread, strudel, cakes, and cheeses Mayor Kessler had sent ahead.

A door slammed in the house, echoing across the meadow like a gunshot. Josiah started, and reached for his Peacemaker without any thought of what he was doing. The madam, Mrs. Fikes, shouted for Pedro to come. Her voice was shrill, demanding, reaching every inch of the estate, and probably beyond.

A cold chill traveled down Josiah's spine. He let go of the gun.

The Mexican servant stiffened. "No need, Ranger Wolfe, I'll have the goods brought to the house. Leave them here," Pedro said, nervously.

"They're from the mayor in Neu-Braunfels, the . . . madam's cousin." Josiah wasn't sure what to call the captain's wife. The madam seemed an awfully strange thing to call a woman.

Pedro forced a smile. "Come to the main house as soon as you are respectable, but there is no need to hurry."

The captain's wife shouted again. This time, she appeared on the opposite balcony from where Josiah had first spied Pearl; she was leaning over the rail, her right hand at her brow shielding the sun as she looked for Pedro.

"Good. I'll need some time," Josiah said, mainly to himself, watching keenly as Pedro hurried up to the house without saying another word.

There was something about Pedro that just didn't set right with Josiah. He just couldn't figure out what that something was. Or if it really mattered in the first place.

Scrap was lounging in a steaming bath, smoking a quirley, a hand-rolled cigarette, his head resting on the rim of the wood tub. He opened his eyes briefly when Josiah entered the bathhouse, casting him a quick disapproving glance, then closed his eyes just as quickly as he had opened them.

Four tubs sat on a wood-planked floor. A roof jutted out, protecting the bathers from the sun and weather. Three-quarter walls rose up on three sides. The back wall was actually the rear of the carriage house, from which Josiah had entered. There was no other way in or out. Red-hot coals from a well-maintained fire flickered in the bottom of a stone fireplace that had been built on the outside wall. A big pot of steaming water hung from an iron bracket in the center.

Several sets of tables and chairs were scattered about, and there were wood storage closets all along the far wall. Josiah supposed that within the closets there were towels, soaps, and whatever else a man would need to clean himself. He'd been in plenty of hotels that were far less equipped than this place.

A shave was more than necessary, as far as he was concerned, and he hoped there was a good blade and a mirror stowed away somewhere for his use.

A short Mexican, one of the men who'd carried the captain's coffin inside the main house, stood in the corner, obviously to be of service to their needs. He nodded to Josiah when he entered the bath. "*Hola,*" Josiah said, returning the gesture.

A full tub was waiting for him, just like Pedro said it would be. He stuck his finger in the water to test it. The temperature was just right.

"How come you like Mexicans so much, Wolfe?" Scrap asked, sitting up.

Josiah disrobed, piling his clothes just within reach, along with his gun. He didn't answer Scrap until he settled fully in the water. He hadn't told Scrap about Ofelia, and he wasn't going to now. "Not sure that I like or dislike them any better than I do anybody else. What have you got against them?"

Scrap ground out the quirley on the rim of the tub. "I don't know, Wolfe. Maybe it was the Alamo that did it. Sometimes I can't figure you out . . . if you're really a Texan like the rest of us or not."

The water felt good. Josiah wanted to relax. He'd had his fill of arguing with Scrap . . . which seemed like it had been a constant occurrence since they'd left San Antonio. "There's a supper in the main house. We're expected to be there after we get respectable."

"Are you?"

"What, Elliot?"

"A Texan like the rest of us?"

"I'm a Ranger. That's all that matters to you."

"It don't matter to me. Not really. I know what you are."

"And what's that?" Josiah demanded, clenching his fingers under the water. He glanced over to the table his Peacemaker sat on.

"Ain't no sense in gettin' all riled, Wolfe. I'm just pokin' fun at you. You're a Texas Ranger, that's what you are."

"Sometimes I sure don't see what Captain Fikes saw in you, Elliot. I guess I'll have to trust his judgment about you, but I'll be damned if I know why I should. You're one of the most obstinate boys I've ever come to know."

"I'm the best shot this side of Fort Worth. Ain't no more or less to it than that. The captain needed a good, honest shot, and I was it."

Josiah stopped and thought about what Scrap had just said. The only time he'd seen Scrap pull a gun was at the ambush just outside of Austin, and Josiah was so busy fending off the shooters, he didn't see Scrap shoot anything. Didn't matter, other than that the two shooters got away. But every other time in his life Josiah had run into a man who claimed to be the best shot around, well, that man was always practicing shooting, always pulling his gun out of the holster as fast as he could. Scrap hadn't done anything that would back up his claim.

"We'll have to see about that sometime, Elliot. But let's just put this aside for now. I'd like a quiet bath."

Scrap started to say something, but Josiah didn't let him.

"I'm serious, Elliot, I want to take this damn bath in peace. Put it aside."

Scrap shook his head, bit the corner of his lip, then stood up out of the water angrily.

Before he could cover up, Josiah noticed a multitude of scars on Scrap's back. There was no mistaking that Scrap's skin had been permanently disfigured by fire. Hot fire. Nearly all of the kid's back was affected in one way or another. The scars were old and healed over, but they still looked painful.

Josiah turned fully away as Scrap grabbed up a towel and covered his back as quickly as he could.

Josiah closed his eyes, settled down as far as he could into the tub, and tried to let go of his thoughts. But all he could think of was Scrap telling him how his parents had been killed by the Comanche. There was clearly more to that story, probably more than Josiah wanted to know, if the truth be told.

Just about every time he'd had his fill of Scrap Elliot, the kid seemed to give him a reason to like him a little more. Maybe all he needed was someone to watch out for him and show him how to be a Ranger, and maybe more of a man.

CHAPTER 22

Josiah sat on the bench staring at the pond. It was the first time he'd been totally alone since leaving San Antonio. He felt like he could finally breathe, think things through, now that Scrap had stalked off, angry again—still in search of some elusive sort who would listen to his tales and tolerate his wearisome attitudes.

The silence, like the bath, was refreshing.

The Mexican had given him a nice shave and provided him with a clean pair of trousers and a shirt that nearly fit him perfectly. Now he almost felt like the last couple of days hadn't happened, since the dirt had been washed off his skin, out from under his fingernails, and from behind his ears. He almost felt like a new man. Almost. A good meal and then a good night's sleep would complete the circle.

The day was coming to an end, and he wasn't any closer to knowing when he'd return home to his son, Lyle, than he'd been the day before. That was his only concern, the only pull on his soul, at the moment.

Lyle was never far from his thoughts, and there hadn't been any word from Feders. No orders. Nothing. All he could do was wait . . . in this place where he wore a stranger's clothes and did not know the rules or where he fit in.

Mayflies buzzed and swerved about the pond. Frog eyes peered up at him along the banks, uncertain if he was a threat, reacting to every movement he made.

The sun was about to sit its bottom on the horizon, a rolling, bumpy set of hills that stretched on for as far as the eye could see. Cattails swayed in a slight breeze, and across the shallow pond, a heron stalked after its prey, one slow step at a time, watching, listening, for any opportunity to kill its next meal successfully.

Josiah watched the bird for a long time, allowing himself not to think about much of anything. It was a nice change of pace. Until he realized that he was expected to have dinner at the main house.

The sun was nearly gone, and the sky was fading from blue to gray, but not before several fingers of soft pink light reached out from the west, creating a spectacular sunset.

He started to stand up, but immediately sat back down on the bench when he heard footsteps approaching behind him.

He had seen her out of the corner of his eye, blond hair shimmering in the dusky evening light, and knew immediately that he was trapped and needed to flee.

Josiah looked every which way for an escape route, but there was no way he could leave without being seen and taken for rude. Manners, man, manners, he said to himself, standing quickly, and coming face-to-face with Pearl Fikes for the first time.

His chest vibrated and he nearly quit breathing, she was so beautiful. Even in her state of mourning, she was a rare, shining flower in a field of darkness.

The heron squawked angrily as it lit into the air, flushed from its preferred hunting spot. The bird's long blue wings barely cleared the cattails as it flew off, opposite the sunset.

"Good evening," the woman said. "I hope I'm not interrupting anything."

She was dressed in black widow's weeds that were far more simple than those that her mother had been wearing earlier in the day. Her dress fell to the ground, over her feet, her boots hidden, and she didn't wear a hat or veil of any sort. Her hair flowed over her shoulders like a river of gold cascading over a waterfall in some imaginary land. Her eyes were blue, deeper than the color of the heron's wings, and not fragile at all.

There was an ache in her eyes that Josiah recognized. Death always sucked the sparkle out of a mourner's eyes first, then aimed to steal the will to live after it was done grinding away any sight of joy.

"No, ma'am." Josiah removed his hat, and nodded deeply, so much so that the action was almost a bow. "I was just taking a moment to enjoy this pond. I will leave you to yourself."

"No," she said, reaching and touching his arm, stopping him from walking away, "please stay."

The warmth of her touch pierced the long sleeve of the linen shirt he was wearing. She pulled her fingers away quickly.

"I'm sorry, I haven't introduced myself. I'm Josiah Wolfe. I was a Ranger with Captain Fikes." He didn't want to assume the woman was Pearl, but she most certainly had to be.

"I know. Pedro told me. I'm Pearl. The captain was my father."

"I assumed as much."

"We can sit."

Before he thought about what he was about to say, the words jumped out of his mouth, "Is that proper? I mean, sitting out here with a stranger . . . without a chaperone?"

"Please, Josiah, I am long past needing a chaperone. Unless, of course, you're a dangerous man." A smile flittered across Pearl's face, then disappeared quickly, like the bird flying away from the sunset, out of sight, dim light making its wings glow for the longest time.

It had been an eternity since a woman had spoken his name, requested an action of him that he knew he had no choice but to submit to. He was numb. "You have nothing to fear from me," he said.

"I didn't think so. Sit, please. I mean, if you would like to."

Josiah did bow this time, then swept out his hand and said, "After you, ma'am."

"You're an odd man, Josiah Wolfe," Pearl said, settling herself on the bench.

"Thank you . . . I think."

Josiah sat on the bench, as far to the other side of Pearl as he could be, clutching the arm, his other hand flat out on one of his locked knees. The breeze swirled around them, a cool, blanketing rush, offering comfort.

He could smell Pearl, a slight hint of a flowery fragrance that was familiar yet foreign to him. Bluebonnets were bold, while the scent that adorned Pearl's lustrous skin was not intent on attracting anything. It was a duty, a choice, a feminine mystery that Josiah lacked any knowledge of.

Lily was never afforded the opportunity to wear toilet water. Instead, she smelled of their sparse land, of the pine cabin, of their children, and of living. He knew how to react to that scent, even though he had almost lost his memory of it.

Suddenly, he was even more desperate to remove himself from Pearl.

Regardless of intent, he found her scent more than intoxicating. What he really wanted to do was to nuzzle her neck, draw closer to her, no matter how inappropriate that desire was. He was on the verge of losing control of himself, of his thoughts, all of which were a continuing surprise and a matter of serious discomfort.

"Are you well, Josiah?"

"Yes, yes, I'm fine."

"Your face is pale."

Josiah forced a smile. "It has been a trying day."

"I am keeping you from a fine meal. I apologize. Mother will be furious, of course."

"Please don't apologize. Your company is just . . . unexpected."

For the first time, Josiah allowed himself to look for a sign of Pearl's marital status. She wore nothing to indicate she was married, but she could be engaged, promised, in love.

How was he to know? The fact that he even cared made him even more uncomfortable.

Pearl stared across the bench at Josiah, looked down to judge the distance between them, then looked back out across the pond, matching Josiah's gaze exactly. "You are far too nervous for a man of your age and experience, Mr. Wolfe."

Josiah jerked his head toward her, reacting to being called mister instead of by name. He wasn't sure what had precipitated the change, and he wasn't sure he liked the coldness attached to it.

Pearl grinned, staring straight ahead, meeting Josiah's look out of the corner of her eye. "You prefer to be called Josiah, I take it?" The grin faded quickly away.

He nodded. "I fear saying something that will offend you."

Pearl relaxed. "My father was a Ranger, a soldier, and no matter how briefly we were together, my dear deceased husband was a man of similar nature. I am not easily offended, Josiah. Please, relax."

Josiah sat there, uncomfortably silent, staring at circles forming on top of the water. "I am sorry for your loss. Both of them," he added after a brief pause.

Pearl lowered her head. "I did not mean to solicit grief from you, Josiah. I thought perhaps since you knew my father well, then you would know a little about me."

"I had only just recently rejoined your father's company. I am sorry, we had troubles to attend to, and there was little time for familiarity. The captain spoke little of his family to most of the men who rode with him. Sergeant Feders would probably be more aware of his personal situations than I am."

"Peter, yes, I'm sure he would." There was an exasperated tone in her voice.

"Is something the matter?" Josiah was curious if a message had come from Feders that he didn't know about.

"No, no. Peter is a fine man. I am just not ready for a proper suitor at this point in my life. Mother has certainly welcomed his overtures, and pushed me to accept them. There has been plenty of time since Warren's, my husband's, premature death—three years. But, honestly, I am in no state of mind to take up with a man who wants to be just like my father. What am I supposed to do? Sit at home by myself and wait for him to come back in a pine box, too?"

"This is a difficult time for you. I really should leave you to yourself." Josiah stood up.

He didn't really want to leave her, but knowing now that

she had been widowed by some unknown and unfortunate tragedy, and was also the object of Pete Feders's affection, disheartened him as much as learning about her fear and obvious distaste for the Rangering life.

If she did marry Feders, she was absolutely right; she would sit at home for months at a time with one eye on the lane that led up to the house, expecting her dead husband to arrive anytime, just like her father had. He couldn't blame her for her concerns.

Pearl stood, too. "I wish you would stay. I know so little about you, Josiah."

"I'm a Ranger."

Pearl sighed and looked up at him with her deep blue eyes, searching. "I have offended you. For some reason we seem at odds before we've had a chance to know one another."

"I was warned not to take you lightly, and I have tried not to."

"Who would warn you of such a thing about me?"

"Juan Carlos. I believe he meant it as a compliment."

Pearl stepped toward Josiah, coming face-to-face with him and stopping within inches.

Even in the dimming light he could see the worry lines sprouting in the corners of her eyes. She was no more in the early spring of her life than he was. She knew heartache and pain. Life had forced her to look at situations differently, with less naïve hope, as it had him. He was glad she was more than a girl.

"You know Juan Carlos? Where is he?" Pearl demanded.

"I don't know where he is. The last I saw of him was right after our arrival in Austin, in a section of town he called 'Little Mexico.' He saved my life."

"He'll be safe then. That is one less worry. Thank you,

Josiah. I couldn't bear the loss of Juan Carlos, too." Pearl reached out and took Josiah's hand into hers, held it softly for a moment, then let it fall away.

Josiah felt like his chest was going to explode. He had to look away to regulate his breathing. Her fragrance was almost too much to take.

"I think Juan Carlos will be safe wherever he goes."

"Do not be so sure. He has his enemies, just like my father."

"Enemies?"

Pearl nodded. "Last year, before the new governor took office, and the State Police were still trying to do the job of the Rangers, my father rode with them for a short time. It was not for the money. He never lacked resources, as you can surely tell. But he was restless, you must know that. Anyway, Juan Carlos rode with him on a few of the trips. Something must have gone wrong on one of the sojourns they took down near San Antonio, because ever since, Juan Carlos has been like a shadow. He wouldn't tell me what happened."

"I bet it had something to do with Sheriff Patterson. Does that name sound familiar?"

Patterson had mentioned something about the State Police in San Antonio. There had been a lot of tension between the sheriff and the captain, even then, and it had not escaped Josiah's attention. Somehow, Charlie Langdon was involved, too; Josiah just didn't know how. Yet. All he had to go on was McClure's insistence that Patterson was among the riders who fled the ambush. Nothing was clear to him.

"I don't know. Maybe. Did this Sheriff Patterson kill my father, Josiah? I must know what happened."

"I do not think I am the one to tell you."

"You were there when he died?"

"Yes. Maybe it would be better coming from Feders. Or your mother."

"They will try and protect me from the truth. Please don't be like them and treat me like a fragile child. I am far from that."

"I can see that." Josiah sighed, reasonably resigned to telling Pearl what she wanted to know. As far as he was concerned, she had a right to know how her father had died. And the last thing he wanted to do was treat her like less than she was . . . It would be an insult to her father, and to Juan Carlos.

Just as he was about to tell her, her mother's voice echoed loudly over the grounds of the estate.

"Pearl!"

They both froze, said nothing, just stared at each other. Josiah felt like a young schoolboy for the first time in years, on the verge of getting caught in a place he shouldn't be.

Pearl finally smiled. "I should go. It's grown dark. Won't you see me to the house?"

She put out her hand for Josiah to take it. He hesitated only for a moment, but finally complied, holding her hand lightly. He wondered if she could feel him trembling inside.

The evening air had cooled drastically.

Twilight had almost passed as they talked—soft gray evening light, racing into pure darkness. Josiah wasn't sure how much time had gone by, but they had been there for a long time. Long enough for Pearl's mother to become concerned about her whereabouts.

"Pearl!"

"I swear, she still treats me like a child," Pearl said. She stepped away from the bench and headed toward the house, with Josiah uncomfortably at her side.

He thought it odd that she needed an escort, when she had probably made the trek from the pond to the house more times than she could remember, but that was no matter. Josiah was just glad to be near her.

"I'm here, Mother. Please, I'll be there in a moment," Pearl called out as they crossed the lane to the house.

Her mother was standing on the balcony, looking out into the darkness. Josiah could only make out her silhouette in the dark; dressed in black as she was, she was almost impossible to see. But there was no way he could mistake the shadow she cast.

"You're going to worry me to death," the captain's wife said, then turning and going inside the house with a huffy slam to the French doors.

"She's not going to give me a moment's peace," Pearl said with more than a hint of resignation in her voice.

They walked to the door and stopped.

"Thank you, Josiah. It has been a pleasure to come to know you. I hope I will see you again, after the funeral."

"It will depend on my orders."

Josiah felt off balance.

Even more so when he realized that Pearl was leaning in to kiss him on the cheek. He turned away quickly, their lips brushing as he did. The touch, the unintended kiss, startled them both, sending each spiraling away in the opposite direction from the other.

Josiah stood there for a moment, gathering himself, then ran into the darkness, fleeing the house, unsure of where he was going, but certain he needed to get as far away from Pearl Fikes as possible.

CHAPTER 23

Pedro was leading Fat Susie out of the barn, forcing Josiah to stop before he really got started. "No," he yelled. "I won't let you put her down." He bent over, catching his breath, surprised at how winded he was.

"It is the madam's wishes, Ranger Wolfe." Pedro brought the tall chestnut mare to a halt.

The horse was restless, and wary of being led out into the darkness without a saddle and no bit. Pedro was leading her with a simple rope halter in one hand, and carrying a shiny new Winchester '73 in the other. There was no question of his intention.

Josiah stood, and could still feel his heart beating in his chest. "Will she know if I take the horse into town, and let it free? Give her away? The captain loved this horse. You have to know that."

"I know he loved Fat Susie, that is true."

"Let me take her. I need to be free of this place myself. Please. It's not in my nature to beg, but I'm not sure I could bear seeing this horse shot at the moment. She is all that remains of the captain's life that I can see. His home is a beautiful retreat, but for the life of me, I can't see how Captain Fikes lived here."

"Now you understand his need for adventure. He married into his life in Austin, and never quite found his place."

Josiah nodded. "What of Pearl? She surely offered him some comfort?"

"Pearl worshipped the ground her father walked on. When he was here. She hated him for leaving her alone when he was gone."

"I can't let you shoot the horse, Pedro. It's not right," Josiah insisted.

"She will demand proof. You do not know the madam very well."

"Trust me, I'll provide proof. Somehow, I will. I promise. You will not suffer for disobeying your madam, not if I can help it."

Pedro studied Josiah for a moment. There was very little light between them. They were standing in the shadows, their voices low.

Spring frogs croaked behind them, the pond now a chaotic social gathering of night creatures, frantic to find a mate. The constantly repeating, rising and falling, chattering noises and chirps were almost too much to take. Josiah's insides burned with similar emotions and desires. It was like he had just awoken out of the mud after a long winter's sleep himself.

"Very well," Pedro said, handing the rope halter to Josiah. "I trust you, and agree the horse should not perish."

Josiah breathed a sigh of relief. "Thank you." He ran his

hand up Fat Susie's long neck, then scratched her behind the ear. The horse began to relax almost immediately.

Without saying anything else, Josiah swung around at the quickest speed he could muster and jumped up on the horse's bare back.

Fat Susie didn't seemed to mind. Josiah nudged her with his boots, pulled back on the halter slightly, then let it go, giving her her head.

It had been a long time since he'd been on a horse without a saddle, but there was a time when he'd ridden almost every day that way. When he was a boy, and saddles were too costly. Only his father had one. The unbidden skills came back quickly, and he was more comfortable than he'd imagined he would be.

As odd as it was, his youth had seemed to come back and revisit him regularly since arriving at the captain's estate. The memories did not act as a salve, easing his concerns of the day. They only confused him even more.

Given a large dose of freedom, Fat Susie took quick advantage and tore away from the barn with great speed.

Josiah glanced over his shoulder. Pedro had already vanished in the darkness.

Every window in the house was well lit, a glowing fortress in the night. It was easy to see how a man could become a prisoner in such a place, lose his soul to the responsibility of maintenance and stature. Josiah understood the captain's spirit, realized what it was that they'd shared. But in that realization, he also understood that a woman like Pearl could not be courted by him in any way, but only by a man whose spirit in no way resembled that of her father's. Her rejection of Feders was apparent proof. What more could a man like himself offer a woman like her, but more of the same—loneliness and worry?

He didn't know what he was thinking in the first place. He was no more ready to court Pearl than she was ready to be courted.

Fat Susie ran at a full gallop. Josiah was hanging on without a struggle, controlling her very little. He did not care where they went . . . he just wanted to go, and fast.

Josiah tied up Fat Susie on a post and stood staring at the entrance of the saloon. Rarely had he ever felt the need or desire for a drink of whiskey, but this night had proven to be the exception.

The horse had navigated the quickest, shortest route into the heart of Austin. Josiah surmised that Fat Susie would know her way to the saloon blindfolded. This one looked to offer every form of entertainment that the captain was fond of: gambling, whiskey, and women.

Happy music was playing inside, carrying outside on the cool night air, where it matched with another bit of music, coming from another saloon, just as raucous, down the street.

The music was not the normal solo piano player offering a string of lively dancing numbers and ballads, but rather a mix of string and wind instruments, violins, and *pitos*, with a flavor that was less Anglo and more Mexican than Josiah could ever remember hearing. He believed it was called Tejano music, but he wasn't sure.

There was singing coming from inside the saloon, too, all in Spanish, and even though he understood very little of the words, Josiah understood the intent. Enjoy the good times. Forget the past.

People, mostly Mexicans, were still milling about on the street even after the fall of darkness, walking along the boardwalk, with horses and wagons coming and going.

He was not far from the jail block, where a large crowd had gathered earlier, upon their arrival.

From where he stood now, Josiah could see four saloons in full operation, all throbbing with life, each with a different kind of music spilling outside, adding more laughter and shouting to the mix.

Austin was a lively place.

The street was like the pond on the captain's land, the beat of the music so similar to the demands of the frogs that Josiah thought he most certainly could hear them over everything else.

It was the season when everything came out of the darkness to celebrate the long sunny days and the even shorter nights. It was the season of change, what his father used to refer to as rattlesnake season. You had to be careful where you stepped.

The inside of the saloon was lit like it was day.

Bright light spilled out of the windows and onto the street. A few boys just shy of being men, like Scrap, who were most assuredly coming off the trail from pushing cows, walked by happily, almost giddy, and strode into the saloon, backslapping one another, paying Josiah no mind at all. They didn't look like they had a care in the world. They were on an adventure, drinking up life and everything it had to offer.

Josiah couldn't help but notice their youthful exuberance, and the sight of the boys almost pushed him back up on Fat Susie.

He was like that once . . . before the war, and some after it, before he lost Lily and the girls. He was not giddy now, far from it. All he wanted to do was dull the pain he felt deep in his soul and kill the hunger that was raging in his belly . . . and in his heart.

It was, finally, the lure of food, the spicy, familiar, smell of steaming vegetables and beef, that pulled Josiah inside the saloon. His eyes had to adjust to the brightness as he stopped just inside the batwing doors, taking in the view, searching for a path to the closest empty table. There was none, so he eased his way to the bar. A lone stool sat at the far corner, meaning he would have to walk all the way across the cavernous room.

Josiah's entrance had garnered quite a bit of attention. The crowd was mostly Mexican, the exception being a few cowboys, including the ones that Josiah had watched go inside. They were sitting at a table with a few vaqueros, lost in a conversation, speaking Spanish themselves.

A quick hush occurred, a drop in the loudness of the happy Tejano music . . . but once it was determined Josiah was not a threat, and had no intent to disrupt the gay mood of the saloon, the noise and music returned with renewed vigor.

He had jumped into the middle of the pond, joined the uninhibited mood, and was in no hurry to leave. The saloon was so loud he couldn't hear himself think.

The spot at the bar was still open, and Josiah eased onto the stool between the wall and a Mexican who had obviously been drinking for a while.

The man's head was hung down, hands on top of his head propping himself up, eyes open, but bloodshot. He was fresh off the trail, wet mud and cow shit still on his pointed-toed boots, and he smelled like the bottom of a tequila bottle. He nodded at Josiah, and Josiah returned the gesture, but quickly looked away. He was in no mood to make a new friend.

"A whiskey, *mi amigo*," Josiah said to the barkeep.

The barkeep, a short, rotund man with a pitted face and

drooping mustache, nodded knowingly. He plopped a glass in front of Josiah, grasped a whiskey bottle with his stubby but sure fingers, and filled the glass to the brim. He held out his other hand for payment. The barkeep's left hand was missing a thumb.

Josiah laid two bits in the man's hand, then slugged down the drink. "Another." He had seen more than one missing finger in his life. Puzzling over another man's misfortune on this night was not on his duty roster.

He could feel the whiskey burning all the way to the pit of his empty stomach. Since he wasn't a man who drank whiskey regularly, the drink had an almost immediate effect on him, numbing him from the top of his head to his toes.

The barkeep smiled, and poured another drink.

Josiah dug in his pocket and found that he had not replenished the new pants provided to him at the bath with all of his money. His remaining coins were back at the captain's house.

He handed the barkeep his remaining two bits and let the whiskey sit in front of him, intent on making it last longer than the one before.

The bar was nearly twenty feet long, ornately carved, and cut out of fine cherrywood. Another barkeep worked the other end of it, keeping up with the constant demand. A woman sat just inside the bar directing the barkeeps and girls who were coming and going to her with whispers, appearing and disappearing up a staircase just past the end of the bar.

The woman was not old by any means, maybe Josiah's age, or a little older. Her skin was bronze and lustrous, and she had shiny, fine black hair piled high on top her head, bound by expensive-looking gold and silver combs. She wore a plain white linen top dotted with gold buttons, the neckline open to the top of her chest, exposing a deep crevice, offering more than a hint of full, moon-shaped breasts. She was one of the most beautiful Mexican women, Josiah thought, that he had ever seen.

Nothing escaped the woman's attention. Her deep brown eyes continuously perused the crowd, searching for any sign of trouble. Two hulking, well-armed men stood at each of side of the batwinged entrance, watching the woman for any silent command to quell the first sign of gunplay or brawling.

Josiah looked away when her eyes fell on him, just as someone tapped him on the shoulder.

He turned to face a young girl, dressed seductively, her wares mostly open to his gaze. She reminded him of the girl Ofelia used to help her midwife, the one with saucer-shaped brown eyes who was called only *niña*, girl.

He knew this girl's pursuit before she even said a word. She was thin and beautiful, with soft, inviting olive skin exposed in all the right places, but too young for him to even consider seriously.

He would need far more whiskey than he could afford to set aside those ideals. Still, like the first sip of whiskey, the idea of a woman's anxious touch, writhing underneath him, warmed him from the inside out.

"*¿Compañerismo, señor?*"

Josiah shook his head no at the offer for companionship.

The girl smiled. "*Estás cansado, y solo.*"

Josiah shook his head again. He didn't understand what she'd said, and didn't want to. "No, no. Please." He shooed her away.

A look of disappointment crossed the girl's face. She drew a deep breath and walked off, snaking her way through the crowd of tables.

Josiah turned away from the bar, watching her retreat in search of another man with more potential than him, and felt a tinge of regret. She was pretty enough, there was no question about that. He just couldn't bring himself to go after her. Besides, he had no more money. She would have dropped her inviting smile as quick as anything once she found that out.

"She said you must be tired and lonely."

Josiah turned around and came face-to-face with the woman who had been sitting just inside the far end of the bar, directing the girls and men at the door.

He eyed her carefully, curious about her interest in him. Surely rejecting a girl wouldn't get him thrown out of a saloon. He took a swig of his whiskey, leaving two-thirds of a glass. "Too tired, maybe," he said.

"And lonely?"

"Well, there's always that, isn't there?" He finished off the glass, trying not to show his discomfort as the whiskey ripped down his throat.

The woman chuckled. "You have come to the right place then."

"I was just leaving."

"You just arrived."

Josiah stood too quickly, unaccustomed to the whiskey. His head swam a bit. "No, I really think it's time for me to go."

The woman reached out to him across the bar and grabbed his hand, pulling him back as he pushed himself off the stool. She stared him in the eye. "I saw you arrive. It must have been a long and dangerous journey delivering *el capitán* to his *lugar de descanso final*, um, to his final resting place."

Josiah thought the woman's eyes had watered up, but

when he blinked and looked again, he decided he was mistaken.

Her eyes were fixed on him, soft, yet confident. "Please, señor, join me for a meal. It is the least I can do."

"I have no money," he said quickly.

The woman smiled, his hand still in hers. "It's on the house. It is the least I can do for *el capitán*. He was a friend to many of us here."

He looked away, felt her warm touch, then looked back to the pleading in her eyes. To his surprise, he could not resist the woman, did not want to, and nodded yes.

She smiled, and let go of his hand. "Follow me."

Josiah made his way to the end of the bar, weaving through tables, and men standing at the bar, always keeping the woman in his sight. She stopped, grabbed a full bottle of whiskey from underneath the bar, and met him at the bottom of the staircase.

"You don't mind if we have some quiet, some privacy?" the woman asked.

"No," Josiah said.

He watched her make her way up the stairs, taking in the full length of her beauty. Before going up, he looked over his shoulder, saw a disappointed look on the face of the girl who had first propositioned him, and almost decided not to follow the woman.

He wasn't sure what he was getting himself into.

It was like he was outside of himself, being driven by feelings and needs he did not want to understand. He didn't know where he was or what was going to happen. And after sitting on the bench with Pearl, he didn't care. Acting precariously was something new to him, or at least it was something that had been asleep, deep inside of him, for a lot of years.

"Señor?" the woman said from the top of the stairs, waiting, looking even more inviting with a sulky glow coming from behind her.

Josiah nodded, and bound up after her, leaving whatever uncertainty may have existed behind him.

They went down a long hall, lit dimly with sconces on the wall, flickering at eye level. There were several doors, all closed. The noise from downstairs muffled whatever activity was going on inside the rooms, but there was not a question that most, if not all of them, were full.

There was another staircase that led up at the end of the hall. The woman made her way steadily up the last set of stairs, looking over her shoulder on occasion with a slight smile, to make sure Josiah was still behind her. He was close enough to smell a light floral fragrance on the back of her neck.

There were only two doors on the third floor. The woman stopped, fished a gold skeleton key out of a hidden pocket in the tight-fitting full-length black skirt she was wearing, and opened the door farthest from the stairs. Standing firmly in the doorway, she motioned for him to enter.

Josiah complied, pushing by the woman, grazing her full body as he did. The woman did not flinch, did not look away or appear to be insulted by the touch.

A large bed sat in the center of the room, with a thick mattress, covered with lacy pillows and a velvet bedcover the color of a field of violets. There was a vacant fireplace on the far wall surrounded by a few fancy chairs and a table. A chest of drawers with a fine China bowl and pitcher on top of it sat on the opposite side of the bed.

The woman set the whiskey bottle on the table in front of the fireplace, poured two glasses full, without asking anything of Josiah, and offered him one. He took it, clinked it to hers when she offered, and downed the drink in one gulp.

He knew what was coming next, and as nervous, uncertain, and out of practice as he was, the one thing he wanted at the moment was to feel alive, to feel the heat of this woman beneath him.

Pearl had set him on fire, brought him back to life with one grazing kiss. Even though he had just met her, he could only wish it were her with him, alone in a room with an inviting bed. But that was impossible, and would never—ever—happen. He needed to forget about Pearl, forget that she was available, favored by Pete Feders, but opposed to all Rangers. And the last thing he needed to think about was why he had been dead to desire in the first place, what dark sleep Pearl had woken him up from.

His need to touch and be touched was so strong that it nearly knocked him from his feet as the whiskey spread through his entire body, joining the other drinks, pushing him as close to a drunken stupor as he'd been in a long time.

The woman steadied him, opened her arms to him, and before he knew it, Josiah was on the bed, his eager hands knowing exactly what to do, parting her naked thighs with a hunger that he did not think could ever be sated.

CHAPTER 24

They sat, eating by candlelight. Josiah had never tasted beef that was so tender, so delicious. Almost magically, a feast had appeared on a series of silver trays set outside the door in the middle of the night.

The bed was a bundle of twisted linen, pillows scattered across the floor, boots and clothes mixed in. The room smelled of flowers and the woman's musky scent. Hours had passed since they had journeyed up the stairs and into this world of their own making.

The woman sat silently and watched Josiah eat, barely touching her own plate of food. "You must have been starved," she finally said.

Josiah looked up, enjoying some savory vegetables that seemed to melt on his tongue. "I can't remember the last time I had a meal like this."

"Good."

"Thank you." Josiah put down his fork, sat back in the high-backed chair, and wiped his face with a soft white cloth napkin. The food, and the expenditure of emotion and physical desire, had nearly sobered him up. "I will never forget this."

The woman watched every move he made, studying him, almost as if she were trying to anticipate what he was he going to say before he said it.

There was no question that she knew a lot about what made a man happy. Her skills of anticipation and movement were greater than any woman Josiah had ever known.

She was not the first woman of her type that he'd ever been with. It was a long war. But it had been a very, very long time—before he married Lily, never after, and never with a Mexican woman until now. He liked this woman, knew there was something different about her, and wanted to know about her.

"You do not normally do this, do you?" he asked.

"That's not what I was expecting you to say." She was wearing a thin floor-length robe, thrown over her shoulders, her body fully and comfortably exposed to him. The woman bit her lip, shook her head no. "I leave the business to my girls these days."

"The captain was more than a friend to you, wasn't he?"

"Why do you say that?"

"His horse brought me here. I didn't come here on my own."

"I know."

"How so?"

She shrugged with a wicked smile that meant no harm. "I know everything that comes and goes on this street. I know that you are a Ranger who nearly lost his life in San Antonio, and that you are a loyal friend. A quiet man who doesn't question what's asked of him, but would die for the right cause. There are few men who match that description."

"Juan Carlos has been here."

"Yes, of course."

Josiah sighed. "Is he here now?"

"He is close."

"Good. I will not worry about his well-being."

"There is no need."

He nodded, and stared at the woman. "You know more about me than I do you. I don't even know your name."

The woman laughed. "But you do."

"How so?"

He waited for her to answer, but the woman said nothing. Instead, she stood up, walked over to the window, and looked out.

"My name is Suzanne del Toro," she said, her back to him.

"Fat Susie," Josiah whispered.

"*Sí*," the woman said. "Much to my chagrin, *el capitán* called me Fat Susie—and only he could get away with it."

She walked away from the window, climbed back into bed, and beckoned Josiah to join her. He didn't hesitate.

Morning came quickly. Soft gray light filtered into the room as Josiah readied himself to leave. The street below was quiet, the rooms below them empty. There was no music, no hint of anything that had occurred the night before, except the regret that was slowly beginning to creep inside Josiah's aching head.

Suzanne remained in bed, wrapped in a sheet, a sad look on her soft brown face. "I'll never see you again, will I?"

He buckled his gun belt and adjusted it on his hip. "I have to go home to Tyler. I have a son to care for. After seeing to him, I need to join the rest of the Frontier Battalion at the Red River."

"Just like Hank. Always off somewhere."

"Would you really want a man under your feet all of the time?"

"I think you could get under my skin," she whispered.

Josiah blushed. "I'm going to leave you the captain's horse. His wife set out orders to have her shot."

"*Ella es una perra de mal corazón*," Suzanne spit, her lip instantly curling up in a hateful sneer.

Josiah shrugged. "I'm sorry, I don't know what you said."

"She is an evil-hearted bitch."

"She's something, that's a certainty."

"I will gladly keep the horse. My namesake. *El capitán* would be happy that I have her. I had her taken to the livery last night so there is no need to worry about her well-being, either."

Suzanne stood up out of the bed, letting the sheet fall off her naked body. She wrapped her arms around Josiah's neck and pressed herself firmly against him. "*Adios*, Josiah Wolfe. You are welcome here anytime. Do not forget me."

Regardless of the impending regret, he wrapped his arm around her waist, pulled her closer to him, nuzzling his face into her neck, tempting himself even further to kiss her fully on the lips. They had not kissed, had not crossed that forbidden line, which he would not do—unless he knew it was something she was comfortable with; so far she hadn't shown any sign, either.

It surprised him that leaving her was so hard.

"Thank you," he said. "Thank you for everything, Suzanne del Toro. Don't worry, I don't think I will be able to forget you."

He pulled away from her, walked to the door, opened it slowly, stopped, thought about going back and kissing her anyway, but knew he couldn't, then exited with haste.

He hurried down the dark hall and the remaining stairs, the sconces long since extinguished.

Fat Susie—the horse—was nowhere in sight when he stepped outside the saloon. The street was empty, save for another horse, a tired-looking swayback chestnut mare tied to a post several buildings down from the saloon. The sun had barely broken over the horizon, coloring a gathering of tall thunderclouds in the west a deep angry red.

Josiah tried to ignore the sky, and what it might imply about the fortune of the coming day; he was worried less about the warning than about the man who had just stepped out of the alleyway next to the saloon, a six-shooter in his hand, the barrel trained squarely at Josiah's head.

"Don't even go thinkin' about goin' for your gun," the man whispered.

Josiah froze, his eyes glued to the man's gun, a Colt Peacemaker just like his. The man was as tall as him, but probably weighed seventy-five pounds more. It looked like all muscle. His black skin gleamed with perspiration in the morning sunlight, and he looked like he'd been riding for a while. His outfit was dusty from Stetson to boot toe, and his shirt was torn across the shoulder—the Negro looked more than a little frayed, like it'd been a while since he'd had some rest, a good bath, and a decent meal.

Josiah had failed to watch his step, his awareness and mind still lost in Suzanne's bed. If he got out of this mess, there'd be time to chastise himself later. It did occur to him though, pretty quickly, that if the man was going to shoot him, he'd be dead already.

"I wouldn't think of such a thing," Josiah said.

He had very little time to consider his alternatives, but he had to consider that the man might be the Negro who was riding with Patterson, his posse, and the Irish tracker, O'Reilly. He also had to consider that it was possible the Negro was the same man Scrap said he saw riding off after the ambush that took McClure's life. He had to question why the man had not shot him when he had the chance, instead of just holding him there, a gun to his head on an empty street.

"That'd be a good thing, there, Ranger man. Just don't you go movin' about, now. Not an inch, not an eyelash, hear?"

"Are we waiting on something?"

"Be best if you just go an' shut up now, hear? I'll shoot you square between da eyes, I surely will. Makes no matter to me. No sirree, none a'tall. I'll kill you without a worry about nothin'. Now you just wait, and don't move until I says so."

"You got a name?"

The Negro shook the gun, his finger twitching on the trigger, then he jammed the barrel hard against Josiah's temple. "I does, but ain't none of your damn business. Is you stupid?"

"Most people call me Josiah."

"I knows that. You tryin' to be funny?"

"No, that's normally not my nature."

Well, Josiah thought, but didn't say, since he knows my name, that pretty much rules out a simple robbery—which, since he had no money, could have ended quickly, and probably not as badly as this looked like it was going to end.

He took a deep breath, certain now that he better do what he was told, since he assumed he was right, that he was standing face-to-face with one of the men who had been riding with Patterson.

The question remained whether the Negro was a loyalist to Patterson or, ultimately, loyal to Charlie Langdon.

If the man shot Josiah, it wouldn't matter, but in his own mind Josiah thought the two men, Patterson and Langdon, were joined in a greater scheme: one that had left Captain Hiram "Hank" Fikes dead as a doornail. Knowing the truth, why Fikes was killed in the first place, wouldn't go too far in getting him out of the pickle he was in at the moment, but damn, he sure wanted to know what the hell was going on.

"Don't move. Just don't go movin' an inch, you hear?"

Josiah nodded, and felt the cool end of the barrel track along his skin on the side of his face. His only advantage, he hoped, was that the Negro was not much of a student of the Colt Peacemaker.

Josiah had learned early on that keeping an empty chamber in the Peacemaker was a smart practice. With six rounds in the chamber, a sharp blow could dislodge the safety mechanism, permanently damaging it and allowing the gun to fire on its own if it was dropped—or knocked to the ground. If the gun was damaged, unusable, then Josiah would have the clear advantage, if he could get the Negro in the sights of his own Peacemaker.

Surely at this point, any movement at all would cause the Negro to pull the trigger, so Josiah wasn't about to try to knock the gun from the man's hand, but it did give him something to watch for, hopeful for an opportunity that would free him of the man's control.

Only a matter of minutes had passed since the Negro had appeared out of nowhere, but it sure seemed like an hour since the gun had been put to Josiah's head.

The sound of hurried horse hooves digging into the dirt street raced toward them, and drew the Negro's attention away from Josiah for a fraction of a second.

The momentary distraction was all Josiah needed. He didn't know who was coming, but just as Josiah was about to raise his arm to knock the Peacemaker out of the Negro's hand, something whirled past his right ear.

A knife pierced the Negro's shoulder, its intense velocity tearing through cloth, skin, and muscle, burying itself to the hilt in the blink of an eye. The knife sounded like a loud tap on a cantaloupe as it entered the man's body. Blood spurted outward before the black man could react, before he could even let out a scream.

Already in the mode to knock the gun from the man's large hand, Josiah followed through, unconcerned where the knife had come from, or whether it had hit its intended target. It might have been meant for him, for all he knew.

The Peacemaker hit the ground with a thud, fired, and the bullet ricocheted out of sight.

The Negro screamed, reacting to the pain from the piercing knife. His eyes were white with surprise and fear, following the trail of his lost weapon as it bounded out of reach.

Josiah took further advantage of the situation and punched the black man square in the nose as hard as he could, sending him tumbling backward, head over heels.

It only took a second for Josiah to take his own Peacemaker in hand. He trained it on the big Negro before he came to rest, splayed against the wall on the opposite side of the alleyway. "You move, and it'll be the last thing you do." He hesitated, and added, "Hear?"

The Negro nodded, groaning, trying to pull the knife out of his shoulder with one hand, cupping his bleeding nose with the other.

"I got some questions for you," Josiah said as he looked over his shoulder, hoping to see that it was Juan Carlos who had come to the rescue—again. But it wasn't.

Suzanne del Toro stood at the door of the saloon, her eyes looking past Josiah. "Look out," she yelled, digging in her skirt, either for another knife or a derringer. Neither of which would be much help at this point.

Josiah caught sight of the rider on the approaching horse.

It was the redheaded tracker, O'Reilly. The Irishman had two guns drawn, his frothing black horse bearing down on Josiah quickly. The horse swerved, and O'Reilly fired both pistols in unison. Josiah dove to the ground, rolling up against the wall of the saloon and firing his gun at the passing Irishman as he came to rest.

His shots missed, and the tracker returned fire. But the tracker did not aim at Josiah—not at first anyway.

The first two shots were dedicated to the Negro, hitting him square in the forehead with one shot and in the belly with the other, permanently silencing the big black man.

The other shots were over the shoulder, haphazardly hitting the ground inches from Josiah as O'Reilly sought to gain control of his horse and flee as fast as he could.

Suzanne got a shot off with her derringer, but the tracker was out of range. He disappeared around the corner in a cloud of dust, before Josiah could reload.

Josiah finished loading, then stood up, dusting himself off, surprised that he had no wounds.

"You were being watched," Suzanne said. "Are you all right?"

"I'm fine." He looked down at the Negro. "He could have just killed me."

"You're lucky."

"Seems to be a habit I'm getting into. I need to pay more attention."

"You're not accustomed to bad men wanting you dead."

"Not lately, no, you're right. I don't know what these men were after, but my guess is Charlie Langdon is close. He won't rest until I'm dead."

Suzanne caressed his cheek. "You have to learn to be more careful."

"I will."

Josiah looked down the street and saw something he didn't understand. It only took him a second to figure out what he was looking at.

The swayback horse that was three buildings down when he'd exited the saloon was now on the ground. It looked like it was dead, shot in the melee with O'Reilly, or perhaps hit with the ricochet from the Negro's Peacemaker. It was hard to say.

Josiah pulled the knife out of the Negro's chest. "You mind if I borrow this?"

"No, not at all. What are you going to do?"

"Get a piece of proof to keep a good man out of the way of an evil woman," he said, heading toward the dead horse, gripping the knife securely in his hand.

CHAPTER 25

A shiny black funeral coach sat in front of the captain's grand house. Two large draft horses were standing nervously in front of the coach, their coats just as black as the lacquer paint on the ornately decorated wagon of death. The draperies were open, exposing an empty cargo behind thin glass panels. The coffin had yet to be loaded.

Carriages and wagons were parked four or five deep beyond the funeral coach, and a crowd of people was milling about under the portico.

The red, thunderous morning sky now not only threatened rain, it promised it. The sunrise had been wiped away by a wind that drained every bit of color but a dull gray from the roiling clouds. Leaves on the silver maples turned inside out, and anything that wasn't battened down was in severe danger of being picked up and tossed about like it was a feather. Umbrellas were open in legion, straining against the wind, making the entire front of the captain's house a rippling sea of black grief.

Josiah had nearly missed the march to the church, the funeral, and then the burial at the cemetery alongside the church, on a hillside in a family plot of the madam's, overlooking the Colorado River. He had walked, then run, when the clouds became threatening. He made it back to the carriage house just before the rain let loose and began to fall in buckets.

He'd cleaned himself up the best he could, futilely wiped the mud off his boots, changed his bloody shirt, and adjusted himself as best he could, hoping all the while he would be presentable to Major Jones and Governor Coke if circumstances put him in proximity to be judged by them as an acceptable example of a Texas Ranger. That designation meant quite a lot to Josiah, especially in the wake of Captain Fikes's death. He still had that, a designation, a bit of a future to look forward to, and it was in part the captain's urging and belief in him that had brought on that hope . . . as well as put him in harm's way, physically and emotionally. There was always a price for hope, but Josiah was certain that he had more than paid his way forward.

Now he stood under a large oak tree just across the lane from the house, feeling self-conscious about his lack of proper mourning attire, and lack of an umbrella to protect him from the elements.

He would have to show himself eventually, especially if Jones had arrived, like Sheriff Farnsworth said he would. But for the moment he wanted to gather himself, and clear his mind of the previous night, and the realization that he had shared more with the captain than he wanted to consider. And the confrontation with the Negro and O'Reilly still weighed heavily on his mind.

Charlie Langdon was close by and up to something big. He could feel it in his bones. O'Reilly and the Negro didn't act on their own. They were following orders, doing as they were told. Kill Wolfe. At least he thought that was it. The Negro had his chance to kill Josiah, but he'd waited—and when the tables turned, the Irishman killed the Negro. What was he protecting? What didn't he want known? More importantly, why did O'Reilly think the Negro would squeal in the first place?

Josiah knew he'd have to be more aware now than he ever was if he was going to outwit Charlie Langdon. If he didn't, he knew he was a dead man . . . and he'd never see his son again.

At that thought, Josiah started to step out from under the tree after a letup in the rain, but a voice calling his name stopped him in his tracks.

"Wolfe, where the hell you been?" Scrap pushed his way out of a crowd of black umbrellas under the portico and stalked toward Josiah.

Josiah waited under the tree, though he would have rather walked off in the opposite direction, ignoring the brash young Ranger. He didn't feel like he owed the kid an explanation of any kind.

"You've been gone all night. We was worried somethin' had happened to you," Scrap said, coming to a stop a few feet from Josiah, the leaves shaking and blowing above them in the towering tree.

"I'm fine. I needed some time to myself. I went into town."

"Mrs. Fikes is mighty angry at you for missin' her meal. Best table I ever sat at, I can tell you that. You sure did miss something."

"I bet I did."

"Told me if I saw you I was to tell you that she wanted to see you right away."

"Now doesn't look to be the time."

The sea of umbrellas parted, and six men carrying the captain's coffin exited the house, heading directly toward the funeral coach. Mrs. Fikes followed, escorted by Governor Coke. Pearl was right behind her. It took Josiah a second to recognize her escort, dressed properly in a long black mourning coat, top hat, and a face that looked like it had never seen a speck of trail dirt. But there was no question who the man was. Pete Feders. Sergeant Peter Feders.

At least Josiah thought he was still a sergeant. Feders might be a captain by now. He sure looked like he could have stepped up in rank . . . or was going to . . . very soon.

The lane to the church quickly turned to mud. The funeral coach nearly got mired down, but the Mexicans who served under Pedro appeared out of the crowd, rocking the coach forward, unconcerned with their own appearance, ensuring that the captain got to his final destination in fine style.

Scrap had made his way to the church with the parade of mourners, but Josiah had hung back and trailed after the funeral coach surrounded by strangers. He avoided contact with Mrs. Fikes, Pedro, Pearl, and Feders, delaying that event for as long as possible.

He searched every face that came into close proximity to him, determined not to be surprised or ambushed again. It was not beyond Charlie Langdon to send his men into a crowd of mourners and pose an attack.

If there was a hell, Charlie Langdon would surely burn in it.

The sky had opened up, and it rained steadily. All Josiah had to keep himself dry was his hat. Oddly, he didn't care.

The temperature had cooled, and the rain felt good . . . cleansing.

The church overflowed with mourners, and Josiah was not quite inside, not outside, barely able to hear the parting words of the captain's admirers, the two preachers who had led the coffin inside, and the dignitaries who spoke about the captain's contributions to the state of Texas with his bravery, valor, and pure instincts as a soldier and leader. The captain's wife wept openly, supported by the governor when they were called to stand and pay tribute. The governor's own wife had been relegated to a pew behind him.

Josiah spied Sheriff Farnsworth sitting in a packed pew, three rows behind the governor and Mrs. Fikes. Farnsworth had looked Josiah right in the eye as they passed each other, but otherwise the sheriff did not even acknowledge Josiah's presence. No matter, Josiah thought to himself, sure that the sheriff was fuming about his position in the pew, certain that it was below his assumed station in life.

Everywhere Josiah looked, there were men he did not recognize, did not know, wearing their finest suits of clothes, their beards and mustaches trimmed and shaped perfectly.

It amazed him that people felt the need to get all gussied up to enter a church. Not that he was a heathen—but he was still angry at the preacher man who'd refused to minister to Lily when she lay dying. Lily was a true believer. But the preacher broke her heart, protecting himself from the sickness, not allowing God to come into the cabin, to give her a bit of comfort, in her hour of need. After all he'd seen and done, Josiah's days of pondering about God were pretty much over.

People coughed and rustled about inside the church.

Josiah was stuck on the steps in the middle of the crowd,

trapped and surrounded by mourners wearing wet wool coats. The stink was almost unbearable.

The wind was constantly blowing, but it had let up from its initial blast. The rain, on the other hand, continued to come down in sheets, able to fill buckets in minutes. Thunder boomed. Lightning danced overhead. Trees were wrested back and forth, tender new leaves flittering to the ground like it was autumn instead of spring.

It was a bad day to be buried, a worse day to die and meet your maker. Nature was upset, angry, intent on inflicting as much misery as possible, impeding every movement of every human being standing outside the church, soaking them all to the bone.

Through it all, Josiah stood still, his eyes forward, no longer thinking about the captain, or heaven, or God, never taking his eyes off the flow of blond hair careening over the slumped shoulders of a woman he had briefly kissed, and now had most certainly betrayed in such an unredeemable way that he doubted he could ever look her in the eyes again.

There must have been three hundred mourners standing in the cemetery as the coffin was lowered into the ground. Water flowed into the captain's grave, and Pedro finally had to direct two of his men to jump down and bail out the hole before the coffin could be lowered inside.

Josiah's feet were stuck in the mud. He could see through the crowd. The Mexicans jumping down into the hole. The horrified look on the Pearl's face. The preacher man standing at the head of the grave, his hands clasped across his waist, a Bible securely in his grasp, his head down, rainwater dribbling off the brim of his round-topped black wool hat. Beyond the preacher man was more of a crowd, more unknown faces, more gray swirling skies, more drenching rain.

The words "Ashes to ashes, dust to dust" drifted over the crowd, the preacher's voice booming, confident, and certain of the righteous implications intoned at the end of each and every word, steady as a metronome.

Josiah stared straight ahead, watching the mourners around the grave as best he could, even when the call to prayer came, the order from the preacher to bow their heads.

He felt something push against his back, and thought nothing of it for the first second, until he felt a hot breath on the back of his neck.

"Don't move, Wolfe. All you need to do is listen." There was an Irish twang to the voice. It was so hushed and so low, Josiah had to strain to hear it, but he was almost certain he knew who the person was sticking a gun in his back. The tracker. O'Reilly.

"Just keep yer arms to yer side, like they are," the voice continued. "I got a message from Charlie for ya. He says if ya want to see your son again, then you best head east."

Josiah stiffened, flinched when the man mentioned his son.

"Don't go doin' anything stupid now, Wolfe. Just keep your mouth shut. If I don't show back up in a short amount of time to Charlie, he will do something he hates doin'. You know what that is. He said to remember Vicksburg. Only this won't be no accident. Wasn't then either if I know Charlie."

The preacher's voice boomed, "The Lord giveth, and the Lord taketh away." Thunder cracked overhead, matching the boom of the commandment. Rain continued pounding down from the sky, mud splattering, like blood, as it hit the ground hard.

Josiah stared straight ahead, the barrel of the gun digging deeper into his back. Vicksburg was deposited deep in his memory. He had not forgotten it—but as with most of his wartime escapades, the memory had faded with time.

He recalled how the Brigade had stumbled across a farmhouse, and Josiah and Charlie had been given reconnaissance orders. That happened a lot, Josiah and Charlie being paired together, even though Josiah objected as often as was prudent.

They waited until dusk and then sneaked up on the lone farmhouse through the barn. A boy, no more than ten, who had obviously seen them, grabbed his pa's old long gun and fired off a shot at them as they crawled toward the house.

The boy had a good aim, and almost hit Charlie, but he didn't think ahead and hide himself very good. Charlie caught sight of the boy, and didn't think, or stop to think, or probably care that it was a child shooting at them, trying to protect what belonged to his pa, who was probably off to war himself. Charlie fired even though Josiah yelled for him not to. He hit the boy, who was hiding on the roof in the shadow of a dormer, killing him with one shot to the chest.

Josiah could never forget the thump of the boy as he hit the ground or his dead blue eyes, staring upward in defeat, as Josiah rushed forward with help that was too late.

Charlie Langdon didn't shed a tear, didn't even stop to see what he had done. He charged into the farmhouse ready to kill anything that moved. But the house was empty. The boy was alone. His family was either dead, or just lucky to be gone.

"Sure do hate killin' a child," Charlie had said after they'd returned to camp. Then he'd gone off and celebrated.

Josiah saw that boy's face in his nightmares for a long time. There was no way he could forget Vicksburg—and no way he would let Lyle fall victim to Charlie Langdon's evil hand.

"Charlie ain't goin' to wait forever. You and him got some unfinished business. Now, nod if you understand."

Josiah did as he was instructed.

"Good. Once I pull this gun away, count to ten. You don't, these fine people standing around might find themselves in a cross fire, and die 'cause you ain't got no sense. Understand?"

The pressure of the gun barrel withdrew from Josiah's back. He started to count, but stopped at two.

The hot breath returned. "One other thing. Come alone." Then the vile-smelling breath was gone again.

Josiah remained frozen, waited a second or two, then cocked his head slowly, just in time to see a flash of red hair disappear into the sea of black.

When he turned his gaze back to the grave, the preacher was making the symbol of the cross from his head to his chest, staring directly at Josiah.

CHAPTER 26

Major John B. Jones was another Ranger who did not originally hail from Texas. He was born in South Carolina, and the evidence of his place of birth could easily be detected in his speech.

"My sincere apologies, ma'am," he said in a slow drawl after the funeral, doffing his hat to Pearl just inside the portico. He slipped his arm into hers and escorted her inside, chatting in a soft, but direct, voice. Pearl looked numb, her manners mindless. Josiah watched from afar.

It was the first time he had ever seen the major, but he had heard plenty about the man whose charge it was to head up the Texas Rangers that Governor Coke had reinvigorated.

Jones had come to Texas, like a lot of men, via the War Between the States. He joined the Eighth Texas Cavalry, better known to most folks as Terry's Texas Rangers, since they were commanded by Benjamin Franklin Terry, a war hero in his own right. Jones didn't spend his entire enlistment with the Rangers, but he had a respectable career in the war.

There was no question that Jones was, at the very least now, an honorary Texan, after briefly serving in the state legislature. Governor Coke had appointed him head of the Frontier Battalion, assured that the man was as trustworthy as he was demanding.

Jones was a head shorter than Josiah, dressed impeccably in proper funeral attire, his matching thick, solid black hair shining with fresh pomade. His mustache was as thick as a big man's thumb, a perfect V drooping over his lips, trimmed to perfection. At forty years old, Jones had yet to marry, and had a wide reputation for appreciating a beautiful woman in one town and then a new one in the next. The major had his fair share of enemies as well as admirers, as could be expected for a man with such a predatory and untamable drive.

It was no surprise, then, that upon entering the captain's home himself, Josiah found the major in the parlor, conversing with Pearl, who looked like a trapped sheep, penned in the corner, holding a glass of some refreshment or another, looking eagerly over the major's solidly squared shoulder for an escape.

Josiah hadn't intended on rescuing Pearl, but once she made eye contact with him he saw he would have no choice.

Her face was pale and tearstained, even though she had done her best to get rid of any sign of crying. There was no question she continued to suffer from the events of the day, and forcing a polite ear to the major looked to be beyond her capabilities.

As Josiah moved toward her, he thought about how his son Lyle's life was now at risk, threatened. He could barely breathe, could barely think straight. In fact, Josiah's first inclination, after O'Reilly gave him Charlie's message during the funeral, was to jump on Clipper and head for home as fast as possible. But the crowd had waylaid him, and he was stuck in the mass of umbrellas for what seemed like an hour, until he broke free of the crowd of mourners just in front of the captain's house.

The trip from Austin to south of Tyler was a two-hundred-mile ride. Josiah knew the best route for him to take would be a fast ride up the cattle-worn Chisolm, then cross over east to Fort Parker, angle on up to the Moscoso's Trail near the abandoned Fort Houston, head north, and then on to home. It was a three-day trip at the minimum, full-out. He hoped Clipper was up to it.

But no matter the urgency, a trip like that took a little planning. And there were also his duties as a Ranger to consider.

He hadn't received new orders from Feders, hadn't even spoken to the man yet. Not only would fleeing home without speaking to Feders have been a quick end to his reputation, it would also have been bad form not to make himself known to Major Jones. He remained less concerned about the offenses he had committed toward Mrs. Fikes, but he also didn't want her as his enemy.

It was not purely out of ambition that he concerned himself with meeting the major. It was also the rescue of Pearl, and his need for his fellow Rangers and their help—even though O'Reilly had told him to come alone. That was not going to happen.

He was not a fool, not enraged enough by the threat of losing Lyle to completely vanquish his senses. He wasn't going to walk into a trap set by Charlie Langdon without someone covering his back, and his guess was Charlie knew that full well.

The other possibility that Josiah needed to consider was that the message was not true at all, but a ruse to get him out and away from the proceedings at the Fikes home, an emotional response that would leave him more than vulnerable—alone on the trail, to be surrounded by a gang of outlaws from which there would be no escape. Charlie Langdon might not be anywhere near Seerville, or the pine cabin just outside of town. He might be just outside of Austin, lying in wait for Josiah to do something ignorant.

Josiah wasn't sure how he was going to work things out, but he knew, as much as he possibly could at the moment, that he wasn't going to rush off half-cocked. That would get him—and maybe Lyle—killed for certain.

"Excuse me, Major Jones," Josiah said, tapping gently on the shoulder the man cornering Pearl.

Jones whirled around quickly, his dark blue eyes narrowing, the pupils barely visible, casting a gaze that made his face look squirrel-like, his eyes beadier than they normally might be. "What, good man? Can't you see I am in the midst of consoling this poor grief-stricken girl?"

"I beg your pardon, Major Jones, but I believe I have some information that needs your immediate attention."

"What kind of information?" Jones asked, his voice indignant. Then he looked Josiah over head to toe like Josiah was at a guard mount being judged fit for duty. "And who are you anyway to be intruding on this tragic day?"

The rainstorm had continued to rage outside, and Josiah's clothes were soaking wet. His shirt clung to his chest, his boots squished when he walked. Comfort had left his person early in the day—after coming face-to-face with the Negro.

Being presentable was about as important to him at the moment as being polite to Mrs. Fikes, who was standing a few feet away from him, leaning forward on a divan, using it to steady herself as she feigned a conversation with her cousin, the mayor from Neu-Braunfels, A. L. Kessler. Kessler nodded at Josiah, recognizing him, and Mrs. Fikes glared at Josiah like he was the most hated man alive.

Before Josiah could reply to Major Jones, Pearl stepped forward. "His name is Josiah Wolfe, sir. One of your very own, Major. A fine Texas Ranger who rode many miles at my father's trusted side." Her voice was soft, but there was an air of agitation thinly coated on her sweet Texas tongue.

Jones caught his breath, swallowed whatever words were forming on his lips, which most assuredly were not going to be kind, judging from the sudden twist of his face, and said, "I see. My apologies, Ranger Wolfe. We have not yet met in person, but your reputation precedes you."

Then he offered his hand, which Josiah gave a firm shake, which the major returned tepidly.

Josiah withdrew his hand quickly.

"If you two fine gentleman will excuse me," Pearl said, coming to a stop away from the corner, directing her attention toward a path free of human obstruction to the curving, rising staircase, just beyond them and adjacent to the main entrance of the house. "I have had a very long day and feel the need to excuse myself from your company."

Major Jones nodded and lowered his head. "Yes, of course. I would hope to make your acquaintance at some other time. Perhaps under more pleasant circumstances."

"Of course," Pearl said quickly, turning to Josiah. "And I hope to see you again, Josiah, before you depart. I assume you will be receiving a new set of orders soon?"

"I assume so," Josiah answered, ignoring both the major and Mrs. Fikes's twin glares of consternation when he spoke with Pearl.

"Be careful, then, in your travels."

"I will," Josiah said, looking to the door. "Thank you."

Pearl stood staring at Josiah for a moment, then made her way to the staircase, stopping only briefly to again study Josiah, who was still avoiding her gaze, before disappearing completely upstairs. She had obviously detected his discomfort in her presence and was trying to determine its cause. The look on Pearl's face was not difficult to understand, even to a man of Josiah's experience. It was one of confusion . . . and hurt.

Josiah watched her vanish from view, out the periphery of his vision, with a heavy heart, regretful that he felt it necessary to put an emotional wall up to Pearl at an obvious time of need. Guilt was going to be a dark companion.

"This information, Wolfe, had better be important," Major Jones said.

"I believe it is, sir. It concerns the man I think is responsible for the premature and senseless death of Captain Fikes, and I would feel much better if we were able to speak in private."

A half-full bottle of brandy sat on the captain's desk. The room was dark, heavy curtains pulled to a tight close, and there was a musty smell in it, like it had been sealed off for a long time. Three lamps flickered, the smell of kerosene a potent mix from the lack of use. One entire wall was lined with bound books of a number Josiah had never seen in his entire life. He wondered if the captain had read all of them, spent nights alone under the lamp, sipping on a drink, smoking a cigar. It was not an image of Captain Fikes he could conjure in his mind . . . He could only see the captain sitting happily at the gambling table in San Antonio, a pile of his opponents' chips before him. Since arriving in Austin, he had yet to resolve the conflict of the man, the Ranger, he thought he knew so well.

Josiah coughed when he entered the room, an odd scratch forming in his throat. Even though it was an uncharacteristic desire, he made his way to the brandy, poured himself a glass, downed it in one gulp, and let the warmth pervade throughout his body.

The drink had a finer taste to it than the whiskey he'd swigged down in Fat Susie's saloon the night before, but the taste was still an acquired one, and his palate still heartily rejected the expensive brandy. He coughed and shook his head, but welcomed the warming and easing effect of alcohol.

He was tempted to pour himself another, but he restrained himself, certain that he needed to keep his head about him.

Major Jones had been stopped on the way into the captain's library by Mrs. Fikes. Josiah had had no desire to eavesdrop—he wanted to escape the widow's hateful sneer as quickly as possible.

The major entered the library shortly after Josiah sat the empty glass down from where it came. Another man followed Jones into the room and closed the door heavily behind him.

It was Pete Feders. He, too, was shiny and adorned properly for the funeral. He stopped a foot from Josiah, staring at him eye to eye. Being near the same age and build allowed them a certain natural comfort with each other, but the fact remained that Josiah knew very little about Feders, and had learned more about him since arriving in Austin than he might have wanted: that he was a favored suitor, according to Pearl's mother, but Pearl did not seem so keen on the Ranger's affection.

"Wolfe," Feders said, extending his hand. "I'm sorry I haven't been able to meet up with you, but I've barely seen you since I arrived."

Josiah shook Feders's hand, not looking away, holding his gaze for a second longer than he probably should have, his own gaze fixed on the thin scar that ran from the corner of Pete's right eye to his ear. He'd never heard Feders tell how that scar came about, either. It occurred to Josiah, again, that he knew very little of the men he rode with. Hopefully now that the Rangers were re-formed, the Frontier Battalion a true entity, he would gain some familiarity with Feders and the rest of the company, after they gathered together at the Red River camp.

"Is something the matter, Wolfe?" Feders asked, pulling his hand away from Josiah's grasp.

Major Jones had made his way to the brandy, and poured himself a glass. He did not make an offer to the other two, and stood with his back to both Josiah and Feders, lost in thought.

"No, not at all. I'm glad to see you, too. Tell me of your chase after Charlie Langdon, and of Sam Willis's welfare."

"Langdon is still on the loose. Willis is still on his trail. They were heading northeast. I doubled back, thought my presence would be required here."

Josiah nodded. "I figured as much. I was jumped by two of Langdon's men this morning. One of them was killed, a Negro. The other fled, but approached me just earlier."

Major Jones cleared his throat. "Sheriff Farnsworth has some questions about that Negro's death. If it's the same one that turned up on the banks of the river."

"I can answer them," Josiah said. "I was protecting my own life."

"I'm sure that will be all he needs to hear."

"I hope so." Josiah thought about Juan Carlos, about the trouble the captain's half brother had gotten himself into by saving him. He's wasn't about to put Suzanne, Fat Susie, in the same perilous position, so his intent was to leave her out of the story. It sounded like the Negro had been removed and deposited as far away as possible from the saloon the way it was, so there was no need to raise the subject of his indiscretion if it could be avoided.

"Did you recognize this second man?" Feders asked.

"I did. He was a tracker who rode with Sheriff Patterson's posse. The one we met up with the afternoon before the captain was murdered, and we were ambushed."

"We were tricked," Feders sneered, "by that traitor McClure."

Josiah chose not to argue his point or submit his doubts about the Scot's guilt at the moment. It was a small point to make, when his son's life was at stake. "Langdon sent a message. Says I should return home to settle our score if I want to see my son alive ever again."

"It's personal, then?" Major Jones said, pouring himself another glass of brandy.

Josiah nodded, gritting his teeth. "It is. We served in the war together. We have a history." He paused and looked at Feders, who was staring off in the distance. "He told me to come alone or I'd regret it, and I believe he means it. We should make sure no one else knows of our plan, Captain. I fear my son's life if Charlie Langdon knows we are coming his way with the full force of the Texas Rangers."

CHAPTER 27

The sky had begun to clear overhead, and the rain had finally stopped its unrelenting gush. Lightning still flashed in the distance, east, toward home. The late afternoon air had a cool tinge to it, but Josiah could hardly feel a thing. He was anxious to be away from Austin.

He was loading his saddlebags onto Clipper, behind the carriage house, when he heard a recognizable female voice, followed quickly by a man's voice. They obviously thought they were alone, just around the corner, out of sight. Josiah had no interest in slowing his departure by making himself known, but he couldn't help but cock an ear toward the discussion.

"Peter, now is not the time."

"Really, Pearl, if not now, then when?"

"I just buried my father today. Does this have to happen now? Of all days?"

"I'm leaving within the hour."

"Then this can wait until you return."

The man did not answer immediately. Thunder rumbled distantly, a low growl that seemed harmless. "So you will at least think about it?" he asked.

Pearl sighed heavily. "Yes, Peter, I will think about your proposal. But I don't mean to encourage you."

"That's all I can ask for."

Josiah edged to the side of the carriage house and peered around the corner just in time to see Pete Feders stand up off a bent knee.

Josiah stepped back and molded himself against the building once he realized that his shadow fell across the ground as the sun peaked through the clouds behind him. It only took a second to hear footsteps tromping off toward the house.

Josiah relaxed and returned to Clipper, who snorted with disagreement when Josiah tightened down the saddlebags a little too hard.

"You heard, didn't you?"

Josiah spun around and met Pearl's gaze.

She had changed out of her formal mourning dress into a simpler black dress that reached to the ground. Her hair fell freely over her shoulders, and her face, though still pale, had a little luster, or life, to it as she looked at him. He decided the luster was frustration or anger, then nodded. "Yes, I apologize."

She shook her head. "It doesn't matter. I just wish . . ." She stopped mid-sentence and glanced up to the sky.

"That your father were here."

"Yes. It seems like he was never here when I really needed to speak with him. And now he is gone forever. Lost. And what for?"

"All the wishing in the world won't change how things are."

"You sound like you would know how that goes, Josiah."

"I do."

"May I be so bold as to ask why? How you know grief so well that the tone of your voice offers some comfort, even when you hardly dare to look at me?"

"I need to take my leave, ma'am. I need to vacate before the rest of the Rangers, and I must thank your mother for her hospitality before I do."

"Have I offended you somehow, Josiah?"

Words caught in his throat as he fumbled with Clipper's reins. He shook his head no.

Now he felt trapped. The truth was far more despicable than he thought she was capable of hearing, or he capable of telling.

It would have been irrelevant if she would have looked at him like she had Feders, with ire and disregard. But that was hardly what he was seeing. She stared at him anxiously, like she wanted nothing more than for him to sweep her off her feet and flee as far from the house as possible . . . for him to take her with him on the journey he prepared for. That could never happen. Not now. Not ever.

"Please, Pearl, I . . ." He had turned to face her, to look her in the face to tell her good-bye, that it had been a true pleasure meeting her, the only highlight of his day.

Instead, she pushed herself into his chest and his arms opened unconsciously, pulling her closer as she began to sob.

He could smell the sweet scent of her silky blond hair, his nose buried on top her head, feel her trembling body against his, needing him to hold her, protect her. And so he did, holding on to her as tightly as he could, unwilling as she was to let go.

"I'm sorry," he whispered.

Pearl stopped sobbing, pulled her head out from Josiah's chest, and angled her face to him.

This time, they kissed with intent, with unyielding passion that had been building in both their souls from the moment they had seen each other.

Pedro stood next to Mrs. Fikes in front of the main entrance to the house. There was a curious look in the Mexican's eyes, like there was something he wanted to say but found that he couldn't.

Josiah imagined the Mexican found himself in that position quite a lot.

Mrs. Fikes, on the other hand, stood sternly with her shoulders square, looking like there was a myriad of other duties she would like to be standing in charge of other than seeing off a Ranger she held in low esteem.

As Josiah dismounted Clipper, Pearl walked out of the front doors. Feders was not far behind her. It was the surliest, most tense, and most unusual quartet of people Josiah could ever remember gathering for his benefit.

"Well, then, Ranger Wolfe, I hope you have safe travels." It was Mrs. Fikes who'd spoken first.

Josiah didn't quite know what to do—bow, shake the woman's hand, or what—so he did nothing but nod, and said, "Thank you, ma'am. I appreciate the hospitality of the bath and the comfort of the carriage house."

Mrs. Fikes let out a sound that sounded like "Humf" and looked away from Josiah, her nose pointed directly in the air.

Josiah tried not to let the spurn show, since the captain's wife's attitude didn't surprise him, or catch him off guard. It was more of a surprise that she had even come out to see him off in the first place.

"Again," Josiah said, "please accept my condolences on the loss of your husband. He called on me when I suppose I needed it the most. I will be forever in his, and your, debt. Please don't hesitate to call in that marker anytime."

"Hank made questionable decisions at times," Mrs. Fikes said. "Bear that in mind with your memories of him."

"I understand, ma'am, thank you."

Josiah had said one thing but thought another. He knew that if he thought about it long enough, he could probably come to understand why Mrs. Fikes begrudged the captain for living the way he did, but he didn't want to think that long about it. He knew what it felt like to lose someone who shared your bed, and Mrs. Fikes was in no way acting like a stricken woman. She wore her widow's weeds far more comfortably than she should have as far as he was concerned.

Feders stepped past Pearl, who had not taken her eyes off Josiah since exiting the house.

"Keep your wits about you, Wolfe." Feders extended his hand, and both men shook with equal pressure.

One of Josiah's regrets was the fact that he had not had a chance to talk to Feders one-on-one. He still had some questions about what happened when the captain was killed that he hoped Feders could clear up.

Josiah was still not convinced that Scrap's story was accurate, but it had become the standard line, and the Scot's reputation in death was burdened with an act of senseless murder and treason. Perhaps that's the way it should be. In the end, Josiah's quest to know the truth was not about finding out what happened anyway. It was about alleviating his own guilt because he had not seen the ambush coming.

He had played the captain's death, and what came after, over and over again in his head.

The last time he had seen Captain Fikes alive, the captain was sitting with Pete Feders and Sam Willis, huddled together in a semicircle in front of the fire, talking in a hushed conversation. Charlie Langdon sat on the opposite side of the fire, his hands bound in the metal bracelets, his legs pulled together by a tightly drawn rope. He had a conversation with Vi McClure, and some of the best rabbit stew he'd ever eaten, then relieved Scrap from his watch.

Scrap had told him that he'd heard something at the bottom of the hill, probably a critter of some sort—or maybe a member of Charlie Langdon's gang. Regretfully, Josiah had not taken the kid seriously. That, in his mind, was his first mistake, his first ounce of earned responsibility for what was to come.

Just before dawn, he heard voices rising from camp. He was certain the captain was waking up the men—until he heard the first gunshot. Then the camp erupted into a gun battle, and shots came at Josiah from an unseen shooter who had scouted out his position.

Josiah had eased down the trail, returning fire, hitting the shooter—at least he thought it was his shot that killed the unknown man.

As quickly as the gunfire had begun, it ended. Josiah found Scrap in the camp, in a stupor. The kid had pulled his gun on Josiah at first sight, then relented quickly upon recognizing him. Scrap had been grazed by a bullet, but telling him the captain had been shot, he took Josiah up near the corral, to where Feders had covered the captain with a blanket, and where they watched him die.

Scrap said that McClure had let Charlie loose, that he saw them talking, and that the Scot had shot the captain square in the chest, then fled. The kid did not relent from his story, certain of what he had seen.

Before bundling the captain in a blanket for the ride home, Josiah found the key to the metal bracelets in the captain's shirt pocket. Which meant someone else had a key to set Charlie free. It was surmised by all who heard Scrap's story that it was Vi McClure . . . who for some reason had fallen into allegiance with Charlie Langdon and, possibly, Sheriff Patterson and had played a convincing actor's role in the whole setup.

Josiah had not had the opportunity to talk to Feders, or Sam Willis for that matter, to clear some things up, since they'd left each other's company.

Feders had given him orders to return the captain to Austin, then followed after Willis, who had lit out after McClure, Langdon, and the gang who'd set him free. Josiah was certain Patterson was involved, that the ambush had something to do with an incident that had occurred in the recent past concerning the State Police, but he wasn't sure how Charlie Langdon figured into that, either.

When they regained custody of McClure, thanks to some Tonkawa Indians, McClure gave Josiah no more details, but fervently denied killing the captain. Josiah remembered the letter from Feders; it was stuffed in his saddlebag and had been forgotten until that moment. The first few lines were etched in Josiah's memory: "If you are reading this letter, then Little Spots has been successful in finding you. Ranger McClure was left for dead, tied to a tree. He claims innocence."

Later, McClure told Josiah that Willis had taken up a position down the hill, away from camp, as was his custom. McClure said that before going to sleep, he thought he saw something lurking around behind the captain, and like Josiah, McClure had thought little of it, thought it was a critter—but it was probably the man Josiah shot on the trail—or thought he shot at the time.

McClure then went on to tell him that he'd awakened to find Scrap talking to Charlie. Scrap interjected, calling

McClure a liar. The kid always left out part of his story, which all along had bothered Josiah.

McClure said Charlie Langdon was free, and McClure saw a man, probably the man on the trail Josiah thought he had shot, come up behind the captain. The big Scot claimed to have pulled his gun and shot at the man, but as he did, a shot came from behind at about the same time, hitting the captain square in the chest.

There was no way to validate McClure's claim about the shot from behind. It was certainly possible that it happened, but there was no proof. And Josiah was not certain, or could not know, what Feders or Willis saw, or did, at this point.

McClure did name Patterson as one of the men fleeing the ambush, which was no surprise. Josiah had given the information about the San Antonio sheriff to the social-climbing sheriff of Austin, Farnsworth, and had not heard anything further concerning Patterson. Even Major Jones had heard nothing, as they made their plans for Josiah to leave.

What remained, much to Josiah's disappointment as he prepared to leave for home, were more questions. He could not tell Pearl for sure what had happened to her father, nor could he truly discredit Scrap's story, and restore McClure's reputation. Perhaps, that was not his cause . . . but until he knew for certain, Josiah would always feel like he'd had a huge hand in the events that transpired, and would carry a large part of the responsibility for the captain's death. It was a failure almost too heavy to bear.

Feders's voice rang in his head, "Keep your wits about you," and Josiah realized that he had just been standing there, lost in thought, and had not replied.

"Yes, thanks, I will."

"Our plans are certain, then?" Feders said.

"Plans? What plans, Captain Feders, are those? I thought you were staying on for the foreseeable future," Mrs. Fikes said.

Josiah winced at the title. It was news to him that Feders had been raised in rank, but it really came as no surprise.

"I am, ma'am. Ranger Wolfe and I will meet up soon at the Red River with the rest of my company."

"Oh good."

Pearl stepped forward. She had the same look in her eye as she did when Major Jones had her cornered after the funeral, a look that begged Josiah to rescue her. But there was nothing Josiah could do but look away.

"I hope to see you again, Josiah."

Mrs. Fikes let out another "humf" of disapproval.

Josiah glanced to Pearl quickly and said, "It would be my pleasure, ma'am."

He headed then for Clipper, but was stopped midway by another command.

"Ranger Wolfe," Mrs. Fikes demanded.

"Yes?"

"I hope you completed the task I asked of you concerning the captain's horse."

Josiah nodded his head, then made his way to his saddlebag, dug out a small object wrapped in a fancy white handkerchief, a gift from Suzanne del Toro, and offered it to Mrs. Fikes with a steady hand.

"What is this?"

"Proof," Josiah said, looking directly at Pedro—who seemed entirely relieved when Mrs. Fikes opened the handkerchief and found the severed ear of a chestnut mare in the center of it.

CHAPTER 28

Scrap called out for Josiah as he made his way past the carriage house. Josiah was settling in on the back of Clipper, about to urge the horse to pick up speed, to break into a run toward home, but instead he pulled the reins and came to a stop. "Whoa, Clipper," he said. "We better take care of this."

"Where you going, Wolfe?" Scrap stood a few feet from Josiah, shielding his eyes against the bright afternoon sun.

The only remaining evidence of the morning storm was the muddy road that led out of the captain's estate, and the puddles that dotted it that still overflowed, seeking the pull of gravity to deliver a fresh gush of water to the pond. The bench was empty.

"I've got business to attend to," Josiah answered.

"Looks like you're going to be gone for a while."

"I'll meet up with the rest of the company. It won't be too long." Josiah was a little surprised Scrap cared about his departure.

"You get orders from Feders?"

"Our new captain?" Josiah nodded. "I did."

"He can't fill those boots, can he?"

"I can't rightly say. I knew Captain Fikes for a long time. Feders? Not near as long. Not my call. It was Major Jones who saw fit to promote him."

"You don't feel slighted?" Scrap asked.

"Why would I? I have no ambition beyond getting through the day, and seeing to the care and safety of my son. Feders will do fine. If he's not for you, you can transfer to another company . . . or opt out of the Rangers entirely. I have the same option."

"Then what would I do?"

"I don't know. Not for me to say."

Clipper shifted anxiously as Scrap stepped toward him and dropped his arm, his hand dangling within inches of his gun. "I don't trust Feders," Scrap whispered, after looking around to make sure they were alone.

"Why's that?"

"He rode with the State Police before joinin' up with the captain again."

Josiah squinted his eyes, trying to remember if he'd known that or not. He couldn't remember, but thought it was odd for Scrap to bring it up now. "So?"

"I don't know. Those fellas kind of made up the law as they went, did some things that was questionable. The captain didn't take to that too well, why he didn't ride with them long. Told me that hisself."

"Is there something you need to tell me? Did you see something the morning the captain was killed that you haven't told anybody?" Josiah had lowered his voice, too, a reaction to his own deeply considered suspicions.

Scrap shook his head no. "I know what I saw. McClure fired that shot as sure as I'm standin' here."

"Where was Feders?"

"I don't remember."

"You don't remember? Was he in the camp when the shooting started?"

Scrap shrugged his shoulders. "I don't remember seeing him till after we found him with the captain. Things are a little blurry on that account."

"Except for McClure taking the shot?"

"Yeah, uh huh. I done told you that a hundred times."

"All right. I've got to get going. But if there's anything you need to tell me, don't send word through Feders, wait until you see me next if you can."

"You don't trust him, either, do you?"

"I don't know who to trust. All I know is that I need to get going. I'm losing daylight."

"I want to go with you."

"You can't," Josiah said. "I have to do this alone."

Austin faded quickly behind Josiah. The Chisolm Trail was easy enough to find. A good wind had picked up the stink of cows and carried it for miles.

There were a lot of entry points onto the trail, fingers that led off ranches and other trails in between, and since spring was the time when most cattle drives started, the route was busy and noisy. A half million cattle making their way north was not out of the question during the year.

Josiah was glad that a sea of longhorns was heading north. He could ride alongside some of the cattle and the cowboys, drovers, and chuck wagons, mixing in, so he wouldn't be a target if Charlie Langdon had set a trap for him.

He knew full well, though, that there were other dangers

on the trail. Anything could start a stampede; a loud fart or a boom of thunder in the distance could set off a reaction uncontrollable by the best flankers and drag men around.

He'd be lucky to make Round Rock before dark, but he wanted to get as far away from the Fikes estate as quick as he could. He wanted nothing more than to leave his time there behind him, vanquish it from his memory. But Pearl was not going to be easy to forget . . . nor was Suzanne del Toro, or his newfound suspicion of Pete Feders.

It was difficult for Josiah to consider that Feders could very well be responsible for the captain's death, could be the shooter himself.

It was entirely possible, and it more than made sense . . . even with the fractured information Josiah counted as viable. Feders was ambitious. But was he ambitious enough to commit murder? Or was Feders really just greedy, seeing a way into the wealth the captain held? Was Feders really in love with Pearl? Or was he using her to get her widowed mother's purse?

Josiah didn't know.

Scrap had told him Feders rode with the State Police.

Pearl told him that something happened between Juan Carlos and the State Police that caused him to become a shadow. Add in Patterson's reference to the State Police, and the San Antonio sheriff's presence, according to McClure, in the gang that fled after the captain was killed . . . and there was something valid that could be added to the whole idea. Feders had cause, a reason, and could have been the shooter who fired from behind McClure. Feders could be a cold-blooded killer . . . and Josiah had left him behind, unquestioned, chasing after Pearl's heart.

Josiah could only shudder at the thought of what might happen to the captain's daughter if Feders *was* the killer—

and didn't get his way, didn't get her hand in marriage like he had asked.

The thought was almost demanding enough for him to turn back, but he couldn't. Lyle was all that remained of his previous life, of Lily, of the life he so desperately wanted back. He couldn't bring himself to sacrifice his son for a woman he barely knew. No matter how frightening and selfish that proposition seemed at the moment.

By the time night fell, Josiah was past the towns of Round Rock and Brushy Creek, and the large circular limestone rock that marked the most favorable crossing point. Even though it had been a little treacherous considering the spring season and the afternoon rain.

A herd of cattle was settling in a shallow valley, glad, it seemed, like Josiah, to rest after a long, hard day. He'd found the trail boss and told him of his presence upwind of the herd. He'd declined a meal, though the chili and biscuits made his stomach waken and disagree with his decision to spend the night away from the comfort of a chuck wagon, and the chatter of strangers.

He had no idea who those strangers were, and the less he exposed himself to unknowns, or put himself in a position to tell his story, the better. It was too much of a risk to hope that Charlie Langdon wouldn't have men looking for him from Round Rock to Tyler.

That night, Josiah settled in on his bedroll, hidden between two bull-sized boulders. Like every night, he kissed his dead children good night, allowed their memory to comfort him, and promised Lyle that he would be home soon.

He did not sleep well at all, stirring at every sound, at every coyote yip and owl's hoot.

He was wide awake as the gray dawn cut the night away. He gathered his belongings and packed his saddlebags, glad the darkness had passed without incident.

As day broke, he was well on his way toward Belton, a favorite stopping-off point for a lot of cowboys. There were plenty of merchants to restock, plenty of saloons that offered entertainment of the kind Josiah had once thought he would never partake in again, but now had.

Fat Susie had visited him in his dreams, and he'd been unable to send her packing from his head. There was more to the woman than how she lived her life every day. Regardless, Josiah was certain that he wouldn't stop in Belton. If he did, it'd only be for a brief respite, to water Clipper, and then he'd get back on the trail.

He rode hard, his eyes constantly searching the horizon, his surroundings, for any sign of ambush, any sign of Charlie Langdon's gang. So far, there had been no sign of any threat. But Josiah did not let down his guard, did not get comfortable with the assumption that they were not lying in wait for him. Not this time.

Belton came and went. He would avoid the toll on the Chisolm Trail to cross the suspension bridge in Waco, avoid the herds of cattle backed up to cross the Brazos River. This time of year would be dramatic, the clank and tapping of longhorns heard for miles in every direction, the stench almost unbearable. Instead of paying the toll, Josiah would slow his pace and go directly through Waco.

He was able to get lost in the crowds of Waco, a brief bit of comfort from being out in the open for so long—even though he was annoyed at being slowed—but he did not let the memory of O'Reilly putting a gun to his back in the funeral crowd stray too far from his mind.

It had been a long, hard ride, and Josiah finally gave in

to his physical needs. He stopped to water Clipper, and to restore himself, grab a bit of food and fresh water. His senses were strained, as he tried to take in every sight, sound, and smell possible in Waco, trying to see Charlie Langdon or his men before they saw him. He was glad there were no uniform or badge requirements for Texas Rangers.

He escaped Waco unseen, and caught up with another herd of cattle. He stayed alongside the cattle for as long as possible, then headed on to Fort Parker, to see if there was any word waiting for him from Feders or Major Jones.

That was part of the plan to outwit Charlie and his gang.

If there were no new orders, news that Charlie Langdon had been captured, then he was to proceed forward, to home, and play out the rest of the plan to bring Charlie Langdon to justice, once and for all.

Josiah's father had always called Fort Parker by another name, Fort Sterling. His father was not a big believer in the Parker story, the captive Cynthia who went back to live with the Indians after she was rescued. There was a lot of anger among the men who'd fought in the Indian Wars, prejudice that would not die. Josiah, however, had inherited a contrary bit of rationale from his mother and always questioned both sides of the fence, even Cynthia Parker's right to live as she chose. It caused a lot of conflict between father and son in the early years, but they eventually came to see eye to eye on most things in life.

War changes a boy into a different kind of a man.

His father would be enraged that Quanah Parker, Cynthia's half-breed son, had grown into such a powerful leader, Josiah's father's point proven right that Cynthia should have been treated like the savage she had become, and killed upon sight.

That was a disagreement that was never settled. Josiah called the fort by its popular and more known name, Fort Parker, and he was glad to see the gates standing open in welcome as he approached.

He was close to home now, the memory of his father cast aside, his hope about his son's well-being far more important than an old battle that could not be won.

The land was beginning to transform from hard limestone outcroppings situated among grassy meadows, properly suited for grazing cattle, to the hilly, deep-ravine pine forests he knew so well. Josiah was heartened by the familiar greening landscape, glad to hear a blue jay chatter in the distance, glad to be riding Clipper on soil he understood.

At a slow, comfortable trot, looking forward to a moment's rest before completing the last leg of his journey, he entered the fort, which was just a scattering of cabins built haphazardly, surrounded by a tall fence.

The first thing he did was check in with the post commander, a rotund man with balding silver hair, Colonel Leonard Gibbon.

Gibbon, who looked like a no-nonsense kind of commander, gave him the bad news that there was no news. Charlie Langdon had not been caught, and there was not word of Lyle's whereabouts, no missives from Feders or Major Jones.

There had been no mail at all given to the fort commander to hold for Josiah.

He was slightly disheartened, his hope tarnished a little, but only because he was tired, because he had not slowed one bit in his effort to get home as quickly as possible. There was still a plan to follow.

Clipper had not complained on the trip from Austin to Fort Parker. The horse had not hesitated once, and had run as fast and hard as Josiah could push him. But when Josiah walked out of the commander's cabin, he noticed that the horse was beginning to look weary. Clipper needed a fresh stall, some oats, a good scrubbing, and some serious rest. Thankfully, there was a livery across the compound, just inside the back gate.

Josiah led his horse to the livery, tied Clipper to the post next to another horse, and stood there for a minute. The other horse looked familiar, the saddle even more familiar. It was a solid black stallion, a white star on its narrow nose, with a hand-tooled Mexican saddle appointed with silver buckles and studs tightened across its back, the likes of which were rare in these parts. Josiah could only remember seeing a similar saddle once before . . . recently . . . on a horse just like this one.

"Is that you, Wolfe?" someone shouted from the darker reaches of the livery, a stall Josiah could not see clearly into.

A man walked out into the center of the livery, toward him, and Josiah nodded, relaxing the hand that had dropped to his side and gripped the Peacemaker when he heard his name called out.

"I heard you were coming this way, and I've been looking for you day and night," Sam Willis said.

Willis put his skillet-sized hand on Josiah's shoulder, looked at him woefully, and said, "I'm afraid I have some bad news for you."

CHAPTER 29

There was no time to give Clipper the proper amount of rest that he was so obviously in need of.

The cabin was half a day's ride from Fort Parker, and the horse would just have to make the trip . . . or die trying, because there was no way Josiah was going to spend another minute at the fort once Sam Willis confirmed his worst fears: Charlie Langdon was holed up in the cabin outside of Seerville, with Ofelia and Lyle held hostage inside.

Before hitting the trail, Josiah sent word to Austin, asking Major Jones to send more Rangers than they had initially planned on needing. Feders and a handful of men were supposed to be behind him by half a day, not too close and taking a different route—just in case Charlie had spotters set along the trails leading to Fort Parker. They wanted it to look like Josiah was riding alone, just like Charlie had told him to. Only problem now was, there was no way to get word to Feders, no way to warn him except to leave a message with Colonel Gibbon, which Josiah did, before tearing out of the fort and heading north on Moscoso's Trail as fast as he could.

There was no time to lose. No time for Josiah to reexamine Feders's role in the captain's death . . . He'd just have to hope he was wrong, that Feders was a model Ranger, doing his job this very minute.

The wind rushed at Josiah's face as he and Clipper left the fort. He was pushing the horse harder than he could ever remember pushing him. The weather was not of consequence, other than that it wasn't storming, raining. It could have been the most perfect spring day, and Josiah wouldn't have noticed once he got on the trail and headed toward home.

Moscoso's Trail dated back to the early expeditions of Hernando de Soto, the first European to discover the Mississippi River. It was not as widely used by cattle drivers as the Chisolm, but it was used by stagecoaches. The narrow, weedy trail connected South Texas with the Labahia Road and, north into Arkansas, with Trammel's Trace. Josiah had ridden the Moscoso's hundreds of times, knew it well enough to travel it blindfolded, which was a good thing . . . since his eyes were glazed with anger and dread, dosed with tears—which he attributed to the wind.

Sam Willis could hardly keep up with Josiah. His black horse frothed at the mouth, and its hard muscles glistened with sweat. Sam, who was a big man, nearly as big as McClure, was bent forward, riding as hard as he could, pushing the horse just as hard as Josiah pushed Clipper.

They had little time to talk. Josiah was not interested in much of anything else other than the news he'd been given, but Willis did tell him that he had followed Charlie and his gang north, lost them a few times, because they had split apart around Austin, which made sense to Josiah, considering his own encounters with O'Reilly and the Negro. Willis found Charlie's tracks again just south of Round Rock, and followed them to Seerville, keeping a good distance, not willing to stop and send word for fear of losing them again.

By the time Willis realized the gang had settled at the cabin, it was too late to help Ofelia protect Lyle. Willis was outmanned six to one. His trip to Fort Parker, along with searching for Josiah, was to get some help and make it known to others where Charlie Langdon was and what he was up to.

Charlie knew the lay of the land in and around Tyler and Seerville just as well as Josiah did. He knew where the cabin was, and knew Josiah would not have thought to worry about the Mexican midwife needing to protect herself and Lyle with anything other than the shotgun that sat just inside the front door.

The familiarity of the land, of the trail, of the knowledge he held deep in his memory about everything that surrounded him, gave Josiah little comfort. He could only hope that he wasn't too late to save Lyle, and ultimately, he was grateful that he wasn't riding alone . . . no matter the risk.

Vultures circled just over the next ridge. Seven or eight ugly redheaded eaters of sour, dead flesh, they also served as a signal, a sign, that at some point, somewhere, a struggle had taken place and a life had been taken. How often did a badger or a deer die of old age? Nature didn't work like that, and Josiah knew it.

Thankfully, they weren't close enough to the cabin for the object of the vulture's desire to be there. But they weren't far, about four miles now.

Clipper didn't slow. Willis and his horse lagged behind, running as fast as they could. It was as if Clipper could sense Josiah's panic, his need to get home as quickly as possible.

Josiah kept his eyes peeled for any sign of movement, any shadow that might turn out to be one of Langdon's men, hiding, ready to take a shot at him, but he could only worry for so long about being shot out of the blue. Each mile he rode was a mile closer to Lyle.

He crested the ridge, and looked up and saw that more vultures had joined the kettle. When he looked back to the trail he saw why.

A man, naked from the waist up, vacant of socks and boots, dangled from the limb of a towering southern red oak tree.

The tree was nearly eighty feet tall, its trunk three feet around, and the man had been placed so he was hanging square in the middle of the trail. He wasn't moving; he was as still as a dead moth caught in a spider's web.

A vulture was sitting on the dead man's shoulder, tearing a piece of flesh from his cheek, helping itself to an easy meal. The big bird flushed upon seeing Josiah, lifting off silently with one graceful thrust of its wings.

Josiah brought Clipper to a stop about fifteen feet from the man. He was tempted to shoot at the bird, to run off the lot of them, but he knew it would be no use. They would soar in the sky until the man was six feet under, his scent buried, and then they'd be off, scavenging for some other victim of unfortunate circumstances.

Josiah recognized the man then, saw that he'd known him when he was living, and had questioned more than once what side of the law he truly stood on. That question wasn't going to be answered anytime soon, but it was puzzling why the sheriff of San Antonio, J. T. Patterson himself, had been hanged on the Moscoso's Trail, only a few miles from Seerville. The sheriff was a long way from home, but pretty darn close to where Charlie Langdon and his gang were holed up.

Willis eased up alongside Josiah. "Looks like he's been there for a while, but I was just through here a day ago and didn't see a thing then."

Patterson's face was gray, his head hung limply to the side, victim of a perfectly coiled rope. His bare chest and arms were covered with shallow slits in the skin from a sharp knife. Josiah had seen this before.

The wounds on his chest were not caused by the seekers of carrion. Slow cutting was a technique Charlie Langdon used in the war to get information out of a prisoner about troop movements, the inner workings of the ranks, or anything else he thought was relevant to win the next battle.

The technique was effective, and one that Charlie obviously still used to find out what he needed to know to survive.

The cuts had congealed . . . blood had stopped pumping through the sheriff's heart after a quick snap of the neck. It had probably been a relief, the torture finally over.

Josiah exhaled deeply. "I expect we ought to cut him down."

"No, I don't think so," Willis answered.

Josiah started to object, and turned to Willis, curious why he would protest such a thing. But he swallowed his question.

He was staring into the barrel of a Colt revolver, and he noticed at that moment that Willis's eyes were black as a storm cloud, and held no emotion at all, other than cold, hard hate.

Josiah reluctantly dismounted from Clipper, his hands high above his head, realizing he had been tricked into leaving Fort Parker.

This was the third time in recent memory that he'd been at the barrel end of a gun, and he didn't like the thought of it. Juan Carlos had saved his life at the Menger Hotel, and Suzanne del Toro had put a knife in the Negro's chest outside of the saloon.

But there was no one to come to his aid on the Moscoso's Trail. He was on his own and knew deep in his heart that he was as close to his own death as he'd ever been. His skin tingled, and his eyes were focused on Willis, waiting for him to make one small mistake. Like Charlie Langdon, Josiah had perfected a set of survival skills in the war.

"Now slowly unbuckle your belt and ease your gun to the ground," Willis said.

Josiah did as he was told, quickly eyeing Clipper, and the Sharps carbine sticking out of the sheath. He was five feet from his horse, and the carbine was on the opposite side of the saddle. Willis could probably get at least one shot off, more than likely two, if Josiah rolled under Clipper to retrieve the Sharps. He was too far away. At the moment.

"Now," Willis continued, aiming his Colt at Josiah and pulling his own rifle from its sheath, "take off your boots. Just in case you think you're going to get a chance at me with a knife or a derringer."

"Why are you doing this, Willis?"

Sam Willis squinted, his forehead pulsing with ribs of fatty skin. "Don't go asking a lot of questions, Wolfe. We're short on time. Charlie knows there's a company of Rangers ridin' in your shadow."

Josiah nodded, acknowledging Willis's confirmation that he was working with Charlie Langdon. He tried not to show any surprise that Langdon had somehow figured out the plan he and Feders had hatched back in Austin. They'd hoped to rescue Lyle with a swarm of men. Now it looked like Josiah might have to face down his former deputy one on one.

"You're on the wrong side of things, Willis. It's not too late to change that." He pulled off a boot, and his Bowie knife fell on the ground.

Willis laughed. "It's way too late for me to change anything. Kick the knife over to me." He was still sitting on his horse.

Josiah thought back to the night the captain was shot. McClure told him that Willis slept away from the camp, like he always did. Scrap didn't say anything about the man in the camp, but said Willis had gone after Charlie and McClure by the time Josiah had reached the captain.

He kicked the knife toward the black horse. "Your friend died with a murder on his shoulders. But I never thought he shot the captain. I think you shot the captain, killed him in cold blood. I just don't know why you would do such a thing. Kill Hiram Fikes, then betray your best friend."

"I ought to shoot you here and now, just get it over with," Willis said.

"Why don't you?"

"Charlie ordered me not to. I'm supposed to deliver you to him."

"That's a risky proposition."

Willis rocked his rifle up and down in an urgent nod. "Take off the other boot, Wolfe."

"All right." Josiah leaned down, grabbed the toe of his boot, and tugged a little, but not hard enough to pull it off his foot. "Why'd you do it, Sam?"

"You really don't know, do you?"

"I'd been off the trail awhile before the captain called me down to San Antonio." The boot came off his foot, but he held on to it, not emptying it like he'd had the other one.

"Me and McClure and Patterson rode with Fikes and Feders in the State Police. For a short while things was fine. But there was always this Mexican with Fikes, and Patterson don't like Mexicans, thought they all were liars and thieves, didn't trust the one Fikes was so fond of one bit. Anyway, one night we was playing cards in a saloon down in Refugio. There'd been rumors that Charlie Langdon was out and about, but they didn't pay much mind to the rumor. We'd heard it before and it turned out to be false. I did, though. I knew Charlie in the war, knew he'd come back and tried to live the straight and narrow, being a deputy of some sort, but he couldn't quite live that way. A lot of us had that problem, adjusting back to the laws of ordinary men. War gives certain people a taste for things that never goes away."

Josiah stared at Willis and tried to remember if he'd served in the Brigade, but he was certain that he hadn't. Josiah would have recognized him long before now. McClure said he was from Kentucky, and Willis probably was, too. Brigades mixed, met up at different times. It was entirely possible that Willis knew Langdon and would not have known Josiah.

"So, Patterson," Willis continued, "wouldn't sit at the same table with the Mexican. 'Bout that time, ole Charlie Langdon pulls off a bank robbery across the street from the saloon in Refugio, and everybody heads out after him. We were State Police after all, no matter what anybody thought of us. Anyway, Charlie got away, mainly 'cause I let him, once I realized it was him, after cornering him behind the saloon by myself. When we headed back to the saloon, all the money from our table was missin'. Patterson blamed the Mexican, got into a big row with Fikes, and that pretty much set the stage for their feud, since the captain always took the Mexican's side."

There was a reason the captain trusted the Mexican; they were blood, and the captain knew Juan Carlos was no thief. Josiah wasn't going to tell Sam Willis that, though. "But the Mexican, Juan Carlos, didn't steal Patterson's money, did he?"

Willis shook his head no. "You ever drive cattle, Wolfe? Spend day after day downwind of those foul creatures, knowin' your life ain't going to get any better? I joined up with the State Police, and it wasn't much better, and didn't pay worth a darn. Besides, once I met up with Charlie again, he thought it was a good idea to have a man inside, and I could make twice the money. Especially after Fikes tapped McClure and me to join up with the Rangers."

"You were a traitor."

"Not the only one. A fellow named O'Reilly was a deputy for Patterson. That's how I got the key to let Charlie loose. There was more than him, too. Fellas that served with Charlie one way or another."

"What about McClure?" Josiah asked.

"McClure? He didn't know nothin'. Nothin' except he was startin' to question what I was up to. McClure always had high ideals, big dreams. I suppose it was because of how he was raised, but money never seemed to matter to him like it did to me."

"So the shot that killed the captain came from your gun?"

"Yes. I didn't plan for McClure to take the blame, but when I saw it happen that way, I thought it was perfect to let that snot-nosed Elliot scream after everybody that McClure had killed Fikes. Now, if you don't want to be joinin' your captain in the great beyond, I'd suggest you toss that boot to the ground and put your hands behind your head. We need to get you to Charlie so you two can reminisce about old times."

Josiah dropped the boot softly. It landed on its heel and stayed standing up. "Why is Patterson dead?"

"He was with a posse of men who were more loyal to Charlie Langdon than they were to him. I guess Charlie got tired of carrying him around. Found out everything he wanted to know."

"What's that?"

"Hell if I know. You can ask him yourself, but I wouldn't count on gettin' an answer."

Josiah stared at Sam Willis and exhaled loudly. McClure was innocent, and Josiah had even questioned if a man like Pete Feders could be guilty of murder. Maybe he wanted him to be . . . so Feders would leave Pearl to herself, to him, if he survived. Rage boiled from the tips of his fingers all the way to his toes, and he knew that if he was going to save himself, it was now or never.

CHAPTER 30

Josiah did not break eye contact with Sam Willis as he grabbed up the boot, dove to the muddy ground in a roll, and caught the knife Suzanne del Toro had given him, wrapped in her white handkerchief as a parting gift, as it fell from inside the boot.

Clipper reared up when Sam fired a shot. The bullet thudded into the wet ground inches from Josiah's feet. The horse then spun around and effectively put itself in between Josiah and Sam, just long enough for Josiah to get a solid grip on the knife, aim it, and throw it at Sam as hard and directly as he could.

The knife spiraled through the air and hit its target dead-on, the blade piercing Sam's pant leg just under his knee. A loud yell was followed by another shot from Sam's gun, this one going wild, straight up in the air, as he reacted to being stabbed just under the kneecap.

Clipper hustled out of the way, the gunshots sending the horse skittering off, until it came to a stop just beyond the southern red oak.

The carbine was more than thirty yards from Josiah's grasp.

He quickly scanned the ground for his Peacemaker. He was standing ten feet from it and ten feet from Sam Willis, who was still sitting on his horse, grabbing his knee and in the process of pulling the knife, cussing like the wounded soldier that he was.

Josiah had about ten seconds to decide what to do next. It didn't take him that long. He ran as fast as he could toward Sam and dove sideways, slamming his body as hard as he could against Sam's wounded leg.

Willis was either too flustered or in too much pain to get off a decent shot. Another wild shot exploded from his gun, close to Josiah's ear, and Josiah suddenly felt like he was in a deep well; he could hardly hear anything, and he could smell only gunpowder and carbon.

He bounced off the horse, tumbling to the ground in a thud, and Sam Willis toppled off the side, screaming, yelling, cussing. Neither man moved for a second or two, but Josiah was up first, and grabbed his Peacemaker, cocked the hammer, and aimed the gun at Sam Willis.

Willis had lost his grip, and his gun lay half a foot from his grasp.

"Leave it," Josiah commanded, shielding himself at the rear of Willis's horse. "Or you're a dead man."

"You ain't got the guts to shoot me, Wolfe. Charlie said you was soft, and he's usually right about things like that." Willis grimaced, stretching his hand for his gun, ignoring Josiah.

"I'm serious, Willis."

Willis grabbed the butt of his gun, pulled it into his grip, and then in a sudden burst of energy swung the barrel toward Josiah, pulled the trigger, and fanned the hammer.

Josiah saw what was coming and reacted. The first bullet hit Willis just above the belt, square in the stomach. The second bullet hit Willis in the chest just under the heart. The man bounced on the muddy ground, a combination of convulsions caused by being shot and his body finishing out the motion of shooting at Josiah. The third and final shot caught Willis just under his right eye. An explosion of blood and bone and a quick, final gasp were followed by the stillness of the swift hand of death.

Josiah walked over to Sam Willis, and the reality of his actions was quickly apparent. "I'll only kill a man when I have to, Sam. I bet Charlie Langdon forgot to tell you that part of the story about me," he said, rolling the man over with a solid push of his foot, so he wouldn't have to see his face ever again.

Horse hooves approached from behind Josiah, coming up the trail at great speed. He didn't have time to hide in the bushes, and turned around just in time to see two horses coming around the bend. He relaxed his finger on the trigger of the Peacemaker. It was Feders and Elliot.

"Wolfe," Feders said, bringing his horse to a halting stop in front of Josiah. "We heard shooting and feared the worst."

Scrap Elliot brought his horse to a stop next to Feders. "Damn, Wolfe. Is that Patterson?"

"It is," Josiah answered. "And that's Sam Willis there. He's the one that shot the captain."

Feders nodded. "I'm not surprised. There's no time for

recounting things, Wolfe. We need to get back to the cabin. We got there before you and took out two of Charlie Langdon's lookouts. We've got the cabin surrounded with six Rangers from our company that we gathered up in Austin. Charlie's inside with three other men, claims if we come one step closer he's going to shoot the boy and the Mexican woman."

"He will," Josiah said. His hands trembled at the thought. "You were supposed to wait for me."

"Come on, Wolfe. That's your son in there. Your emotions could have sparked a showdown and left all of us dead. I wasn't going to let that happen. I was always going to get here ahead of you," Feders said. "But I do have another plan."

Josiah stared up at Feders. He looked no different than he had riding out of San Antonio at the side of Captain Hiram Fikes. Same hat, same horse, same riding clothes, as far as Josiah could tell. Rangers wore no insignia to set themselves apart in rank. You just knew who was who, and what was what.

"That's good to hear, Captain Feders," Josiah said, locking eyes with Feders, a slight smile flashing on both men's faces. "Because I'm about all wrung out."

The cabin sat in a slight valley. A two-stall barn sat off to the north, about twenty yards from the front door. A weedy, unplowed field and meadow sat behind the barn, rolling down to a creek that was skirted by a shallow bayou and piney woods. Josiah could see his entire plot of land from the vantage point he, Feders, and Elliot were crouched upon. It took all Josiah had in him to ignore the cemetery edged up along the woods.

"You're sure you're up to this, Wolfe?" Feders asked.

Josiah nodded that he was, staring at the cabin, not seeing anything moving inside.

A thin coil of smoke rising into the air from the chimney was the only sign of life. The pine smoke smelled good, reminding Josiah, along with all of the smells of the land, that he was finally home.

"There's a man in the barn. One behind the wood stack. One there in the field, lying prone." Feders pointed to the right of the cabin. It took Josiah a minute to see the man, but he did.

Scrap was on the other side of Josiah. "I'll be behind you."

"You sure about that, Captain?"

Scrap gritted his teeth and glared at Josiah.

"The kid's a crack shot, Wolfe. You're going to have to trust us."

Josiah nodded again, and sighed. "All right."

Feders turned his attention back to the cabin. "There's three more Rangers scattered about at the edge of the woods and the bayou, standing watch just in case Langdon has reinforcements coming in, or tries to make a run for it."

"You sure this is going to work?" Josiah asked.

Feders shrugged. "I'm not sure that we have any other choices. But I don't really think Charlie Langdon wants to kill a child in cold blood. The Mexican? She might already be dead. We haven't seen her since we surrounded the cabin. There was some shooting when we took out the lookouts and let Charlie know that he was trapped."

"You don't know Charlie Langdon like I do. He planned for this. He's got an escape route figured out . . . always has."

"I've known plenty of devils like him, Wolfe. Don't

worry. He won't be expecting you to do what you're about to. And, we've got your back—this has to work."

"All right. Let's do it."

Josiah dismounted from Clipper about fifty yards from the cabin. He immediately raised both arms over his head. "Langdon. It's me, Wolfe. I got an offer for you."

His voice carried on a soft breeze. The sun was bright overhead, staring down from the center of a cloudless sky. There were no sounds other than grass brushing against grass in the slight wind. No screeching hawks, no horses whinnying, no vultures flapping their giant wings to stay aloft—those birds were probably feasting four miles away. There was nothing but silence, nothing but the heartbeat of a man, intent on saving his son's life.

He stood there staring at the cabin—his Peacemaker left behind, his belt empty, his saddle sheath vacant of the Sharps carbine. He held no weapons, not even a knife hidden in his boot. Feders had insisted, and Josiah had reluctantly agreed with him.

There was no word from inside the cabin. Not even a flutter of the curtain in the window next to the front door.

"You hear me, Langdon? I got an offer. A trade. Me for the boy and the Mexican woman. We ride out of here then."

The front door cracked open. "How stupid do you think I am, Wolfe? There's Rangers all around this place. You think I'm gonna risk gettin' my head blown off by a buffalo gun, thinkin' I'm a free man on my way to nowhere?"

Josiah heard Lyle squeal inside the cabin. He couldn't tell whether the boy had been hurt or was playing happily.

"Me for the boy, Langdon. I'm unarmed, I swear. Kill me right here and now if you want, but don't hurt the boy. He's of no consequence to you just because he's my blood. He's an innocent."

"Lot of innocents die, Wolfe. You know that. Saw it often enough. Killed 'em yourself."

"Only when I had to."

"You always were hesitant on the trigger. Never did feel comfortable with you on the drive."

The door cracked open a little more, and Josiah could see the silhouette of a man standing off to the side. He'd know Charlie Langdon anywhere.

"I'm standing here in front of you now, Charlie," Josiah said. "Not at your side, not covering your back. Those days are long gone. Take my life. I'll gladly give it for my son's."

"Tell you what I'll do. I'll ride out of here with your son, and leave him and the woman when I'm certain I'm not being followed."

"That's not the offer."

"Well, that's the deal. Other than you're coming along, too."

Josiah heard a twig snap behind him, and knew Scrap was settling into his position. "All right, then," he said, stiffening a bit. Sweat beaded on his forehead, and for a brief second, he was afraid, then he pushed the fear away with the confidence he held in Feders's judgment and plan.

"You have no choice," Charlie said.

The door to the cabin opened wide then, and Ofelia was standing in the center of it. She blinked from the harsh sunlight, and Josiah could see a dried streak of blood on her face that reached from her eye to her neck. Somebody pushed her out onto the porch, the barrel of a rifle stuck securely in the center of her back.

It was then that Josiah first heard the noise, a familiar but distant tinkle. The sound was so faint he could barely hear it over his rapidly beating heart. He took a deep breath and scanned the shadows beyond the porch for the origin of the new sound, but saw nothing.

Other than the blood and fear on her face, Ofelia looked to be fine. Josiah didn't recognize the tall, straggly man with the rifle in her back, but that wasn't a surprise.

"You just stay right where you're at, Wolfe," Charlie hollered from inside the cabin.

The breeze shifted, and Josiah heard the tinkle again. Only this time it was louder, like there was more than one, a chorus of rattles. And then he knew—knew for certain what it was that he was hearing.

In his absence, a rattlesnake had set up a nest in a hole under the porch. It happened every year. The spot was too perfect for a snake to pass up. One of his chores was to keep the porch and surrounding areas free of the deadly critters, but he hadn't given the chore any thought until now.

He wanted to shout out and warn Ofelia, but he held his tongue, and watched carefully as the tall cohort of Charlie's urged her down the steps. They made it down without issue, without sensing anything was amiss, though the man did look around on the ground when he stepped away from the porch.

The snake was not yet fully riled, had yet to show itself, and Josiah hoped it would wait.

Charlie appeared in the doorway. Lyle was stuffed under Charlie's left arm like a bag of potatoes, a Colt stuck to his son's head. There was another man behind Charlie. He held a gun to Lyle's head, too.

One false move, and Lyle was dead for sure.

Josiah was completely panicked. His eyes focused under the porch. As Charlie stepped down, Josiah saw the snake peer out from under the boards. The rattler grew loud, enraged that it had been disturbed.

"Stop!" Josiah screamed, Charlie's order to stand still forgotten as he rushed forward.

Charlie heard both warnings, Josiah's and the snake's, but was down to the next step before he realized what the warning was for. It looked for a brief second like he thought he was walking into a trap, a trick, but he realized quickly that he was in danger from something other than a Ranger.

The man behind Charlie jumped back up on the porch, pulling the gun away from Lyle's head as he did. Charlie skidded to a stop just off the step, and was about to do the same, jump back up on the porch—but the rattlesnake struck, tearing through Charlie's pant leg, biting into the flesh of his calf.

Charlie yelled out in pain as the snake buried its fangs deep into his flesh. He held on to Lyle as best as he could, but the pain and the surprise were too intense, and the gun fell from his other hand, tumbling to the ground.

Josiah was in front of Charlie in a matter of seconds. He ripped Lyle out of Charlie Langdon's clutch and dove off to the right, his son safely in his grasp.

Charlie was screaming, grabbing at the snake, rolling on the ground, when a loud report from Scrap Elliot's rifle shot echoed across the valley, announcing the end to Charlie Langdon's reign of lawlessness.

Josiah held Lyle as tight as he could, feeling every inch of the boy, who was screaming and crying wildly, to make sure his son hadn't been shot, that he was all right. Lyle continued to cry, a welcome sound to Josiah's relieved heart and mind.

After a long minute, after the rush of Rangers surrounding the cabin, and hearing Captain Peter Feders order everyone to lay down their weapons, Josiah stood with Lyle in his arms—who until that very moment had not realized that it was his father who had come to his rescue.

Lyle stopped crying, smiled, and threw his arms around Josiah's neck, and for the first time in a long time, Josiah smiled, too.

EPILOGUE

Josiah loaded the last crate onto the wagon. Ofelia sat with Lyle on her lap, waiting on the seat up front. Clipper was fully rested and tied comfortably to the back of the wagon.

"I think that's the last of it," Josiah said. "I'm glad you're coming with us, Ofelia."

"I have been here all my life, señor. It is past time I saw more of the world."

"Austin is a different kind of place."

"That will be the best thing for the both of us. There are many bad dreams here."

"And many happy ones."

Ofelia nodded, and forced a smile. "They will always be here, the happy ones, but there are more down the road. Ones that can touch you."

This will always be my home, Josiah thought. He took a deep breath, and drank in the sight of his land and cabin for the last time. He had already visited the cemetery, had bid-den Lily and the girls good-bye, all the while asking their forgiveness for leaving them. But he had to go. He would have never felt right about leaving Lyle alone at the cabin again. Besides, he felt more alive now than he had in a long time.

He wasn't sure what lay ahead, what his life would be like in Austin, but it offered him more than the family homestead could now.

Charlie Langdon had survived the snakebite and gunshot wound—Scrap's orders from Feders had been to hobble the man, not kill him—and was set to stand trial in a week. Charlie had been properly delivered to the jail in Tyler by eight Texas Rangers, including Josiah himself. The hangman surely wasn't too far behind . . . but that was an event Josiah had no desire to see. His duty was done.

Juan Carlos had been cleared of all his implied crimes, but there was no word about the old Mexican's whereabouts. Josiah hoped he would see the captain's half brother again sometime in the future, but he wasn't certain of it.

Captain Pete Feders had gone on to the Red River camp, where he was forming the new company. Once Josiah got settled in Austin, he was to join the rest of the Rangers, including Scrap, on the edge of the Indian Territory.

He did not allow himself to think of Suzanne del Toro . . . but he could not help thinking of Pearl, and he more than hoped that he would see her again, even though she was complicated, uncertain—and one of the most beautiful women Josiah had ever seen.

He climbed up on the wagon, smiled at the thought of Pearl, flicked the reins, and called out, "Let's go. Come on, let's go."

Turn the page for a preview of the next book in the Josiah Wolfe, Texas Ranger Series

THE SCORPION TRAIL

by Larry D. Sweazy

Coming soon from Berkley Westerns!

PROLOGUE

September 1852

Twelve-year-old Josiah Wolfe was acutely aware of every sound in the woods. The long gun he carried was his father's—and it was the first time he had ever been allowed to carry it away from the house on his own. Beyond target practice, he had hardly ever handled the gun, much less hunted with it, but his father was ill, struck with a fever that had lingered longer than anyone thought it would, and the meat in the larder was growing thin.

His ma gave him the charge to bring home some squirrels or rabbits—something, anything, to get them through until his father recovered.

There'd been an anxiousness in his ma's blue eyes that he'd never seen before, a tenseness in her voice when she saw him off and said, "Now, you be careful out there on your own, Josiah. I need you to come back whole. I need you to come back," she'd repeated with fear frozen in her throat. His father coughed from the bed behind her, too weak to raise his head. "I couldn't bear to be like those

Parkers." She watched him until he disappeared down the lane.

There was not a child in East Texas who did not know the names of Cynthia Ann and John Richard Parker. The children, Cynthia, age eight, and John, age five, were kidnapped by the Comanche in 1836, after a violent raid on their home. Fort Parker had been built by the eldest Parker two years earlier, and it was surrounded by twelve-foot walls that enclosed four acres, with six cabins inside. Most of the inhabitants were extended family from Illinois. The raid in which the Parker children were taken was quick and bloody—conducted by a large party of Indians, mostly Comanche, but there were also Kiowa, Caddo, and Wichita involved.

Fort Parker was less than a day's ride from Seerville, the closest town to Josiah's father's small parcel of farmland, and even though the massacre had taken place four years before Josiah Wolfe's birth, he carried a healthy fear, mistrust, and curiosity about anything that had to do with Indians. The kidnapping was lore. A spooky story used to correct bad behavior.

Just the utterance of the word "Comanche" made Josiah shiver, even though Indian Territory was a long way away and the Comanche and other tribes had been all but run out of East Texas. No child wanted to be the next Cynthia Ann or John Richard—and no parent in the vicinity was fully confident that such an attack could never happen again.

There were still Indians that refused to give up the raiding, and some strays stole cattle and still traded with the Mexicans down south.

John Richard had been ransomed back from the Comanche, but had run off to rejoin them not soon after. No one had ever seen or heard from Cynthia Ann again—though there were newspaper reports that she'd been spotted trading with a companion, a Comanche, on the Canadian River. The memory of her white life, it seemed, had been stolen from her, and most folks believed that Cynthia Ann would be better off dead than living among the Indians.

With the world on his shoulders, and surely not wanting to disappoint his father or his sweet but forever nervous ma, Josiah had headed out into the woods, assuming the role of provider, of doing for others what they could not do for themselves.

At first, he was confident, but as the morning edged along, and he got farther from home, he became more fearful. He had shot one scrawny little gray cat squirrel that barely covered the bottom of his satchel. The bigger fox squirrels foraged later in the morning than the gray cats, so there was still hope. But then the need for meat took Josiah deeper into the forest than he had ever been.

He wished it was spring instead of fall.

In spring there'd be plenty of cat squirrels bouncing around the hardwood forest close to the cabin. But all of the wishing in the world wouldn't turn back time. There was a chill in the air, and the days of late were regularly overcast, and growing shorter. Now that the harvest of corn was in, Josiah had been obliged to return to school—which did not make him too happy.

A game trail caught his attention, and he eased along a hidden winding path that cascaded down a steep ravine.

He clung tightly to his father's long gun and navigated his way through the towering hardwoods, a thick grove of pines, then into a floodplain that was dried up and sandy.

Silt covered the first six feet at the base of every tree along the meandering river that was at the end of the trail, remnants of the spring floods. A red-bellied woodpecker chortled three times as it lit out overhead, then it landed on a nearby tree and started to work, quickly hammering away in search of ants or other insects to eat.

Every creature on earth must be hungry, Josiah thought. He stopped and caught his breath. He could feel his heart beating in his chest, and another pang of hunger gurgled in his belly—breakfast had been a bit of grease-soaked bread.

After he had stood still for five minutes or so, a big squirrel buck jumped from one tree to another. But it was nearly a hundred yards away. Josiah raised the gun, steadied himself, and tried to balance his weight so he wouldn't go tumbling backward once he pulled the long gun's trigger. The light was dim under the canopy of leaves that had yet to fall, and the sky above was roiling gray, the clouds tossing and turning in a north wind that seemed to be growing stronger by the minute.

The buck was busy jumping from one tree to the next, and with each jump it was farther away from Josiah, and the certainty of a piece of meat was quickly running out of range. Josiah took a deep breath, sighted the squirrel as best he could, and pulled the trigger. The blast shattered the peaceful silence that blanketed the river bottom. The squirrel fell to the ground with a loud thud. The shot was square-on.

The discharge had propelled Josiah back a bit, but he did not fall—he knew what to expect. The smell of black powder tickled his nose, and it gave him a feeling of satisfaction and comfort. He'd have two squirrels in his bag—a couple more and he could head home and present his parents with a few days' worth of meals. Hopefully, his father would recover quickly and they could go hunting together.

He made his way to the squirrel, unconcerned about how much noise he made. All of the creatures had now been alerted to his intention. The buck was truly the biggest squirrel he had ever seen. It had to weigh three or four pounds. It made the gray cat look like a mouse when he tossed the buck in the satchel with it.

Blood covered the fingers of his right hand, so Josiah went to the river to clean himself up. He had laid the long gun down on the ground a few feet behind him, but he clutched the satchel tightly between his arm and ribs. He could smell the squirrels, the blood, and it quelled his appetite, almost made him queasy, but he would not for a second part with the kills—some critter might grab them and run off.

Bent over, staring down at the water, washing his hands, then his face, Josiah could see the reflection of the clouds overhead—but after a second, after wiping the last bit of water from his face, he nearly quit breathing.

There was a man in the reflection, a man standing over him with his father's long gun in his hands. Even worse, setting panic free to scream through his veins, was the realization that the man was an Indian. Josiah was almost certain it was a Comanche.

He froze until the Indian nudged him from behind with his foot. "Up," the Indian demanded. "Up."

Josiah did as he was told. He was trembling, and he was afraid he was going to pee himself like a little baby, but he didn't. He turned and faced the Indian. The Indian had shoulder-length black hair, a buckskin shirt, and a breechcloth with leggings. There were streaks of paint on his face, black curvy lines trailing from his hard eyes, and Josiah didn't know what they meant. All he knew about was war paint. But why would a lone Indian be here in war paint? he wondered. That would mean there were more Indians. He broke out in a sweat at the thought.

The Indian motioned for Josiah's black-powder bag, and for his cartridges, too. Josiah instinctively shook his head no, and started to back up. He stopped when he was ankle-deep in the water, not taking his eyes off the Indian. It was then that he noticed the blood running down the Indian's thigh, noticed the gaping bullet hole, and the scowl of pain that was marbled across the man's face.

"Give," the Indian demanded, motioning again for the ammunition.

Josiah shook his head no again, squared his shoulders, and stood firm, but before he realized what was happening, the Indian swung his father's long gun at him. The butt crashed into the side of his head before he could move, before he could scream. He only felt a brief burst of pain before everything went black.

Josiah slowly came to a little while later, lying on the bank of the river. A loud sound had startled him awake, his head ached with pain, and he could taste a bit of blood. It was late afternoon now—the sky grayer than it was in the morning, with a cold rain sprinkling down and a fierce wind rattling the leaf canopy overhead. It sounded like a train was running over the tops of the trees. Josiah sat up, rubbing his head, his eyes searching at every turn for the Comanche.

But he was gone . . . along with his father's long gun and the satchel of squirrels. Josiah stood up slowly, then gathered his bearings, made sure that he was correct—that everything was gone, including the Indian.

He began to run, run as fast as he could, toward home, toward his father and his ma, as far away from the woods, and the Indian, as possible.

He could only hope the Indian was alone, and not waiting for him, not waiting to follow him home. And then, fear upon fear broke loose in Josiah Wolfe's twelve-year-old soul, when he realized that his mother could not protect herself any better than he could, or the Parkers had, when they were overwhelmed by angry, raiding Indians.

He ran faster than he had ever run before.

CHAPTER 1

July 1874

"Ofelia, have you seen my boots?" Josiah Wolfe demanded.

Morning light bathed the porch in a warm glow from the rising sun. It was a small comfort that the house faced east, toward Tyler, toward Seerville, toward what had been, until recently, home.

Ofelia Martinez smiled, and ignored Josiah. She was sitting on a porch swing holding Josiah's two-year-old-son, Lyle, on her lap playing pat-a-cake. "*Acariciar a una torta, acariciar a una torta, hombre del panadero.*"

Breakfast had already been cooked, eaten, and cleaned up. There was still a lingering aroma of strong coffee and bacon wafting out from inside the small house.

Lyle squealed with laughter, then said, "Pat-a-cake, pat-a-cake, baker's man!"

"*Sí,*" Ofelia said, giving Lyle a hearty hug.

"Ofelia!"

"*¿Qué, señor?* What?"

Josiah was standing in the doorway. His face was red, an odd contrast to his cornflower blue eyes and the thick shock of straw-colored hair that stood uncombed on the top of his head. He was tall and lanky, and his head nearly bumped the top of the door when he came and went. He had to watch his head when he had a hat on or he would knock it off. One more thing to get used to in this house.

"Where are my boots?"

Ofelia broke into a healthy laugh. She was short, what some might call squat, her dark brown Mexican face was lined with wrinkles, and her hair was grizzled and unruly, gray refusing to turn white, even though it probably should have years before.

Josiah had known Ofelia since he was a boy, and she was the closest thing to family he had left in his life. She had been a midwife in East Texas almost her entire life. Mostly to Mexicans like herself, but Josiah's father and ma didn't carry around much prejudice—Mexicans came and went frequently on their little farm, helping out for what wages they could earn, and what wages Josiah's family could pay.

The Wolfes never owned a slave—his father found the practice distasteful, even though he never said so outside of the confines of his own home—but that did not stop Josiah from signing up with the Texas Brigade when the War Between the States came to Texas. He was a son of Texas, and there was an expectation that he fight, like the rest of the Wolfe family had before, in the skirmishes of the land, like the Cherokee War his father fought in, and became a hero in, before Josiah was born. Josiah had been more than happy to carry on the fighting tradition when the time came.

Ofelia had been with the family during happy times and

sad. She had been there after the war, when Josiah returned broken, then was saved by Lily, the girl of his dreams, giving him a family, and new hope. She had been there, too, when both Josiah's parents died and were buried on the back forty of the Seerville farm. Most importantly, and most recently, Ofelia had been there when the fevers came and took Josiah's three little girls, and ultimately death claimed his wife, Lily, in childbirth, leaving a newborn baby, Lyle, in the arms of a man who knew nothing about child-rearing. Ofelia had been there through it all. So when Josiah decided to move to Austin, he was more than a little relieved that Ofelia agreed to come along and watch after Lyle while he continued on Rangering. He owed her the world.

"They are on your feet, Señor Josiah." Ofelia laughed again, so much so, her whole body shook from head to toe.

Lyle joined in, even though it was obvious that the little boy, who favored his mother, with curly dark hair and brown eyes, didn't know why he was laughing. He looked at Josiah and Ofelia quickly, from one to the other, trying to determine, it seemed, if he was causing the laughter. Lyle was too young to know the past, or understand the present, and Josiah was intent on keeping it that way for as long as possible.

Josiah burst into laughter then, once he looked down and found his boots exactly where he had put them. "Well, that figures, doesn't it?"

"It does, señor, it surely does."

"My apologies, Ofelia."

"No need, *señor*, you know that."

"It's just hard . . . to leave so soon."

Ofelia nodded, wiped the tears from her eyes that had accumulated from laughing so hard, and stood up, lugging

Lyle up with her. She easily handled the boy, like he was a sack of potatoes, balanced on her hip like a commodity that fit perfectly against her body.

"It will be easier to get the house in order without you underfoot. Besides, it is best to get you back where you belong . . . among the living. I will be fine here. The city has much allure, and I have some distant relatives here as well. It is not like I will be all alone, señor."

"I don't know how I'll ever be able to repay you."

Josiah held out his hands a few inches from Lyle. The boy eagerly jumped into his father's arms.

"We have already discussed this, señor. I will stay until it is time for me to leave. We will settle up then."

Josiah nodded. "It's a deal. All right. No more of that, I promise."

"*Bueno*."

"Good!" Lyle shouted. "Good!"

Josiah and Ofelia both broke into a hearty round of laughter again.

One thing was for sure: Lyle would be much better at speaking more than one language than Josiah was. And all things considered, since he was obviously going to be raised a city boy instead of a country boy, it was a good thing for Lyle. The world was changing faster than Josiah could keep up with.

"*Bueno. Bueno*," Lyle continued as, followed by Ofelia, Josiah walked back into the house, readying himself to finally leave.

Josiah Wolfe had been in a new city more than once in his life, but it was still nearly impossible for him to conceive that his recent move to Austin was now a permanent one. He was no longer a visitor, or a Texas Ranger riding into town on business just to leave again when trouble was quelled or an arrest made.

The Texas capital was now his home. It was a far cry from living on the land he was born on in East Texas, where he knew exactly what to expect with the seasons and weather, where every step he took could be retraced to his boyhood, to his own painful—and joyful—memories. The new scenery was a relief from the tragedy he'd left behind.

City life was going to take some time to get accustomed to, but it was the choice he'd made and he knew he'd have to live with that decision.

It was for the best, he was sure of it, even though his heart caught in his throat as he tightened the saddle on his horse's back.

Clipper, his Appaloosa stallion, stood firm. Josiah and the horse had been through a lot together. Outside of Ofelia, there was no other creature on earth Josiah trusted more than Clipper.

He climbed up on the horse, took a deep breath, settled himself in, then nodded solemnly at Ofelia, who was standing on the porch with Lyle still attached to her hip.

"*Adiós*, Papa. *Adiós*."

Josiah waved, then turned and rode off slowly without saying good-bye. He had promised Lyle and Ofelia that he would be back soon. That was as close to saying good-bye as it came for Josiah Wolfe.

Austin was a crowded, noisy, town. Josiah missed the whip-poor-wills at night, even the baying of a lone coyote—all replaced with flat-out citified silence, at night anyway.

Daytime in Austin was louder than ever, day in, day out, people coming and going, horses whinnying, and train whistles blowing. It was the trains that unsettled Josiah the most. His house was less than a block away from the tracks, and it shook regularly.

He would be glad for the reprieve from the noise and from the shaking house, he thought as he made his way through town at an easy pace on Clipper's back, taking in the coming day, in no huge hurry to get where he was going.

There was a lot to take in, a lot to learn about his new home, but Josiah knew enough to kind of understand what was happening around him, and that was important as far as he was concerned.

The Houston and Texas Central Railway had come to Austin in late 1871, a Christmas present to businessmen and those too eager to take advantage of the new opportunities the railway afforded. The capital city became the westernmost railroad terminus in Texas. Construction boomed, and the population, helped along with an influx of freed slaves, had doubled since the first steam engine roared into town.

Along with the growing communities of Negroes, there were Mexicans living near Shoal Creek, and a healthy mix of Germans, Irish, and Europeans was scattered about the city in small enclaves.

A new governor, Richard Coke, had been elected and taken his seat in the capitol in January, and there seemed to have been a new leaf turned. The past, specifically Reconstruction, was thought to be over, but old social lines were still not crossed.

Very few Anglos dared venture into places like Little Mexico, the quadrant of streets and businesses just off Republic Square—even at midday. Josiah had visited there once, before moving to Austin, and made the brief acquaintance of a woman, Suzanne del Toro, but he had not visited her since moving to Austin permanently. He didn't have the courage to make the visit. Though he did search the crowds for her face, hoping to get a glimpse of her—no matter how guilty the search for or thought of her made him feel.

The Anglos had their own section of town, just across the river, that was just as dangerous as Little Mexico and was certainly off-limits to the majority of polite folk in the city. Most big cities had their own version of Hell's Half Acre, and Austin was no exception.

Even a Yankee had his place in the city . . . on the outside of the proper social circles, which constituted the hardest enclave to penetrate, if that were ever achieved. Money or fame usually broke down those doors, at least wore them down, opened them if there was enough of both. Josiah had neither.

The only thing he had going for him was his Texan birthright, his stature as a Texas Ranger, installed as a sergeant in the newly formed Frontier Battalion. He had connections to the powerful, but was reluctant to use them, or even acknowledge them in public.

There was no mistaking that he was welcome in the home of the now-deceased Captain Hiram Fikes—at least by the captain's daughter, Pearl, if not by the captain's widow. Pearl's mother feared Josiah as a potential suitor of her daughter, and though she may have been right, Josiah was well aware that the new captain of his company, Pete Feders, had asked Pearl to marry him. She had used her grief and mourning to hold the decision at bay, and Josiah was glad of that . . . but he knew he stood no chance of winning the girl's heart, and he wasn't entirely sure he was ready to try . . . though he thought she was the most beautiful woman in the living world.

Josiah eased Clipper to a stop near the center of the capital city, a few blocks away from the Democratic operations of Richard Coke. He could have easily taken another route to the Red River camp, where his company of fellow Rangers was assembled for training, but he hadn't.

He had one last stop to make before leaving town.